UNDER THE CAPE

An Anthology of Superhero Romance

Edited by Rachel Kenley

For more information contact:
Riverdale Avenue Books
5676 Riverdale Avenue
Riverdale, NY 10471
www.riverdaleavebooks.com

Design by www.formatting4U.com
Cover by Scott Carpenter

Digital ISBN: 9781626015586
Print ISBN: 9781626015593

First Edition, July 2020

Dedication

For the heroes of the Corona Virus Pandemic

Including and especially:

medical professionals,
hospital workers,
first responders,
delivery drivers,
grocery and retail workers
teachers

and everyone who kept us going
and put their own safety and health
at risk during this time.

Thank you all for being the heroes we needed

Table of Contents

Introduction i

SUPER SWEET STORIES

Flying Fast, Falling Hard, Kim Strattford........................1

Where There's Smoke, E.D. Gonzalez 23

Trust Paradox, Naomi Hinchen 47

Time for No Mercy, Elizabeth Schechter 77

No Words Needed, David T. Valentin...........................93

Swiftly in Love, Stella B. James..................................115

SUPER HEAT STORIES

Supergay, Julie Behrens..141

The Little Push, Christopher Peruzzi 173

Foolproof, Louisa Bacio 199

Just Be Yourself, Rachel Kenley 229

Law, Love, and the Whippoorwill, Austin Worley......261

Author Bios 305

Introduction

I am writing this toward the end of May 2020 as the world continues to manage the Coronavirus pandemic. It seems important to state this at the beginning of an anthology with the theme of superheroes since our definition of 'superhero' has changed in recent months. Today, we talk of heroes being the medical professionals, first responders, delivery and grocery workers who are keeping our topsy-turvy world going. And, like all true heroes, when you call them heroes, they say, "I'm just doing my job." Isn't that at the heart of so many heroic acts? People doing the right thing at the right time and most especially when it's not easy.

Love and relationships are never simple–add superpowers along with the need to answer the call when a villain appears, and you've got a recipe for some serious conflicts which the authors of these stories have fun exploring.

In the Sweet section (no sex), we start with Kim Strattford's *Flying Fast, Falling Hard*, where it will take more than superpowers for our heroine to get over a previously broken heart. Deciding to form a dynamic duo in public and private is not a decision to be taken lightly in E.D. Gonzalez' *Where There's Smoke* as well as Stella B. James' *Swiftly in Love*. Naomi Hinchen's heroine faces the age-old question of how much can we reveal to a new lover in *The Trust Paradox*. Good and bad are relative and dramatically switched in Elizabeth Schechter's *Time for No Mercy,* and in *No Words Needed* by David T. Valentin, a young man can't decide what's more overwhelming–discovering he has powers or that his crush may like him too.

Then, we dial up the heat and watch as the leads in both Julie Behren's *Supergay* and Louise Bacio's *Foolproof* look at a previously held truth when they fall for someone they thought was a villain. Surrender can be so much fun. In *The Little Push*, by Christopher Peruzzi, being on the same team doesn't automatically mean you'll get along. Being loved for who we truly are, no matter what we can do, is at the heart of my story *Just Be Yourself,* and we end with Austin Worley's novelette *Love, Law and the Whippoorwill*, where power and superpowers make for an exciting match.

The world always needs heroes and they deserve their happy endings too. Happy endings are in short supply these days, which is part of why this anthology has been a joy to put together. It's given me something fun and hopeful to focus on. I don't know what specifics I'll remember looking back on this crazy time, but I am grateful this was a part of it. I hope it brings you some much needed enjoyment and diversion.

Enjoy,
Rachel Kenley

SUPER SWEET STORIES

Flying Fast, Falling Hard
By Kim Strattford

Tom Sullivan was a pretender. That was clear from the moment Marta Livacek met him. His shiny smile, his oh-so-normal background. He'd proven squeaky clean when she'd had the archivist of the Alliance of Superheroes check him out—a necessary prelude before inviting him to join.

He came from Missouri. He'd majored in physics at Washington University and become a pilot for the Air Force. And when he'd flown through some odd smoke after a strafing run on a terrorist camp in Slobovia, he'd been changed.

He didn't need a plane to fly anymore.

His power was real—that wasn't the problem with him—but he was cocky and impulsive, and she'd seen a hundred other metas like him. He was in this for the ego, not to help people.

"Marta," Sullivan said, appearing out of nowhere. Flying meant no footsteps, but she was usually good at hearing the change of wind that meant a flyer was coming up on her. It annoyed her beyond words that he'd gotten by her.

"You're early."

1

"I figured that was a less egregious crime than being late."

She crossed her arms over her chest and leaned back in the big chair—bigger than the other chairs that ringed the table because she was in charge of the alliance. "How about being on time? No crime there."

"What did I do to piss you off?" He sat down in the chair next to her without being asked. That also annoyed her.

"I don't get pissed off, Sullivan. I don't allow myself to. Self-control is key when we've got the powers we have."

"And what powers do you have, exactly?" His smile was a snotty one, and she could hear the unsaid, *Other than being an uber bitch?* "Here you are the leader, and you don't appear to be meta in any way."

"Someday, you and I will have a go in the gym, and I can show you just how little use meta really is compared to a well-trained body and a disciplined mind." She leaned forward. "But that pleasure will have to wait. The members have voted you in."

"And you had to tell me that yourself?"

She let one side of her mouth slip up—it was a creepy smile and she knew that because she practiced it in the mirror. Everything about her was creepy—the black uniform and mask she wore when working, the way she moved, her silence as she fought. She'd never taken on a superhero name—let people call her whatever they wanted: she didn't need some fancy title to strike fear in bad guys' hearts. She'd just be herself, and she wouldn't go away until someone got lucky and took her out.

The way they'd taken out her husband Peter, a cop, on his way home from a long shift when he'd seen a car run a red, nearly hitting an old man in the crosswalk. He'd given chase in his patrol car. He'd caught up.

They'd gunned him down.

She hated guns. She hated criminals more.

She'd found a sensei—took her a while, most wouldn't deal with a desire to train coupled with the anger and grief she'd carried—who molded her into something hard, something lethal. Something that was nothing like this grinning boy-man who could fly but so far showed little else in the way of skills. That said, flying was useful—and he could go damn fast—and muscles could be developed.

"I'm telling you myself because there are conditions. You can fly, sure, but you can't fight any better than my dead aunt."

"Then your dead aunt must have been pretty good." He wasn't grinning any longer. Marta had hit the poor boy's ego.

"You'll need to work at it before you become anything more than a prospective member. I have a list of trainers and who's offered to teach you what." She handed him the tablet.

He read it, then looked back up at her. "Not you?"

"You're not ready to be trained by me."

A little more of his boyish charm slipped away. "Okay, lady. Let's go to the gym now. I'll show you how not ready I am."

She gave him a full smile, the one that meant she was actually amused. "You don't want to do that."

"Oh, I do."

"It's your funeral." She got up and headed for the gym, not checking to see if he was following.

3

He flew, of course. Big show-off. He passed her and was in the gym warming up on the punching bag when she walked in. His moves weren't bad. He had potential. She might not trust his motives—or that he'd be in this for the long haul—but she could see he wasn't a lost cause.

And sparring with her would help him understand that he needed work.

She stood with her arms crossed and watched him.

"Not going to warm up? Big mistake, Marta."

She shrugged. He didn't need to know that every move she made was a warm-up. That sitting didn't have to be resting. That walking could be an exercise in discipline. That reaching for something, extending the arm, rising on tiptoes, could be more than just grabbing a mug someone had left too high.

Her sensei had wanted her to always be ready. Always being ready meant never relaxing. It took her forever to fall asleep at night, and she usually woke up many times—the sound of anything unusual was enough to pull her violently from sleep.

He left the punching bag, did a few stretches, and then walked over. "Whenever you're ready. Ladies first, do your worst, and all that."

She didn't move. "You're the guest here. You start this."

He telegraphed his first punch so clearly that she barely had to move to slide out of the way, easing her body and head back, her feet never leaving the ground. His next two punches were equally amateurish.

She waited until he frowned and seemed ready to fight with a bit more strategy before she whipped

4

around in a tight, fast turn and knocked him halfway across the mats with a sharp kick to his side.

His grunt as he hit the ground was extremely satisfying. He got up, rubbing his side, clearly having no idea how carefully she'd pulled the kick, how his ribs would be cracked if she'd wanted to really hurt him.

He came at her more slowly this time. She'd give him that: he learned from his mistakes.

It didn't help him. She blocked his punch, twisted his arm—not enough to break his wrist—and sent him crashing to the mat again. She danced out of the way, making the "come on, come get me" gesture with her fingers that had infuriated her when her sensei had done it to her when she'd been learning to fight.

It clearly got to Sullivan, too. He charged her, this time feinting left, then going in for the real hit. She caught his fist with her open hand, twisted and let his momentum carry him around her. A chop on his back face-planted him into the mat.

His back would hurt like hell, but she'd held the hit—it could have been much worse, the kind someone wouldn't die from, but also wouldn't get up from.

He was breathing hard and didn't try to stand. She sat down next to him and touched him on the temple. "This is half your problem. You're cocky—you think you'll always win. We don't. We just fight until that moment comes when it's over for us."

"Bleak outlook," he managed to say between huffs of what sounded like pain.

"Realistic outlook." She pushed herself to her feet. "Do you need help?"

If she thought he did, she wouldn't have asked.

5

She'd have just hauled him down to the infirmary and treated him.

"Nope. Nope. I'm good. Probably do a set of weights before I go."

She laughed, a spontaneous sound she was shocked to have made.

"Wow, you do have a sense of humor after all." He rolled to his back and looked up at her. "Thought maybe you'd forgotten to get in line for that, overachieving in the fighting as you are."

"Humor is useless." Peter had been funny. He'd made her laugh a lot. Where had it gotten him?

"Sometimes, humor is the only weapon we have." He sat up with a groan. "Like now. Holy crap, lady. Don't pull your punches or anything."

She let an eyebrow go up and gave him the one-sided creepy smile again. "Oh, Sullivan, I was going easy on you."

His look of dismay gave her way too much satisfaction, but she enjoyed it anyway as she left him to get up on his own.

* * *

Marta Livacek was an enigma, and not just because Tom was getting nowhere in his charm campaign. It seemed like no one charmed her. She stayed at the edge of group functions, her smile a half one. He'd only seen her laugh once, and it'd been after she kicked the crap out of him in the training room.

Hell, he might be the only person who'd ever seen her laugh in the alliance's polar headquarters. Her husband probably had seen her laugh—Tom knew her history, and it was grim. But it had been 10 years ago. Grieving was one thing, but she'd made this into a vendetta. The first thing she'd done was to catch the lowlifes who'd shot her husband to death, so she could have moved on.

He suspected she didn't want to let go of her hate and anger. She might think she was under control, but he'd seen others like her when he was a pilot. They cracked up eventually—no one could hold onto that much negative emotion without consequences.

"Big thoughts?" Felix, the gargantuan half-man, half-something else but Tom wasn't sure what—loaded more weight on the barbell Tom was hoisting. Felix had taken a shine to Tom and reminded him of some of his pilot buddies back in the day, only a lot bigger than any of them.

"A little spotting would be nice." He tried to remember the right way to breathe when hefting weights—he'd done all this in flight school. You had to be stronger than people thought when you were pulling aerial miracles out of your ass in high-G. But he'd never tried to get as strong as Marta wanted him to be.

After a few fights for the alliance, he knew why she wanted him strong. He was starting to think his best use was as transport or high-altitude surveillance—he'd lost every fight he'd been in.

"Impressive." It was her voice. It wasn't that sexy a voice so why did it give him chills? And not just the creepy, "must you sneak up on me all the time?" kind.

"Thanks," he managed to get out as he pressed the barbell up a little more.

"Tom's doing great." Felix was the only one who

never sounded like she scared him. "I keep adding weight, and he keeps lifting it."

"Don't break him."

"Would...you...care?" Tom set the bar down on the rest and tried not to look like he wanted nothing more than a cold beer, a hot shower, and a corner to collapse in, and not in that order.

Marta shot Felix a look Tom couldn't read, and the big guy skedaddled.

"Wow, you have them all trained, don't you? So, are you kicking me out of the tree fort? Did you bring a pink slip?"

She laughed again. It was a startlingly engaging sound. "Amazingly, no. You've been working hard, and that's not gone unnoticed."

A sneaky way to avoid saying that she'd noticed. He let his mouth turn up into a smirk to show her he was wise to her ways.

She rolled her eyes and walked to the window that looked out on the ice. "I like how you've gelled with the teams you've worked with."

"Thanks." He sat up and grabbed his towel. "But what do you really want?"

She turned to look at him, and he was caught by the sharpness of her features. On anyone else, they'd be too severe, but somehow, she made them work. Maybe it was because they went so well with her nearly omnipresent scowl.

"I didn't think you'd work out."

"Yeah, I kinda figured that out on my own, toots."

This time her laugh was more a puff of air—a sound of disbelief. He'd noticed no one else teased her

8

or gave her guff right back to her. Did she like that he did?

"Well, I guess I just wanted to say I'm changing my mind." She headed for the door.

"Thanks." He waited until she was almost out to say, "Had to come by personally and tell me that? Right this minute? It couldn't wait till later?" He gave her his best cocky, "I'm a pilot, ask me how" grin.

She glanced back at him, her own smile a smirk now. "I know how needy you flyboys are."

Then she was gone and a moment later Felix wandered back in. Tom held up his hands in surrender. "We're done for the day, buddy. I can't take any more."

"I know. I just wanted to say...she likes you."

"Uh huh. And pigs will fly with me next mission."

"No, really. I can tell."

Tom snapped his towel at Felix's massive thigh. "That's your superpower now? Matchmaking?"

Felix shook his head and started his own workout, leaving Tom to cool down, his mind racing—his friend's words were having way more impact than they should.

There was no way Marta liked him.

Was there?

* * *

Marta made her way carefully down the track of the hill, trying to ignore how much every muscle in her body seemed to hurt after the blow the alliance had just struck at the latest group of super-powered—if also super-stupid—villains. She winced as she stepped wrong—they might not have been loaded in the brains department, but these guys had packed a lot into their punches. And she'd been in the thick of it, of course.

"You know I could fly you down."

Damn it all to hell—how did Sullivan always sneak up on her? She didn't turn to look at him, more because she thought it would wrench her neck than to be snotty. "Nope, I'm good."

He didn't leave. "You don't look good."

"Looks can be deceiving." She attempted to limp a little less. She abandoned the charade when he landed next to her. "What?" She tried to give him her best glare, but knew she failed when he shook his head.

"If you don't want me to fly you down, I'll walk you down."

"Don't you have an after-action report to do?"

"Yeah. It'll be really long. We came, we kicked their asses, and we all limped home."

She realized he seemed to be favoring his left leg. He'd been in the thick of it, too. Probably more than he should have been, even though Felix told her he was a workout and sparring machine. He was definitely stronger and a better fighter than he'd been when he joined.

"You're hurt, Sullivan. Fly down. Walking is stupid."

"Oh, please, Marta, tell me you're listening to your own words?"

She started walking again, unwilling to let him see he was right—and worse, she knew it.

"Okay, then, we'll hoof it." He took a deep breath. "You know I didn't have to join the alliance, right?"

"You'd have stayed in the Air Force?"

"That's not what I meant, although that was an option—only they got really squirrely with some tests they wanted to run on me, and I decided retiring was a better option than being some sort of test bed for a new kind of warfighter."

"Why? Has there been a downside to flying for you?"

"Other than putting up with you?"

She laughed—damn it all. Why did she find him funny?

"No, actually, for me there hasn't been. But I don't want this power proliferated willy nilly. I know you've seen my psych profile—I'm a well-adjusted guy. But not everyone is. Power corrupts, and flying is big damn power in my book."

"I'll concede that you're right." She could tell he was smiling and said, "Stop that. Random chance dictates you'll be right occasionally."

"I could have been a movie star." He laughed when she shot him a look. "Seriously. You know I've never hidden who I am behind a mask or a name. Never even wore a uniform until I got on your super special team."

She glanced over at him. He filled out the dark gray uniform really well. Not that she cared other than as the leader, wanting the team to present well.

Oh hell, the man had a nice ass. Was it a crime to admit that if only to herself? "Why no Hollywood, then? They didn't offer you enough money?"

"They offered me tons of money, Marta. But it was... empty. I joined the service because I wanted to make a difference. I joined the alliance for the same reason."

"Sure you did. You don't get off at all on the fan-

11

pages or the fawning women. You get to enjoy it all the more since you don't hide who you are. Living out in the open can be a brave move—or just that of someone who craves attention."

"Lady, I'm sorry I'm not as screwed up as you— that I don't have some tragic origin story to give me an out for being a dick to everyone."

She stopped and forced herself to be calm before she spoke. "You don't get to speak of my past that way."

"No one does. Everybody just tiptoes around it like you're special. You think I never had to go see a spouse of a fellow pilot—tell them their husband or wife wouldn't be coming home that night because a plane went down? You think you're the only one who's ever felt that pain?" He reached out to touch her shoulder, but she stopped him with a look. "The only thing that makes you special is how you wallow in it. It was 10 years ago. Do you think your husband would have wanted this for you? Sure, he'd be proud of what you've done, how you've brought us all together. But to be this alone—this closed off? I can't imagine he would have approved."

He took off, leaving her alone on the path before she could tell him to go to hell. It seemed to take forever to get down the hill and to the shuttle.

Everyone was waiting for her. Some of them looked hurt—nothing life threatening, but in pain. They all seemed exhausted. And none of them said a thing as she limped to the door and said, "Let's go."

She'd made them wait because she was too proud—too closed off, Sullivan was right—to accept a ride down. And not one of them but him was going to give her the rash of shit she deserved.

Maybe she'd gone too far in the scary department.

She sat down in the co-pilot's chair and didn't look
around as the rest followed her aboard. They'd think she
was her usual, anti-social self. They'd never guess she
felt bad—that Sullivan had made her feel bad.

"Here you go, boss." A tablet was pressed into
her hand. Sullivan had compiled everyone's after-
action report into one while they waited for her to get
her ass down to the ship.

She didn't meet his eyes. "Thanks."

"No problem."

He left her alone—everyone did—for the rest of
the flight.

* * *

Tom saw Marta sitting in one of the window seats
that looked out on the icy expanse outside HQ. She
had her knees pulled up to her chest and looked very
small...and alone.

He took a deep breath, then walked over. Walked,
not flew, so she'd hear him coming and be able to stop
him before he made a total ass of himself.

She didn't. She just said, "You wanted me to hear
you."

"Yep. You must be sick of me getting by your
special radar or however you hear all the things you
do." He grinned, but she didn't look up to see he was
gently teasing.

She also didn't say to go away, so he sat opposite
her and leaned against the wall, his knees up, but not
pulled in like hers were. Not so...defensive.

"You okay?" he asked.

She nodded.

"I know you're not a woman of many words on a good day, but is there something I've done to make you go unusually taciturn?"

She laughed softly. Then she finally turned to look at him, a smile that was almost sweet on her face. "You're the only one who makes me laugh."

"Felix doesn't?"

She shook her head. "He makes me smile, though. I count him as a true friend."

"I guess I don't fall in that category, not after my pissed-off speech on the hillside?"

She took a deep breath, and he wondered if she was trying to control the urge to clobber him, but when she looked up and met his eyes, hers were calm. "You told me the truth. That makes you something."

"Yeah, a pain in your ass."

She laughed again. He really liked the sound. "The two aren't mutually exclusive: friend and pain in my ass."

"I guess that's true." He sort of enjoyed that idea, because he wasn't sure he could stop being a pain in the ass—it was sort of a signature style after so many years—but he also wanted to get to know her, to find the woman beyond the pain and the creepy mask and controlled voice. "Okay, I'm going to go way out on a limb, but things are quiet, and you look like you could use a diversion. Is there anywhere you've always wanted to go but just haven't been? My treat for lunch."

Her smile turned into the slightly derisive one. "You're going to fly us there, I take it?"

"No, I thought we'd take the bus. There a stop around here?"

Her grin was adorable, not a word he ever though he'd use to describe her. "I appreciate the offer, but I have work to do." She got up in one lithe movement that set his mind down the unfortunate path of wondering just how limber she really was. To get it off that track, he asked, "If it had been Felix—or someone, anyone else—who invited you, would you have said yes?"

"No one else would have asked." She touched his shoulder, her eyes very soft, and then she turned and walked back toward the operations room.

He touched his shoulder, thought about how her backside looked in that skin-tight uniform, and tried his best to wipe the sappy-ass smile off his face.

* * *

Marta stood with the rest of the alliance, staring down at the device left by the terrorists they'd just rounded up.

A device that was counting down. That they'd tried their best to disarm and failed.

"Felix."

He moved to stand beside her.

"Move it to shuttle one."

He shared a long look with her, then picked up the device and carried it to the closest of their waiting shuttles.

She hadn't expected this bomb to be in the camp, much less armed and ready. She hadn't been prepared. She'd been thinking about cities she'd never been to, foods she'd like to try even if she'd never told Sullivan that his offer was never far from her thoughts—that he wasn't either.

She forced Sullivan-induced whimsy from her mind. Thank God this thing was a conventional bomb. "All right, guys. There may be wreckage falling down. You know what to do. Felix, you're in charge until a formal vote can be held." She hurried onto the shuttle and hit the panel to close the door, but heard Sullivan yell, "Felix, you'll do great—and you're an awesome friend in case we don't get back," and then he dove through the slowly closing doors.

"What the hell is wrong with you?"

"Nothing." He got up, hurried to the pilot's seat, and strapped in. "How much time do we have?"

She checked the device's timer. "Five minutes."

"Then sit down and let me do my thing."

"I can fly this."

He didn't look at her. He was madly turning all the right levers and buttons to get the shuttle up as quickly as possible, higher and higher, to where they stood the best chance of not having the blast's shockwaves impact the surface. The other members would use their various skills to keep the pieces of the shuttle from harming people or property.

"You're crazy," she said, not looking at Sullivan.

"And you're an idiot for not asking for help. Are you that suicidal?"

"We're going to die. The autopilot on this thing is iffy. We have to stay with the shuttle until the device goes."

"Yes, you'd die if you were alone. But you've got me. And we're going to see just how fast I can take off and skedaddle with oh, say, two seconds to spare." He shot her a grin that was both excited and a little bit terrified. Mostly the former, though.

16

Damn it all, why was he so cute? And why was she thinking about that when they had a job—maybe their last one—to complete? Maybe their last one, but maybe not. She realized she really wanted it to not be their last one.

For the first time in a long time, she cared if she lived or died.

"And for the record, Marta, since we're not going to die, we *are* going on that date."

"Date? It was lunch. On you."

"Well, now it's dinner. On me. In my world, that's a date."

"Your world is a place of delusions." She got up and checked the device. "Three minutes."

"We're fine. How long will the shuttle door take to open?"

"Fifteen seconds at least."

"Okay, going to depressurize now. Get an oxygen mask on. And can you fasten the device down? Don't want it falling out that door if the shuttle hits some turbulence."

She slipped an oxygen mask on, then pulled out the cargo hooks from the floor and wound them around the thing until she was sure it wasn't going to fall out. "Got it."

"Did you pick a city?" His voice sounded funny coming through the mask speakers.

"Seriously? We're busy here."

"Not at the moment. You're practicing your bondage skills, and I'm flying this pretty little ship. Been a while. Have wanted to fly it since I got here." He patted the panel. "Sorry, honey, that our first time is your last time."

17

She found the tenderness he was showing the shuttle unaccountably charming.

"So? What city, Marta?"

"Prague. It's home." Why did she tell him it was home? And when did she pick Prague? She'd been going back and forth between Bangkok and Paris in her silly fantasies where she actually said yes to him.

"Love it. It's a date, then. You'll steer me on the Czech menu, yes?" He started to laugh. "Like you need any encouragement to tell me what to do?"

"Like you ever do what I say, Tom."

"Whoa, first name. You really do think we're going to die, don't you?" He started setting some switches, getting the autopilot ready to take it the few seconds they'd need. "Time?"

"Forty-five seconds." She could feel the temperature dropping as the plane depressurized. It became harder to breathe, to push the air in and out.

"Open the door, Marta. But put a harness on first, yeah? Hate to lose you before our date."

She rolled her eyes—the gesture lost on him, but it made her feel better—and wrapped the harness around her before hitting the exit panel. The normal warning alarm sounded, then the doors began to open, but he'd depressurized enough to keep her from having to fight not to be sucked out. "Thirty seconds," she yelled as the temperature dropped some more.

She unhooked the harness and watched the timer. "Twenty-five."

He was setting more switches, keying in commands, and she admired the way he didn't miss a beat, the calmness that seemed to radiate from him as he did what she realized he was very, very good at.

18

The alliance was lucky to have him.

She was lucky to have him. "Twenty."

He kept the plane ascending, and she trusted him to know how far was too far for them to survive. Trust: what an unusual concept. She was so used to relying on herself to make the plans—or at least double-check them if they weren't hers.

"Setting auto pilot now. Will monitor for next ten seconds, then join you."

"Roger that, Eagle One."

She heard his laugh over the speakers. "Holy cow, Marta—you have a sense of humor."

"Yeah, yeah, don't spread it around."

He laughed again. "Guess you believe we're going to get out of here."

"Guess I do. Gonna be awfully pissed off if you're not up to the task, flyboy."

"When aren't you pissed?" His voice was gentle, not mocking.

"Right now I'm not. About to die with a crazy man at the controls and I'm...happy, I guess."

"Happy is good, darlin'. Autopilot holding steady, by the way." He unstrapped his harness and joined her, and when the timer hit five seconds he said, "Show me what you've got, baby," with a laugh as he hoisted her up, their faces very close.

She wrapped her arms around his neck and her legs around his midsection and buried her face in his shoulder. "I'm going to write you up for creating a hostile work environment."

He laughed, a sharp burst of sound. "And we're out of here." There was a jolting feeling of being launched from the shuttle and then a moment of peace, followed by the sound of the shuttle blowing up. Sullivan had turned so he was facing the ship but was bent in an awkward way, and she realized it was so she wasn't in the way of any debris. He groaned but kept flying.

"Are you hit?"

He didn't answer, and she tried to reach around.

"Yes, I'm hit. No, it's not a problem. You falling because you suddenly can't keep your hands to yourself will be a huge problem, however. Knock it off."

"Fine. But I'm checking it out as soon as we land."

He turned them, and they watched as pieces of the shuttle hurtled toward the ground, all but one caught by alliance members. The one they didn't get landed in a lake, not on anything important. She smiled. They could do this without her. That was a comforting thought.

"I've gotta get down, Marta. I may have lied about how badly I'm hit."

"You idiot." She pointed to the ground. "Terra firma. Now."

"Yes, boss." He flew really fast.

It was more fun than a roller coaster. As they neared the ground and he slowed, she whispered, "Thank you."

"No thanks necessary, ma'am." She could hear the silly grin she liked so much by the way his voice sounded. "Just doing my job."

"You watched way too much TV as a kid."

"You are not wrong on that."

They landed, and he sagged and nearly dropped her. She pulled free of his arms and landed lightly on her feet, managing to catch him and ease him down so she could see his back.

It was peppered all over with little bits of shuttle. "Tom, this must hurt like hell."

"I won't lie. A big dose of painkillers before you pull all that crap out of me wouldn't be refused."

She nodded to Felix, and he picked Tom up in a fireman's carry. Undignified as hell, but would cause the least pain to his back. As she followed them to one of the other shuttles, she reached out and touched Tom's hair.

It was soft. Curly hair so often wasn't. Peter's had been straight and dark, not the sun-streaked blonde that Tom had.

"You did not just stroke my hair." Sullivan's voice bounced as he was carried.

"You're right. That wasn't me."

"Liar. It felt good, by the way." He seemed to give up talking, just rode out the ride with as much dignity as it was possible for a hero to have when he was riding ass up on a brute.

"Told you she liked you," she heard Felix say.

She smiled but resisted comment.

"Yeah, we've got a date and everything. You were spot on, buddy."

Felix glanced back at her. "That right or is he delirious from pain?"

She tried to give Felix the Marta stare of doom. She could tell by his silly grin that she failed miserably. "Yes. Prague. Dinner. On him."

Felix gave her the sweetest smile imaginable, then he seemed to pick up the pace. "Better get him fixed up right for you, then. No time to waste."

Tom groaned with the extra jostling from Felix's near quick-march. "Dude, we're not going tonight."

Felix looked back at her, seemingly for confirmation.

She felt like she was working through a yenta or

21

something. "Felix, slow down. I'd prefer him alive when I subject myself to his company."

Felix laughed, then looked surprised. "You made a joke."

"I do that occasionally."

"No, you really don't." Felix climbed into the shuttle, settling Tom gently face down on a row of seats. "Good luck, buddy," he said, patting him on one of the few places on his shoulder that didn't have pieces of metal embedded in it. Then he walked out and yelled, "Need a pilot here."

Nobody came fast enough, so he said, "To hell with it," and settled into the pilot's seat. "Take a seat, Marta."

She sat on the floor beside Tom's seat, and said softly, "You were lucky. These are all small pieces and they didn't go very deep. If something bigger..."

"Don't borrow trouble, Mar."

She smiled at the name. No one called her that anymore.

Tom reached around, and she realized he wanted to hold her hand. Really? There was a limit—but then he found her hand, and squeezed quite hard, and she felt bad, realizing he was in pain.

"Distract me," he said. "Tell me about Prague. Am I going to like it?"

"Well, you seem to like me, so I guess so."

"If it only seems that I like you, then I'm doing something wrong." He tightened his grip on her, a squeeze that he eased off immediately. "I really, really like you."

She squeezed back, then tousled his hair very gently and could see his surprise by the way his smile changed. "I figured that out all on my own, flyboy."

Where There's Smoke
By E.D. Gonzalez

Smoke dodged another laser blast. The beam exploded into the wall behind him, hurling debris that sent the henchman ducking for cover. To Smoke, the wreckage may as well have been slogging through molasses, while he danced in zero gravity. In the time it took the debris to hit the museum floor, he'd pushed the shooter—one of the villainous Snow Bear's many fur-lined flunkies—into a reproduction of a cave bear skeleton. Bones clattered around the hall as Smoke howled with laughter. You couldn't buy irony like that!

Snow Bear took advantage of the distraction and slammed Smoke into the wall. Smoke's giggles grew wheezy as Snow Bear pressed a thick arm against his throat. The fur from his white overcoat would have tickled under other circumstances.

"You're new in town, aren't you, little man?" Snow Bear snarled, all teeth.

"In point of fact," Smoke replied, coughing, "I'm new to your whole country. If you're the caliber of supervillain to be found in America, I may as well go back to Scotland."

Snow Bear growled and tossed him into the giant sloth display. Ah, of course—the speedster gets knocked into the sloth. The irony was a lot less funny now. With a burst of speed, Smoke shook it off and zeroed in on Snow Bear. The white-clad villain was now climbing the stairs to the exhibits on the curved balcony above. Smoke started to follow, but a metallic glint snagged his attention. Something was hidden to his right, something inching toward him—

Another henchman with another laser gun. And another one on the opposite side, too. He hadn't noticed the henchmen staked out behind the columns… or the one crouched beneath the table displaying fossilized seashells… or the dozen on the balcony.

Apparently Snow Bear had kept some of his henchmen back in case of emergency. Smoke put up his fists and searched for an exit strategy. He'd never make it home in time for *fajr* at this rate…

One of the henchmen on the balcony collapsed with a choked cry. Two more followed. Smoke blinked twice, as if that would clear up this turn of events. He didn't know the cause of this mysterious affliction, but he would make the most of it. He disarmed the henchmen surrounding him in two seconds. On the floor above, Snow Bear reared back, anger written loud and clear in the set of his massive shoulders. Then he rallied, aiming his laser gun for Smoke's head.

"No."

Flames burst to life on the upper level. Smoke stifled a gasp. Within the flames floated a human face, drawn tight with fury. Two black-gloved hands clamped down on Snow Bear's shoulders. Snow Bear had a split-second to look surprised before he was knocked flat and out. Smoke stared at the still form, feeling uncharacteristically slow.

The newcomer blazed through the remaining second-story goons. Their laser blasts affected him about as much as a light rainfall. His own blows hit strong and true, eliciting a chorus of grunts and shouts. Smoke squinted. The museum was dark aside from the lasers and the fire. He caught fleeting glimpses of the stranger. Large frame. Long hair. A black (or was it navy blue? Forest green?) costume. Metallic gold accents and cape.

Precision. Strength. Courage.

"Restrain those goons before they wake up," the man yelled at him.

Impatience.

Smoke tied up the first-floor henchman in funny positions. By the time he finished, the man on the balcony was finishing off the last henchman. With an almighty thwack—though Smoke couldn't quite make out what caused the sound—the henchman went down. The fire surrounding the stranger's head faded to a warm glow around the temples and then disappeared, leaving nothing but a man's silhouette, black on black. Smoke was tempted to take off his glove and brush his fingers against the other man's skin. Would it be hot to the touch, or would it yield only a normal, human warmth?

"That was very impressive," he said instead.

"Thank you."

"Would you care to compare fighting techniques over a cup of coffee sometime?"

The man's head dipped and rose, like he was giving Smoke the once-over.

"I'm not that kind of superhero," the man said.

"What kind are you, then?"

"If you're as lucky as you seem to be, you'll find out someday. Good night."

The man vanished into the shadows. Smoke could have followed him, but he didn't. He grinned a battle-ready grin.

America was looking better all the time.

* * *

Smoke stopped four more crimes-in-progress over the next week: two ordinary robberies, a supermarket hostage situation orchestrated by Bread Man, and the Warthog's latest attempt to take over the city, this time with exploding mechanical piglets. His mysterious rescuer hadn't shown up at any of them. Smoke didn't particularly need him. Guys like the Warthog and the Bread Man were incompetent enough that he defeated them both in one afternoon and still had time left over to do his grocery shopping. Actually, the grocery shopping was harder. What did Americans need with all these different types of orange juice?

He missed the other man. He was the first superhero Smoke had met since relocating. America was much bigger than Scotland; all their heroes were so far apart. It made it difficult to get together for a post-battle nosh. And so, instead of heading to the nearest Thai place for victory noodles, Smoke went straight home from the grocery store, changed into Sadiq Nasir and prepared mujaddara for one.

He turned on the television while he ate, if only to drown out the sound of the neighbor watching an American football game. From the tone of his shouting, his team was losing today. Too bad. The news was on, playing a brief update about Snow Bear's failed attempt at a museum heist.

"Snow Bear was apprehended this evening in Medford, where he allegedly tried to recruit henchmen at a local strip mall. He was already wanted for an attempted burglary at the McLaughlin Museum of Natural History earlier this week. That crime was thwarted by two of Boston's newest superheroes, Smoke and the Damager..."

Damager. His rescuer's name was Damager.

Wow, that was a stupid name. Bloke was lucky he was so good at being alluringly mysterious.

* * *

As Sadiq skidded into work on Monday, just barely on time as usual, a couple of his co-workers congratulated him on his recent victories. Sadiq thanked them with a smile. He didn't see much point in a secret identity anymore; there weren't many Scotsmen of Middle Eastern origin running around Boston. It was actually kind of nice, being able to deploy super-speed at work when he wanted. He didn't do it often, but it did come in handy when his boss, up-and-coming fashion designer and total butterfingers Melyssa Cool, upset her mug, and he was able to pull her new dress designs away before the tea ruined them.

"Christ on a cracker, that was close." Melyssa took a moment to heave a breath and shake away her remaining nerves. "Thank you so much. I saw you on the news last night. You're really on a roll lately."

"Thanks, but I didn't do it alone. A fellow calling himself the Damager turned up. You wouldn't happen to know anything about him, would you?"

"Just what I hear. I should think you'd be in a better position to know him than I would."

Sadiq gasped in feigned outrage. "You think all superheroes know each other? That's a little judgy."

Melyssa laughed and told him to call *Vogue* about scheduling a photo shoot next month.

The rest of the morning was normal. He fielded requests for interviews, tracked down some missing material shipments, and reassured investors (or the same investor… four times in a row) that everything was going delightfully. In between all of the running around, Sadiq found time for a quick internet search on the Damager, but the only thing he learned was that the man was the old-fashioned type who kept his true identity on the downlow. Sadiq could understand that, but it was a disappointment.

By the time his co-workers came to get him for lunch, he'd put Damager out of his mind. The entire office always ate out for lunch. One of their favorite places was Kurtzberg's Deli, a narrow, unassuming building two streets from their office. It was as famous for its bagels and roast beef sandwiches as it was for its gray-haired proprietor, whose first name no one seemed to know. Sadiq had asked him about it once. All he got for his troubles was a wink and a smile and a little extra pastrami in his sandwich.

Metal tables and chairs, nearly all of them occupied, crowded the little restaurant. Sadiq, Brad and Marcy lost the draw for the only two chairs still available.

"That's one nice thing about using a wheelchair," Nicolette said, grinning. "You bring a chair with you wherever you go."

"How much will it cost me to sit on one of the arms?" said Brad.

Sadiq was about to suggest they go eat in the park when the door slammed open. The bell above it rang wildly. Everyone's heads snapped around to look. A figure in a tan and yellow costume with a stylized wheat stalk as a belt buckle stood in the doorway. The gun in his hands was even more ridiculous: a baguette with a muzzle sticking out one end and the trigger at the other.

"No one get up!" he boomed. "I am the Bread Man, and I use dough to steal dough! Now hand over the bread!"

Sadiq actually groaned out loud. The Bread Man, again? Seriously?

Bread Man startled at Sadiq's grumbling. Outrage and fear flickered across his masked face in quick succession before finally settling on haughty annoyance.

"So, we meet again, my expeditious enemy."

"Seriously?" Sadiq couldn't help saying it out loud this time. "I already defeated you and your stupid dough gun this week. Don't we have better things to do?"

"Ah, but this time, things will be different! I've perfected a new and improved dough formula that will—"

Yeah, whatever. Sadiq was bored. He slammed Bread Man into the wall at superspeed. Bread Man squeezed the trigger on his way down. A thick stream of dough shot into the air. Some adhered itself to the ceiling, but most fell back to the floor with a wet plop. Police sirens wailed outside.

"You call this new and improved?" Sadiq said.

Bread Man straightened indignantly. "Can't you tell? I added raisins to the dough."

Sadiq shot an electrical charge to short circuit the gun and then everything went black.

Next thing he knew, he was waking up on a metal surface. When his ears stopped ringing, Kurtzberg explained Bread Man had apparently anticipated this move and equipped his gun with a defense mechanism which responded to Sadiq's limited electrical powers with a blast that shot him out the front window and into the hood of a police car.

Sadiq spent the next 10 minutes repairing Kurtzberg's window. After work, he changed into Smoke and set out in search of a clue to where his doughy nemesis might have gone. A helpful busker said he'd seen the Bread Man running towards Boston Common, but that lead went nowhere. The trail was colder than the salami Kurtzberg had placed on the back of his head to bring the swelling down. Smoke hadn't appreciated it at the time, but he missed it now. Between the collision with the police car and all the unsuccessful searching, his head was pounding. He stopped by the Make Way for Ducklings statue and sat on Mrs. Mallard. Her cool bronze head felt good on his temple.

"Should have brought my camera."

Smoke opened one eye. He expected to find an amused civilian. Instead he found a grinning masked man who sort of looked like his museum rescuer.

Oh!

"You're a hard man to find," Smoke said, leaping away from the ducks.

"That's the idea."

Out in the open, with streetlights and starlight mingling in the open air, Smoke got his first good look at the Damager. He was black, stocky, and just a little taller than Smoke, though of course, they both wore boots. His long braids were gathered in a ponytail, and his mask—black, just like his costume—covered most of the upper half of his face. His eyes stood out like embers in a cold fireplace.

He was kind of hot, and not just because he could set his head on fire.

The Damager spoke again, this time in a more serious tone. "You had a tussle with the Bread Man at Kurtzberg's this afternoon?"

"Tussle is a generous word. I'd say it was more of a blip."

"What happened, exactly?"

It didn't take Smoke very long to relate the details of his brief encounter with what had to be Boston's most ridiculous supervillain. He left out the bit about being electrocuted, but judging by the Damager's smirk, he must have heard about it already. Lovely.

"Why are you so curious?" Smoke asked, a mite more peevish than necessary.

Damager held out something small and oblong. Smoke squinted at it. The object was dark, and Damager's glove was dark so he couldn't quite make out what it was supposed to be.

"It's one of the raisins that Bread Man added to his dough gun," Damager said.

"Okay. What about it?"

The Damager crushed the raisin in his fist and opened his hand again. Tiny metal fragments glinted in his palm in a little puddle.

"Acid bombs," said Damager. "Each one has a reservoir of acid strong enough to eat through metal."

"But not you and your gloves, I take it?"

31

Damager cleaned his hand with a tissue and grinned. It was a nice grin. Much better than the smirk, though that wasn't so bad either. Smoke gave himself an internal shake and turned his attention back to the matter at hand. In the Damager's hand. The Damager's big, strong hand…

"If Bread Man brought bombs, why didn't he set them off?" Smoke asked.

"Maybe he didn't hit what he wanted to hit, thanks to you."

In which case he'd be back, and probably soon, in the hopes of accomplishing his mission before anyone discovered the raisins' true purpose. Smoke grinned.

"Fancy a late-night sandwich, then?" he said.

* * *

If Kurtzberg was annoyed at being woken up by a couple of superheroes at one in the morning, he covered it by being annoyed at his building's heating system.

"It takes all day to warm up in here and then you have to turn it off and go home," Kurtzberg said, jabbing the thermostat with a gnarled finger. He and his family lived on the floor above the deli. "I've lived here my entire life, and not one day has this thing worked right."

"Don't worry about it," the Damager said. "I'm hoping we won't be long."

Smoke resisted the urge to conduct the search at superspeed. Better to slow down and let Kurtzberg search with them. He'd know better than either of them if something was amiss.

Despite visiting Kurtzberg's regularly, the place was unrecognizable at night. The poster-sized photos seemed to leap from the walls, the shadows around their black frames creating an odd, disjointed effect. Smoke was hyper-aware of every corner and every line of grout between the floor tiles.

They searched the tables and chairs, the shelves of food items for sale, the neatly bisected display counter—one half with meat-based dishes, the other half vegetarian. As Smoke stuck his nose into the supply closet, he asked Kurtzberg what he knew about the Bread Man and why the supervillain might be targeting him.

"Maybe I didn't put enough liverwurst in his sandwich."

"Now there's a thought," the Damager said, pausing in his search. "His name is the Bread Man. Bread is important to him. If he thought someone else was showing disrespect toward bread-kind, it could be enough to send him on a rampage."

"But said he was here to rob the place," said Smoke.

"And as we all know, supervillains always tell the truth." Smoke glared. Damager winked and grinned. Blast him. "I'm just saying, that if he was really on some kind of bread vendetta, wouldn't he want everyone to know it?"

"Maybe he's waiting for the right moment to make a big, splashy statement," Damager suggested, but he seemed less sure now.

They continued their search in the kitchen. It was even more cluttered than the storefront. Great shining appliances dominated the narrow space. An old-fashioned telephone hung from a stark white wall. On the opposite side, where the wall was brick, was a smallish green safe.

Damager rapped his knuckles on the safe door. "What's in there?"

"Nothing. It's to confuse thieves." Kurtzberg opened the safe. Empty. "The money from the cash register goes in the real safe upstairs until we take it to the bank. Everything else valuable, we keep in a safety deposit box."

"And those valuables are?" asked Smoke.

"Some jewelry, some dishes. And a written copy of our bagel recipe."

"Your bagel recipe?"

"Well, it's our recipe *now*. My grandfather got the recipe from the Polish guy he opened the deli with. When my grandfather bought him out, the buy-out included the bagel recipe. Everyone who works here has the recipe memorized, but we keep the original paper for old times' sake."

"So, this recipe is something special? No one else has it?" Damager said. He and Smoke exchanged a look, their minds racing down parallel tracks. Kurtzberg just looked offended.

"You've clearly never tried our bagels. Of course, it's special!"

"Special enough to steal," Smoke concluded. "Bread Man assumed the recipe was in the safe, or at least somewhere in the restaurant and tried to use the raisins to get it."

"There's a sentence you don't hear every day," said Damager.

They stood in silence, processing. Kurtzberg waggled the safe door back and forth, staring into its barren, black depths. Smoke tapped a finger against his lips.

"How many people know where you keep the original recipe?" Smoke asked.

"That I know of? Just me, my wife and our family. But they could have told any number of people. It's not a state secret."

"Then you won't mind if a few more people learn about it?"

* * *

Kurtzberg put on a magnificent show for the morning news, complaining how he no longer felt safe keeping his precious, valuable, irreplaceable bagel recipe in his kitchen safe.

"First thing after work, I'm going down to the bank and locking it up tight," he all but yelled into the microphone. The footage cut away after that to a brief clip of a reporter standing outside the deli and asking the camera when Boston's bread supply would be safe again. The segment re-aired in the evening, too. Hopefully Bread Man caught at least one of the broadcasts.

After the first broadcast, Smoke and Damager began shadowing Kurtzberg, watching, waiting, alert for any sign their adversary had swallowed the bait. When the Damager first arrived for duty, his shadowy costume endearingly out of place in the light of day, Smoke felt his heart sprout wings. He ruthlessly squashed that feeling. He refused to get butterflies about the fact that he was spending the day with the handsome superhero. And Smoke *knew* he was handsome, no matter what that mask might be hiding. The butterflies, however, refused to leave entirely, though they did agree to disappear into chrysalises for a while. That, Smoke supposed, was the best he could hope for.

Guarding Kurtzberg was not the most exciting

way to spend a day, even with Damager by his side. More than once, Smoke had to stare into the sun to keep his eyelids from drooping. He and Damager made flirtatious small talk here and there, but there were only so much bonding two fellows could do when one of them insisted on concealing his true name, life, interests and occupation. So, Smoke spent a lot of time counting the nanoseconds until Kurtzberg would close the deli and make good on his promise to go to New England Community Bank.

The bank stood on Franklin Street, between the Norwegian consulate and an upscale Japanese restaurant. Smoke was only familiar with this area of town because of the clothing store down the street, which had been on the verge of selling Melyssa's clothing line until the CEO killed the deal because their zodiac signs were incompatible.

Smoke told Damager that story, just to pass the time.

"I always knew you fashion people were loopy," Damager said, laughing.

"I'm both flattered and insulted. Flattered by you thinking I'm a 'fashion person' when I'm just a glorified secretary and insulted by you comparing me to some geriatric CEO who thinks chemtrails are dropping AIDS into our drinking water."

"I don't think anybody's 'just a' anything, especially not the people at the bottom of the ladder. I bet your whole workplace would fall apart without you."

The butterflies ripped out of their cocoons and scattered. Smoke scrambled for a normal response. "They do get cranky if no one's there to fetch the coffee first thing in the morning," he said, face warm.

Finally, as the sun dipped westward, Kurtzberg left the business of closing the deli to his sons and struck out for the bank. His protectors followed along the rooftops and fire escapes. With every step Kurtzberg took along the crowded sidewalk, Smoke expected the Bread Man to make his move. But no, that mush-brained troglodyte waited until Kurtzberg was almost at the bank, where security was far closer to hand than it was around an old deli.

A bus remodeled to look like a loaf of bread came screaming around the corner. Smoke was on the street in a second. He stopped between the bus and Kurtzberg.

The bus doors burst open. Bread Man leaped onto the sidewalk, bread gun at the ready.

"Welcome, hero! I see you've finally cleaned all that egg off your face," Bread Man said cheerfully. "But even you can't stop me from rising to the top of my profession! Now if you'd be so kind as to hand over the—ghhk!"

Bread Man went down. The Damager shook out his fist.

"Dude's got a hard head," he remarked. Smoke snatched Bread Man's gun away—a little bit tentatively, after what happened the last time. The gun sat inert in his hands as a slew of henchmen, each with a picture of a bread ingredient on their shirt, stormed out of the bus: Flour, Sugar, Baking Soda, Salt, Egg…

Smoke nudged Kurtzberg towards the bank. "If you would be so kind as to go inside and call the police? There's a good man."

Fighting alongside Damager—really alongside him, not a floor apart—thrilled Smoke. In the moment, he was preoccupied with settling into the unfamiliar

37

rhythm of working with a partner. By the time they knocked out the last henchman… well, it didn't quite feel like they'd been working together for years. But with a couple more fights like this one, it might.

The whole time, Kurtzberg and the people inside the bank were glued to the glass doors, watching the fight like it was award-winning television. Kurtzberg ventured outside again as Damager hauled their adversary to his feet. Though dazed, Bread Man recovered enough to spit, "This was all a trick!"

"Of course, it was a trick, you idiot," said Kurtzberg. "I don't even have the recipe on me."

Bread Man raised his fist. Damager yanked him back by the mask. Already loosened by the fight, the mask came off in his hand, releasing a shock of light brown hair. Bread Man ducked his head, but it was too late. Kurtzberg's eyes narrowed.

"Hey, wait a minute. You're that sleaze bucket dating my son, aren't you?"

Smoke spent the rest of the time before the police arrived keeping Kurtzberg from turning Bread Man's face inside out.

***

Smoke and Damager watched from a fire escape as the police pushed Bread Man into a squad car.

"Looks like he'll be on the cooling rack for a while," Smoke said innocently.

"Yeah," Damager agreed. "If only he wasn't so dense."

They both held out for as long as they could, but the police hadn't even left the scene before they burst into laughter. Smoke's eyes always seemed to shut of their own accord when he laughed this hard, but this time he fought to keep them open. He wanted to see what Damager looked like when he laughed, and he wasn't disappointed. His eyes, like most people's eyes, looked so much better when they were smiling.

Smoke took a breath. "Seriously this time. I'd like to be a cliché and get to know the man behind the mask."

The Damager sighed. "I'm afraid I'll have to be a cliché in return and disappear mysteriously into the night."

Smoke nodded, his throat tight. He could understand that. Perhaps Damager wasn't out to everyone in his life. Perhaps he didn't want to risk his heroic career for romance.

Perhaps he'd changed his mind and didn't think Smoke so attractive after all.

"I'll see you around," Smoke said. His smile was less sincere than before, but it was the best he could manage.

Damager's answering smile was faint but earnest. "Count on it."

* * *

Smoke did not see him around.

It wasn't like he was living as a shut-in, either. He went to work during the day and occasionally went out with friends in the evenings. He battled quite a few supervillains, all on his own. A couple of his co-workers commented on his victories, but for the most part, they'd grown used to having a superhero in the office. Sadiq didn't consider himself a glory hound, but he missed having someone to celebrate with. If only he'd gotten a job in DC or Los Angeles, where most of America's superheroes seemed to congregate.

But no, if he lived there, he'd never have met Damager. That just wasn't acceptable, no matter that his romantic aspirations had been dashed.

After Jummah that Friday, Sadiq turned his phone back on and found several messages from Melyssa, to the effect of *the office fridge finally died and everyone's stuff is ruined, please bring something edible on your way back.*

Kurtzberg's was the closest place that accommodated everyone's dietary needs, so he turned his steps in that direction. He swung his umbrella idly at his side. The weather had warned of showers throughout the day, but right now the sky was a light gray with a few inviting patches of blue. If the rain continued to hold off, maybe he'd take a walk through the Public Garden after work. Boston could get along without Smoke for one evening.

Sadiq scanned Kurtzberg's as he entered, just as a precaution. The place was practically empty. A large black man sat reading at a corner table. At the counter, an Asian woman took two salads from Kurtzberg as he waved goodbye to her little girl. Sadiq nodded to Kurtzberg as mother and daughter left, but he didn't get close enough to order yet. What would everyone want? Brad didn't like seafood, Lila didn't eat meat on Fridays, Nicolette only ate dairy on even-numbered days...

"Hey."

Sadiq turned. His eyes met those of the man in the corner. His hair fell around his broad shoulders in long, loose braids. A pile of books and a plate with a half-eaten sandwich took up about half the surface space of his table. The man offered him a nervous smile. Sadiq was about to ask if they'd met, but oh, those smiling eyes...

"I was hoping you'd come back here, so I set up shop," Damager said. "Kurtzberg's been keeping me in pastrami and lox."

"Don't you have a job?" was all Sadiq could think to say.

"I'm a professor. My students are on summer vacation, and so am I." His smile grew shakier. "Hey, if I'm overstepping, or if you don't want to see me..."

"No, no! It's just, my boss is expecting me back soon. Will—did you want to talk to me about something?"

"Yes, but it can wait. I'll be here."

"Will you? How do I know you won't change your mind?" *Again.* He'd had hope before, only to end up spending the following days staring vacantly at the walls while his neighbor cursed at his television.

The Damager took off his watch and handed it over. It was cheap, but there was an inscription on the back: *For Devon. Good luck and love always!*

"My parents gave me that when I left for college," Damager—Devon—said. "My dad passed the next year. So, I'll definitely be wanting that back."

Sadiq pocketed the watch with all the care it deserved. "I get off work at 4:30."

Then he walked up to the counter, heart hammering, fingers carefully tracing the watch face.

Devon was a much better name than Damager.

* * *

When Sadiq got back with the food, a greater catastrophe than a mere refrigeration failure had seized the office. A designer of Melyssa's acquaintance had been photographed on a yacht with three swimsuit models, none of whom were his wife. Sadiq spent the rest of the day answering braying telephones, informing bloodthirsty reporters that Melyssa did not comment on her colleagues' personal lives, and reassuring one paranoid investor that Melyssa was in no way involved with any intra-industry orgies.

By the time they got that squared away, Sadiq hardly had time to rush home, try out every permutation of every outfit he owned, settle on pale jeans and a dark T-shirt, and rush to Kurtzberg's as sunset dyed the clouds pink. Everyone in the deli looked up as the bell above the door clattered. The only person Sadiq cared about was sitting in the corner, right where he'd left him.

Devon's plate had been cleared away and replaced with a Styrofoam coffee cup. He was still on the same book—*The Silmarillion* by Tolkien—ambitious, as he'd been that afternoon, though the bookmark had moved significantly.

Devon smirked at him. "You have superspeed and you're late? What kind of clichéd BS is this? I gave you a watch and everything."

"Yes, well, fashion people don't go on summer vacation." Sadiq gave back the watch. Ten after five, the traitorous thing said. "Except for the ones who enjoy yacht orgies."

It should have been fun banter, but there was a tinge of desperation in Devon's snarking. Sadiq held out a hand. Devon's hand, wonderfully glove-free, was rough and warm and just a little sweaty.

42

"I don't believe we've been formally introduced. I'm Sadiq. Nasir."

"I know." The Damager startled and laughed sheepishly. "I might have looked you up after our first meeting."

Sadiq grinned. "Great minds think alike."

"I'm Devon. Gonçalves."

Sadiq pulled out a chair. It shrieked against the white-and-blue tiled floor. Around them, business continued as usual.

If Sadiq had thought to worry that his first date with the Damager wouldn't live up to his expectations, he'd have been reassured when Devon nearly dropped his bookmark into his coffee. They were both equally nervous wrecks.

They chatted for hours. Devon taught university-level math and occasionally Portuguese. He liked playing football, but couldn't stand to watch it. *Good*, Sadiq thought, his mind racing too far ahead as usual. *When we move in together, I won't have to put up with you shouting at the screen like my neighbor.* Sadiq's nerves calmed as they exchanged birthdays, sibling names, and favorite kinds of bagels, but he knew he'd never be at peace until he asked the one question that had been running around his brain for days.

"Why'd you change your mind?"

"Which time?" Devon said. His smile was just self-deprecating enough that Sadiq forgave him for everything immediately. "My whole life, all I've wanted to do is be useful to people. That's always been the most important thing. I never really thought about dating anyone seriously. I didn't even understand why anyone would want to. But then you flirted with me at the museum… and everywhere else. And it's so stupid, but I got this image in my head of driving on a rainy night and not being able to see the road, and then all of a sudden, the windshield wipers came on. That's what it felt like talking to you. Things getting clearer. At first, I was excited about it, but then I started thinking about what it might mean. Was I really ready to rearrange my entire life around the guy who sits on ducks in the middle of the night?"

Sadiq didn't protest that description. It was fair. Rude, but fair.

"So, I backed off," Devon continued. "I figured life would go back to normal after that. Instead, everything continued to be different, but now for the worse. And I thought to myself, what's so bad about change, anyway?"

"I thought you just didn't like me," Sadiq admitted. He softened the blow of those words with a laugh and a quick flip through the book on top of Devon's to-be-read pile. *The Ultimate Hitchhiker's Guide* by Douglas Adams—all five books in one.

"That was the one thought that never crossed my mind." Devon leaned in close and whispered, "I don't light my head on fire for just anyone."

* * *

Kurtzberg was clearly a romantic at heart, but his romanticism had a limit, and that limit was closing time. At 7:00 sharp, Sadiq and Devon were turned out onto Boston's steamy summer streets. It was a little late for the walk in the park Sadiq had envisioned earlier, so Devon offered to walk him home instead.

"Oh, my parents would love you," Sadiq quipped, and then he wanted to punch himself. It was way too soon to be joking about meeting parents!

But Devon just asked, "Your parents live around here?"

"Only if you count Glasgow as 'around here.' Which I do, since I can run there and back in a couple of minutes."

"Not bad. But can you do this?"

Devon glanced around to make sure no one was watching and stabbed his hand with a pen. The pen shattered. The hand was just fine.

"So, if pens start falling from the sky, you're all set. Big deal," Sadiq said, grinning.

"Hey, it could happen. What if Boston's next big supervillain is the Pen Master and he or she attacks the city with writing implements? Who'll be laughing then?"

The playful debate lasted until they arrived at Sadiq's apartment door. For the first time in his life, Sadiq wished he'd moved slower.

"Thanks for coming to find me," Sadiq said, playing with his keys. To the rest of the world, they would have looked like two ordinary fellows, if one ignored the super-speed drumming of Sadiq's fingers against his thigh, and the fact that Devon was swinging a satchel of five fat books like it was a bag of popcorn.

"Maybe we can meet up again sometime?" Devon said.

"As ourselves or as our other selves?"

"Preferably both. As ourselves, we could hit the Freedom Trail over the weekend?" Sadiq nodded his agreement. "And as our other selves, maybe we could form a team."

45

"You really want to?" Sadiq didn't even bother to hide his excitement this time.

"Why not? We kick ass. It'd be a shame to deny the city's supervillains the beatdowns they deserve. We could coordinate, like surf and turf, or ebony and... uh, bronze?"

"Nice save." Sadiq jangled his keys. "If either of us is changing names, it's not going to be me."

"First you diss my powers, now my codename. Is this how dating is supposed to go? Because I feel like it isn't."

"I'm a fashion person, remember? Coordination is right in my wheelhouse."

"Fine, fine. I'll think of something." He thumped the satchel against his leg a few times. "How about Fire?"

"Isn't that a little generic?"

"Maybe. But you know what they say: where there's Smoke..."

Trust Paradox
By Naomi Hinchen

"So how was your week?" says Mark. I cram a forkful of fettuccine into my mouth before I can blurt out the truth. *Well, I stopped a bank robbery, a couple of muggings, and a mad scientist trying to turn the city council into chinchillas, so... pretty typical. Hey, want dessert?*

"Oh, you know," I say after swallowing my mouthful of pasta. "Same old, same old. I got caught up at work." In a manner of speaking.

"Ugh, me too," says Mark. "Mostly because my boss is an asshole who can't set a realistic deadline."

"Uh-oh. Is he making you crunch again?"

Mark rolls his eyes. "Someday maybe he'll learn that when we say, 'this will take a month,' yelling louder won't get it done by Friday. But I'm getting really into the new learning algorithms…"

When he's not griping about his boss, Mark lights up when he talks about his robotics work, sitting up straighter and gesturing wildly with his fork. I enjoy his enthusiasm, even if I can't share it; fighting killer androids as often I have tends to dampen the appeal of robots. But I don't mind letting him wax poetic about neural nets for a while.

"…and it turned out that the problem was with the servos the whole time!" he says. "So, don't mind me,

47

after a week of this I'm pretty much running on caffeine and inertia."

"As opposed to the way you are the rest of the time?" I say innocently.

"Ouch," says Mark. "Touché. But yes, worse than usual. I was seriously tempted to call off date night and sleep all weekend." He smiles, revealing the hint of a dimple. "But who knows when we might get our schedules to align again?"

I try not to visibly wince, because that one's on me. I've canceled on Mark at the last minute twice already, when unavoidable saving-the-city business came up. Sometimes I think Murphy's Law has it in for superheroes in particular.

"I'll do my best not to disappoint, then," I say.

"Who said I meant you?" says Mark. "It was worth the overtime for this ravioli."

I snort and swat him on the arm. Very gently, because at full strength I could punch through solid steel. "I hope you and the ravioli are very happy together, then. Remember to invite me to the wedding."

"Really, though," says Mark. "I know it's only been a couple of months, but... this is going well, isn't it?"

"It is," I say. "I promise I haven't been avoiding you on purpose. My life is just like that."

That must have been the right thing to say, because the smile is back. "Good. I like you a lot, Melanie. I want to be sure you feel the same way about me."

I can't help the small, pleased flutter I feel at the words. I want to say *I like you a lot, too*, but somehow what comes out of my mouth is, "You haven't known me for very long. For all you know, I'm hiding a deep, dark secret."

Dammit, I need to stuff my mouth with pasta again and stop myself from talking. I take a sip from my water glass instead.

"Are you trying to find a nice way to break it to me that you're an axe murderer?" he says. "No, wait, you're a werewolf. Or, I know, you're an internationally famous pop star in disguise."

I spray the entire table with water as I break into helpless laughter. Probably more than the joke really deserves, out of context.

Mark grins ruefully. "Okay, I admit, my little sister used to watch a lot of Hannah Montana."

So close and yet so far. I imagine explaining it to him. *Actually, I can't carry a tune in a bucket, but you're right that you might recognize me in a different outfit...*

"Yeah," I say when I can speak again. "You got me. I'm Hannah Montana."

We're up to the tiramisu when Mark starts fiddling with his napkin again. "I did have something I wanted to ask you," he says. "I know we haven't talked about exclusivity yet..."

And right then I hear a muffled beeping. Oh, crap, it's the Super Society alert. See what I mean about Murphy's Law?

"I'm not seeing anyone else," I say. "If that's what you wanted to know. But hold that thought." I dig my phone out of my purse. If they're calling me outside my patrol hours again, the world had damn well better be on fire.

Alien invasion. Didn't we have one last week? Still, that really is an all-hands-on-deck situation.

"Sorry, I have to go," I say.

"Right now?" says Mark.

49

I stand up, tugging my skirt into place. "It's work, sorry." I drop a couple of twenties on the table for my share of the bill. "I'm the girl they call when the servers are on fire."

I can see a little crease forming on Mark's forehead, and I wonder for a panicky second if he's figured out that I'm bending the truth. But all he says is, "It's a little late to be going to the office, isn't it?"

I shrug helplessly. "I leave them alone for a few hours and the place goes to hell." I drop a quick kiss on his cheek. "I'll call you later."

Really, we were lucky to make it to dessert.

* * *

"You're late, Asteria," says Captain Terra.

"It was date night," I say, launching into the air to dodge a squirt of slime from one of the aliens. They look like giant glistening slugs, except with legs, and most of the team is already coated in goo an inch thick. I wonder if anyone's thought to try sprinkling them with salt.

"It's the nature of the job," says Captain Terra sternly. "The safety of the city is at stake. We don't have time to wait around for your personal life."

I roll my eyes. Fortunately, I'm encased in cobalt-blue magical power armor and Terra can't see my expression.

"Don't listen to her," calls Mighty Mammoth, currently towering 10 stories high and squashing slugs underfoot. "She's just jealous because she doesn't have a personal life of her own."

"I heard that," Captain Terra calls back. "Mammoth, you're on slime cleanup duty later."

"Ouch," I mutter. "Harsh."

"It's not a punishment," Captain Terra says serenely. "It's an object lesson in courtesy to one's teammates and respect for the chain of command." She punctuates this by parkouring off a building and kicking an alien in the face.

Terra is a baseline human with no enhancements or special abilities, but she holds her own among teammates with mutant powers, magic and cybernetic implants. This tells you everything you need to know about why she's team leader.

She lands on her feet, not even out of breath, and says, "Asteria, go help Lady Jupiter clear out Aspen Street. Get any remaining civilians out of the way."

"Roger that," I say, and take off again.

I spot Lady Jupiter in her skintight purple leather, repelling aliens with her mental shield, and land smoothly behind her so we can stand back to back.

"Asteria! Hey, girl," says Lady J. "We can't even go a week without the planet being invaded, huh?"

"Tell me about it," I say, shooting an energy beam at the nearest slug. "I was on a date."

"The same guy you've been seeing?" says Lady J. "How's that going?"

Lady Jupiter is probably my closest friend these days, which is sad when you consider we don't even know each other's real names. Not that this has ever stopped superheroes from gossiping. In some ways it's like high school all over again.

"Good, I think," I say. "He wants to be exclusive."

"Ooh," says Lady J. "You like him, huh? Are you going to tell him?"

"Tell him what?" I say.

51

"You know what."

Of course, I know. It's the elephant in the room in a superhero's every relationship. "Not yet," I say. "It's too soon to think about that."

"Maybe, but you *are* thinking about it."

That's the downside of being friends with a telepath. They always know more of your business than you want them to.

Lava Man charges in from the other side of the street, scattering slugs before him in a wave of fire. "Hey ladies. What are we talking about?"

"Asteria's deciding whether to tell her boyfriend she's a superhero," says Lady J shamelessly.

"You can't make it work long-term without honesty," says Lava Man sagely, hurling a fireball that takes out two slug-aliens at once.

"It's too soon," I say. "I can't tell someone I don't know that well yet. Remember Alphaman?"

Lady J shudders. "All too well, thanks. Hey, look out behind you!"

"Who's Alphaman?" says Lava Man.

"Before your time," I say. "He had to resign."

"Resign? Why?"

"Well, he picked up this girl in a bar one night, and somewhere in the course of things he let slip his secret identity…"

Lady Jupiter snorts. "Let slip, my ass. What do you bet he was all, 'Hey baby, I'm Alphaman. Want to see my super stamina in action?" She's probably right. Alphaman was kind of a bro.

"And the next day she sold the story to the *Daily Sentinel*," I say. "It was all we talked about for weeks."

"Last I heard he had changed his name and moved to Nebraska," says Lady J.

"Telling your boyfriend isn't the same as telling a one-night stand," says Lava Man. "There's got to be trust or the relationship will never work."

"Uh-huh," Lady J says. "And how are things going with you and Destructor these days?"

The visible part of Lava Man's face goes redder than his mask. "Look, I'm not saying it was *easy* finding out Kyle was a supervillain. But he's practically reformed now! And he'll be out of prison in another month!"

With relief, I let the subject turn to Lava Man and Destructor's star-crossed affair, a train wreck we've all been watching with morbid fascination, and which successfully distracts Lady Jupiter from *my* love life.

* * *

There's no right time to tell someone you're a superhero.

Long-term partners have to find out eventually, because they deserve to make an informed decision about the risks of proximity to a superhero. Besides, once you move in together the other person will inevitably figure it out. It's like not telling your partner you're a werewolf—eventually they'll connect the fur clogging the shower drain with your tendency to cancel plans at the full moon.

But *when* to come clean is the hard part. You can't just spill your secret identity to any Tom, Dick or Harry on OKCupid, who might turn out to be a supervillain or a journalist or a garden-variety vindictive asshole. You need to know them well enough to trust them and that takes time.

But wait too long and you risk destroying *their* trust in *you*. There's a limit to how strong a relationship you can build with someone you're constantly lying to. And the longer you've been together, the less thrilled your partner will be to learn that you've been keeping secrets. In the worst cases, this ends in divorce— because however soon is too soon, after you've put a ring on, it is definitely too late.

So, there's the paradox. Tell them before you've built trust and risk finding out they're not trustworthy, or build trust first and risk destroying it?

How long do you wait? Is it about how long you've been dating? How serious the relationship is? I haven't found the sweet spot yet. Maybe there isn't one.

* * *

Hours after leaving Mark at the restaurant, I crawl in through my apartment window, exhausted and covered in space slug slime. I want to collapse into bed for about 24 hours, armor and all, but experience tells me that the slime stains will *never* come out of my sheets.

Instead, I run a hot bath. I close my eyes, touch the amulet embedded in my chest, and allow my magical armor to discorporate. Unfortunately, the slime doesn't disappear with it. It's now dripping from my date clothes, which I'd forgotten I was wearing before the call came in. Grimacing, I shuck off the outfit into a pile on the bathroom floor, where it soon forms a gooey brown puddle that smells like compost in the sun. Ugh, I'm too tired to deal with this. I'll scrub the tiles in the morning. Or possibly tear up the floor and start from scratch.

I more or less fall into the bath, where I lie soaking in the warm water until I nearly fall asleep right there. As I drag myself out of the tub and in the general direction of my bed, I remember I told Mark I would call. Well, I can't call him now, it's... some ungodly hour of the morning. I really should at least text him, I suppose, after rushing out of there.

When I gingerly retrieve my civilian phone from the slimy mess of my discarded clothes, the little blue message light is already blinking. A dozen Slack pings from work—I really do have a day job that calls at all hours—and a voicemail from Mark.

An awkward throat-clearing. "Hey, Melanie. I guess you're not home yet." A pause, then in a rush: "Look, since dinner got cut short, do you want to try doing something this weekend? I know your schedule is crazy and all, but... you know, you didn't get to eat the tiramisu, so if you wanted to try that dessert course again sometime, there's a really nice bakery over on Third Street. Call it a do-over. So, uh... let me know."

That's better than I was hoping for, actually. I must have it bad if I'm finding this level of awkwardness cute, but my spirits rise a little at the prospect of a do-over date. Maybe this time we'll make it all the way to the end.

I know. I should really know better than to tempt fate like that.

* * *

The rescheduled date starts out well enough. We pick up dessert at the bakery which, true to Mark's recommendation, does an amazing chocolate éclair, then take our picnic lunch to the park. It's a beautiful Saturday, and for once I have a no-strings day off. A couple of friends on the Super Society are covering my on-call shift and have sworn not to call me for anything less than planet-threatening.

We spread the picnic blanket out by the big rock that looks like a horse's head. Plenty of other people have come out to enjoy the sun, and we're close enough to the playground to hear children shrieking with laughter on the swings.

"This is nice," I say. Normal, is what I don't say out loud. Mundane. I've learned to appreciate those qualities.

I open the picnic basket. "Okay, did you want the turkey sandwiches or the ham and cheese?"

Mark doesn't answer. I wave a hand in front of his face. "Mark? Earth to Mark?"

He shakes his head, like a dog shaking off water. "Sorry, I was distracted for a moment. Can you hear that?"

Now that I'm listening, I do hear it. "Sort of a... thumping?"

"Yeah. Maybe there's a busker somewhere playing the drums?"

"No," I say, frowning. "It sounds like something bigger." Almost like giant footsteps...

A moment later, the screaming starts.

I'm on my feet right away—it's a reflex now—mentally cataloguing *something growling* and *was that an explosion?* and *oh God, the playground, there are kids here...*

"What was that?" says Mark.

"I think it's a supervillain attack," I say.

"Oh, you have got to be kidding me," moans Mark.

Just then the source of the footsteps crashes through the nearest fence and turns out to be a *dragon*. I suppose it's not that big as dragons go—and yes, I've seen enough dragons to have a standard—but it's eight feet high and a good 10 yards long, plenty big enough.

I grab Mark's hand and drag him behind a sturdy oak tree. Not that this will be much protection if the thing breathes fire (and with the smoke trailing ominously from its nostrils, it probably does), but at least if we get under cover, it's less likely to notice us before I can come up with a plan. Which I should really get busy doing. Any second now.

"You can't hide from me!" shrieks a voice. Is this a *talking* dragon? I risk peering out from behind the tree.

It's not the dragon talking. There's a pale, raven-haired woman perched on its back, wearing a flowing purple robe embroidered with astrological symbols. Oh, hey, it's Mistress Mystical. I haven't fought her in a couple of months. I suppose she was due to try something.

She's waving a staff with a crystal ball on the end. No, not waving it. She's sweeping it in an arc in front of her...

...and suddenly the ball glows blue right as she points it at the tree we're hiding behind.

"Aha!" cries Mistress Mystical. "Yes, there is a powerful artifact here."

Oh, shit. Whatever she's planning needs a power

source, so she's scanning for magic items... such as the amulet that gives me my abilities. Which is embedded in my chest, so I can't throw it into the bushes to misdirect her, even if I was willing to risk it falling into her hands. I have to get Mark clear before she pounces on us.

"Let's split up," I blurt out.

Mark looks at me like I'm crazy. "What? That sounds like a good way to lose track of each other."

"Um, the dragon," I say, improvising. "The tree won't hide us for long. I, uh, saw a thing about reptiles on the Discovery Channel. If we run in different directions, we'll confuse it, and it won't know which of us to focus on."

Mark looks doubtful, as well he might. I can't give him time to think. "Run!" I push him in one direction and go running the opposite way. Behind me, I can hear Mark's footsteps receding. With luck, he'll run far enough away to miss this next part.

I make it safely to shelter behind the horse-shaped rock. Once out of sight, I reach under my blouse and touch the amulet. The magical armor forms around me like a warm embrace.

I have to admit, while it's fun to rag on villains for their overdeveloped sense of drama, the good guys are far from immune to a flair for theatrics. I take a certain pleasure in looming up from behind the rock and booming out, "Surrender, evildoer!"

Mistress M plays her role beautifully, too. "Asteria," she sneers. "I should have known that was you I was sensing. Such a waste of power, to wield it so bluntly. Well, now that I have you where I want you, I'll take your power source and be rid of you once and for all." She points the staff at a bench and in a flash of light transforms it into a zebra. Now that's just showing off.

I glance towards the oak tree, but Mark seems to have gone. Good. I roll my shoulders, limbering up for the fight. "You picked the wrong day to mess with me," I say.

It turns out that punching a dragon is really good therapy for a ruined date. Sadly, this is probably not the last time that will be relevant to my life.

By the time I've subdued Mistress Mystical and the dragon, the civilians have mostly cleared out of the park, minus the few rubberneckers who are willing to risk injury or magical curses to get a selfie at a superhero battle. Mark isn't one of them. I hope he didn't spend too long looking for me.

I call him when I get home, if only to reassure him I wasn't trampled by the dragon.

"You were right," I say. "Splitting up was a good way to get separated. I came back to the picnic lawn later, but you must have left. The basket got kind of trampled, sorry."

"Not your fault," says Mark. I bite my tongue before I can contradict him. "I'm glad you're all right. Even if our date got interrupted. Again."

On impulse, I say, "You know what, screw going out. Want to come over to my place and order Chinese while we make out on the couch?"

I can hear the smile in his voice when he says, "Sure, that sounds great."

* * *

We're lounging on my couch with Chinese takeout, flipping through channels, when I pause on a news report about the fight in the park. I hadn't noticed the news helicopters, but they got some good shots of me giving the dragon a righteous smackdown. It's weird watching it from an outside perspective.

"Yeah!" I fist-pump as my image on the screen uses an energy blast to deflect Mistress Mystical's staff, a blast of magic going wild and turning a very confused squirrel bright green.

Mark gives me a strange look. "It's not as if you know Asteria."

Not as far as he knows, anyway. "I can still want her to win," I say. "She's protecting all of us."

Mark looks troubled, and fiddles with his chopsticks. He seems to want to say something but doesn't, so I turn back to the TV. I've put the cuffs on Mistress Mystical, and the report has cut back to the newscaster, when Mark says, "I don't really like superheroes."

I drop my fortune cookie. This is probably for the best, as diving to retrieve it lets me cover my initial reaction. When I come back up, I say "You don't?"

"Never have," says Mark. "I don't like the secrecy. No one is supposed to know who they are, even though some of them could level the city if they chose."

"There are people who use superhuman powers for destruction," I say. "We call them supervillains. That's who superheroes are there to fight, Mark. It seems unfair to put the blame on the Super Society for what they're trying to stop."

"But there's no way for an outside force to hold

them accountable," says Mark. "It's kind of a clique, isn't it? It's up to the supers to police each other if one of them goes off the deep end. How do you know that the people who protect the city today won't be a threat to it tomorrow? And when one of them does go wrong, are the others going to turn a blind eye because it's their friend?"

"Of course not," I say. "They're the good guys."

Mark gives me a tolerant look, as if it's cute how naive I am. And I can't very well tell him I know these people and trust them to do the right thing.

"So, you don't think we should have the Super Society?" I say, my heart sinking. "It's not like super*villains* are going to go away for the asking. If not superheroes, who's going to fight them?"

"We have the police and the military for a reason," he says. "They can recruit people with powers if they like. But I don't like the anonymity. Masked vigilantes running around punching people? They could be anyone."

"Maybe they have good reasons for wanting to be anonymous. They deserve safety, too. They deserve private lives." My voice is starting to rise.

Mark might have a point about accountability in the event someone goes rogue but revealing our identities to everyone can't be the answer. Mark, for example, would be much less safe if my identity became public.

Assuming he still wanted anything to do with me once he found out.

"You're awfully touchy about this," he says, frowning.

"I happen to like not getting murdered by mutant

escapees from a mad scientist's lab, thanks." I take a deep breath and try to calm down before Mark can start to wonder why this topic has struck a nerve. Fortunately, the news is playing a segment on the local aquarium's new baby seals, and I can pretend to be distracted by the cuteness.

But I'm not really paying attention, because the question of when to tell Mark my identity has now taken a backseat to the question of when to break up with him. I can't date someone who doesn't approve of superheroes. I don't have many ironclad relationship dealbreakers, but for obvious reasons, that's one of them.

Still, I can't do it right away. He might get suspicious if I dump him a hot second after he tells me he doesn't like superheroes. I should wait a few days. Maybe a week or so. Just to space it out.

* * *

We're still together a month later.

I can't bring myself to break up with him. I don't *want* to break up with him.

Which means that the question of when I should tell him my secret identity is back on the table. With the added fun of how I can break it to him in a way that will magically change all his opinions on superheroes, instead of causing him to break up with me.

Sure, should be a piece of cake.

The fight with Mistress Mystical is far from the last time the superhero side of my life intrudes on our relationship. There's the time I can't even call Mark because I've been dosed with truth serum and I'm blurting out my deepest secrets. I get Lady Jupiter to tell him I have laryngitis, and she laughs so hard she almost drops the phone. Then the Super Society all get body-swapped with each other. Luckily Captain Terra gets my body, so she doesn't do anything too outrageous, but she says Mark gave her some strange looks while she was pretending to be me. Not to mention the time with the cannibal mermaids—don't ask.

But life goes on. I go over to Mark's place a few times, and it's nice. Domestic. We get takeout and watch black and white movies from his couch. I lean my head on his shoulder and think about what it would be like to have this all the time. Someone to come home to.

Now and then, we manage to go on an outing that isn't interrupted by superhero shenanigans. We drive out into the country for a hike, and when evening comes, we linger on a hillside, looking up at the stars. Neither of us really knows any astronomy, but we don't let that stop us.

"That one is the Teddy Bear," says Mark, pointing at the sky and sketching an imaginary constellation with his finger. "And next to it there's the Bicycle With a Flat Tire."

"Over on the horizon," I say, "you can see the Missing Sock You Lost in the Dryer."

"So that's where it went. I was starting to wonder."

I lean against his shoulder, and he puts his arm around me. I lean back a little so I can see Mark smiling up at the sky, and for that brief, perfect moment I think I could tell him everything. My superhero identity, my powers, the real reasons for the interrupted dates. But I don't want to mar this perfect night.

Mark looks at me and his smile grows wider. "Penny for your thoughts?"

Normally I'd respond with a joke—*I feel like you're lowballing me*—or playfully demand an actual penny before I'll say anything. But tonight, I don't feel like teasing. "Nothing," I say. "I'm happy to be here with you."

He pulls me in to lean against his shoulder again. "Yeah. Me too."

* * *

Except then it all comes crashing down.

We're at a coffee shop, two cups of coffee going cold on the table between us, and Mark is saying, "I can't do this anymore."

I fiddle with the little bowl of sugar packets to avoid meeting his eyes. "For what it's worth, I'm sorry. I know it can't be fun getting ditched all the time, but it's part of the package."

"It's not that," he says. "Well, it is, a little. I don't mind you having an unpredictable schedule or having work emergencies. That happens. Hell, it happens to me, too. It's just…"

"Yes?"

"That is what you're doing, isn't it? Going in to work?"

"Yes, of course," I say, trying to sound baffled that he could think anything else. But my heart has started to pound, and I wonder how much he knows.

"I stopped by your office Friday night. I thought I'd bring you dinner. Offer you a ride home. But the receptionist said you weren't in. Said you had left early, in fact."

I should have expected this, sooner or later. The whole house of cards tumbling down around me.

"So, I have to wonder," says Mark, "why you canceled on me, if you weren't really at work. And what you were doing instead."

"What are you implying, Mark?" I say. "That I'm cheating on you? I'm not."

"I don't know what you're doing, but clearly it isn't what you told me. And it's not the first time. You're always rushing off early or canceling plans at the last minute or trying to make me swallow flimsy excuses. Sometimes I catch you acting strange and you blow it off. There's some bigger picture here that I'm not seeing. What is going on with you? Why are you lying to me?"

I look down at the sugar packets again. "I can't explain. I'm sorry."

Mark runs a hand through his hair. "Look, I'm under a lot of stress right now. There's a big project at work, and my sister might be getting a divorce. I can't deal with wondering what's going on with you on top of that. Whatever it is, tell me." He looks into my eyes, pleading. "Please, give me some kind of explanation that makes sense."

I want to tell him, but I'm not sure he'll take it well. And what if I tell him, and he breaks up with me anyway?

I've hesitated too long. His expression closes up again. "So it's like that." He gets to his feet and throws

65

down enough cash to pay for his coffee. "Goodbye, Mel."

"Mark, wait—"

But he's already walking away, and he doesn't turn around.

* * *

During our watch shift on the Super Society surveillance monitors, Lady Jupiter sits on the couch with me and pats my back as I work my way through a pint of mint chocolate chip ice cream. Sunbeam is there too, straddling the back of a chair and watching me like I'm their new favorite soap opera.

"I really liked him," I say morosely into the carton.

"I know, sweetie," says Lady J. Right, telepath.

"I thought maybe he was getting to be okay with the weird hours and interruptions, but then he dumped me out of the blue. Who does that?"

"Lots of people, unfortunately," says Lady J. "That's not a superhero dating problem, that's a dating problem."

"I'm going to die old and alone," I moan.

"Don't be an idiot," Sunbeam says cheerfully. "You're going to die young at the hands of a maniac with a death ray."

"Not helping, Sunny," says Lady J.

"What you need is a rebound," says Sunbeam. "I hear the Ruby Rescuer is single."

"No," I say firmly. "No other heroes."

"Didn't you date Knight Errant for a couple of months?" says Sunbeam.

I wince. "Okay, first of all, that was an accident. We didn't recognize each other out of our armor. And he's why I have that rule, actually."

"It ended badly?"

"I mean, as breakups go it wasn't that bad, but then afterwards... why do you think he moved to California?" I can't really blame him. Imagine seeing your ex every time you went to work, at a job that requires trusting each other implicitly, with not only your own lives but the fate of countless innocents. Yeah. That's why I don't date other heroes anymore.

I've finished the mint chocolate chip and started on a pint of rocky road when the emergency alert goes off.

"Seems like you might need to punch someone right now," says Lady Jupiter. "Lucky you, a villain somewhere has just volunteered."

It's the most cheering thing anyone has said to me all day.

"Somewhere" turns out to be "right here"—a robot horde is besieging the Super Society's skyscraper headquarters.

"At least we don't have to travel very far to find him," says Sunny. "Silver lining."

"I knew we should have gone for a hidden base," mutters Lady Jupiter, peering down from the window. "Putting HQ in the middle of downtown is like hanging out a sign saying 'Here we are! Come at us!'"

One of the robots is carrying a sort of sedan chair containing a bald man in a lab coat. He pulls out a megaphone and starts monologuing into it: his name is Doctor Iniquity, he's going to take us down once and for all, the other supervillains will flock to him as their leader, what's America coming to when a man can't build killer robots without being suppressed by the nanny state, blah blah blah. I tune it out after a while. The more concerning part is that robots shaped like giant spiders are starting to crawl up the side of the building.

"I'll keep an eye on the cameras from here," says Lady J. "Sunbeam, Asteria, you're both fliers. Think you can pick them off from the air?" I'm climbing out the window almost before she's finished speaking.

One of the underappreciated perks of the superhero life is catharsis. Right now, it feels really good to drop some spider-bots 20 stories to the ground, or blast them with energy beams, or grab one by its spindly legs and smash it into another one.

"Whoa," says Sunbeam from behind me. "Um, maybe rein it in a little, A?"

I look down and realize I've been pummeling the same robot long after it stopped moving, beating its severed head into a heap of scrap metal and wires.

"Oops," I say.

Sunbeam pats me on the shoulder. "Feeling better?"

"Maybe a little."

"Good," says Lady J through my earpiece, "because I need your head in the game. Is it me or is the bad doctor having some trouble with his controls?"

I look down. Sure enough, Doctor Iniquity's megaphone picks up the sounds of him cursing as he savagely yanks at the levers of a handheld controller.

"I'm picking up two different control signals on the same frequency," says Lady J. "Looks like someone is trying to hijack the bots."

"Maybe," says Sunbeam. "But I'm not sure they're an ally. Look."

They point at the next wave of spider-bots swarming up the building. Unlike the first wave, these aren't attacking us—but they are trying to break in through the windows.

I glance down and notice an unmarked van parked across the street. "I think I know where to find the hacker. Sunny, you got it covered here?"

"Oh, don't worry about me," says Sunbeam. "Some more doses of bot-frying radiation coming right up."

I zoom down to street level, land next to the van, and wrench the back door open. I really hope this *is* the hacker, or some poor pizza delivery driver is about to get the shock of their life.

It's not a pizza delivery.

The back of the van is wired up with control panels full of little switches and levers, as well as screens showing a robot's-eye view of the side of the skyscraper. The whole setup has clearly been retrofitted into the van in a hurry, and there's an unruly tangle of wires visible underneath. A man in a gray hoodie sits cross-legged in the back of the van, one hand on the controls and the other holding a can of Mountain Dew.

Then the man looks up, and it's Mark.

I freeze, and he freezes, and we both stare at each other for a moment.

"Are you the one who's taken control of the robots?" I say.

Mark raises his eyebrows. "No, I just happen to be parked across the street with a van full of electronics by sheer coincidence." When I don't respond, he sighs. "Yeah, I didn't think you'd buy that either."

He doesn't seem surprised to see me. But then, he doesn't know it's me. All he knows is that he's been caught by a superhero.

"Can you deactivate them?" I say.

"I could," he says. "The question is, do I want to?"

"You're not working with Doctor Iniquity over there, are you?"

Mark snorts. "Oh, hell, no. I mean, he's technically my boss, but he doesn't know I'm here." Mark's asshole boss, right. At a robotics company. "No, I... borrowed... some company equipment to piggyback on his plan."

"Then what are you doing?"

It's a long shot. I doubt he'll actually tell me. But to my surprise, he says, "I'm after your records."

"Records?"

"You all go around hiding your faces," says Mark. "Taking the law into your own hands. Let's see how you like it in the spotlight."

The pieces fall into place. "You're after the identity database."

The Super Society keeps records of its members. Access is on a need-to-know basis, and usually, even the other members don't need to know. But we keep it for emergencies: in case one of us goes missing, or someone dies in the line of duty and their family needs to be informed. The database isn't connected to any outside network, so anyone wanting access to it would have to get inside our HQ.

Or send a robot inside.

"And what would you do with that information, if you had it?" In a detached way, I note that my voice is perfectly steady.

"Release it on the Internet," he says. "Maybe gift it to a few journalists. It's all coming out, one way or another."

"I can't let you do that."

"You can't stop me. Even if you destroy my equipment, I've already sent the robots their new instructions. And your team seems a bit short-staffed at the moment." He nods at a screen, where Sunbeam is struggling to keep up with the wave of spider-bots. "I only need one to get inside and find your servers."

"But you could stop them. You could send a signal to stand them down."

"And why would I do that?"

"Because you shouldn't be invading our privacy. Because releasing our identities would put targets on the backs of everyone we love. Because once the information is out there, you can't put the genie back in the bottle."

"Don't we all deserve to know who's patrolling our streets? If a suspect gets beaten up by a cop, they can sue the police department. What can someone who's beaten up by a superhero do?"

"Who watches the watchmen?" I murmur.

"Exactly," says Mark.

Through my earpiece, I can hear Sunbeam cursing a blue streak at the spider-bots. "Any time now, A," they grunt. "I can't keep them all out for long."

"I know these people," I say to Mark. "I promise you, we're the good guys."

"Well, you would say that, wouldn't you? Why should I believe you?"

He doesn't trust me. Of course not. As far as he

71

knows, I'm a stranger. There's only one card left to play, and it's a risk. It could backfire on me, hard. But it might be my best shot at winning him over.

"Give us a chance," I say. "Give *me* a chance to prove to you that the city is in good hands."

He looks wary. "How do you propose to do that?"

"If I show you, you'll deactivate the robots?"

Mark frowns, considering. "And you won't arrest me right afterwards?"

"I think we can come to an arrangement," I say. "You'll have helped us defeat Doctor Iniquity, after all."

After a tense moment, Mark nods. "Okay. Give me a reason to trust you."

Trust. That's the key, isn't it? Mark has to trust that I won't arrest him. I have to trust that he'll keep his word and deactivate the robots. And I don't know if this will make him trust me or shatter all trust between us forever, but I have to try. Time for a leap of faith.

I reach up, slowly and deliberately, and take off my helmet.

Mark's jaw drops. Under other circumstances, it might have been funny.

"Melanie?" he says. "You're Asteria?"

I don't know if I've made things better or much, much worse. "This is that bigger picture you weren't seeing. I'm sorry I didn't tell you before."

"You told me you worked in IT," says Mark dazedly.

"I do. I just… happen to have a second job."

"You lied to me. For months."

"I'm still the same person. The way I felt about

you wasn't a lie. And I'm telling you, so you'll understand why I don't want my identity to get out. You saw how much of my life this encroaches on already. I want to preserve as much private life as I can, where I'm Melanie and not Asteria."

Mark is still staring. I take a deep breath and add, "And now, whether you get the database or not, you know one superhero's secret identity. I'm trusting that you'll do the right thing with it."

I stay where I am, holding very still, as I wait to see which way he'll jump.

Abruptly, Mark flips a switch. I turn towards the Super Society headquarters in time to see the spider-bots go limp and drop off the building to the ground. Doctor Iniquity vents a scream of rage into his megaphone.

I let out a long, slow breath I hadn't realized I was holding.

"Okay," says Mark. "I don't know if you've convinced me, but I'll back off the database, and I'll keep your secret. So I'm going to be very annoyed if you turn around and arrest me after all."

* * *

Mark doesn't get arrested. Doctor Iniquity does, without much of a fight. His robots might be scrappers, but the man himself has the hand-to-hand combat skills of a wet noodle. When we report the incident to Captain Terra, I convince her that Mark is a potentially useful civilian ally, and she agrees to overlook his attempted break-in by robot.

Afterwards, Mark and I end up back at my place,

watching the robot attack on the news. Or pretending to watch it, while sneaking glances at each other when we each think the other isn't looking.

I break first. "So, what happens now?"

"I suppose I'm out of a job. And somehow I doubt Doctor Iniquity will give me a reference." Mark's shoulders slump. "I'll probably end up working at a Starbucks. At least there my boss won't be a literal supervillain."

"Don't jinx it," I say. "The sinister Professor Coffeebean may be about to spring his master plan." That gets a laugh out of him. I want to keep being the one to make him laugh. "What I meant was, what happens now with you and me?"

He goes quiet. That doesn't seem like a good sign. "So much makes sense now," he says after a moment. "Like where you were always running off to, and why you disappeared when Asteria fought the dragon lady in the park." He huffs a laugh. "You practically told me once, didn't you? Hannah Montana. I feel like an idiot for not figuring it out."

"Are you angry that I never told you?"

"I don't know. Maybe a little bit. But I can't blame you too much, especially after I told you I didn't like superheroes."

"I hope I can change your mind about that."

"It makes a difference, knowing it's you. And I think that's an argument for going public—let us know the heroes protecting us as people, not just as superheroes. But you had a point. You deserve as much of a normal life as you can make for yourself, too."

"You only ever saw the fringes of my superhero

life. There was a lot I had to hide. Can we maybe... start over?"

"Start what over?" says Mark.

"Us. Now that everything's out in the open. Start dating again, with no secrets between us. On either side, since you seem to have a whole secret life as a hacktivist that I didn't know about."

"Get to know the whole of each other." He smiles. "Yeah, I think I'd like that."

"Some things aren't going to change," I warn him. "Superhero business will still take priority over date night. There will always be another alien invasion, or zombie horde, or army of animate teddy bears."

"Oh, now that story I need to hear," murmurs Mark.

"And this time you'll hear about all the weird stuff, too. Maybe get sucked into it. Stick with me and you'll get kidnapped by supervillains, attacked by monsters, mind-controlled, maybe turned into a hedgehog. It's part of the package. I wouldn't blame you if you ran for the hills."

"I can't guarantee I won't run screaming later, but I want to know all of your life, even if it's weird. So, I'm willing to try if you—" He makes a surprised, but not unhappy noise when I interrupt him with a kiss. When we come up for air, he adds, "On one condition."

"Which is?" I say warily.

He grins with schoolboy enthusiasm. "You *have* to take me flying sometime. If I'm going to have the bad parts of dating a superhero, I want the good parts, too."

I laugh and scoop him up bridal style. "Should I carry you like this?"

75

"Oh! Wow. You're super-strong even without the armor. That's... really hot, actually. Carry on."

I don't know what will happen from here. Maybe we'll make it in the long term, maybe not. But for the first time, I have someone I don't have to hide from.

Time for No Mercy

By Elizabeth Schechter

The door exploded right on schedule. She smiled, seeing her expression reflected in her computer monitor. Whatever ills she had to say about Captain Courage, hero to corporations everywhere, he could always be counted on to be punctual.

"I was wondering if you were going to be late," she called over her shoulder. "Hold on a moment, let me save this file."

His voice was deep, authoritarian. The Captain was a man who was used to being listened to. And it so annoyed him when she didn't listen to him. That was part of what made it so much fun. "You won't be needing it—"

"Where I'm going. Yes, yes, I know the script. Just a tick… there." She turned and smiled up at the very handsome, and now very visibly annoyed hero. He wore skin-tight spandex in bright, primary colors, with little corporate logos embroidered on his broad shoulders. "My, you're looking trim, Captain," she said. "New tailor? Are you cutting carbs?" She pursed her lips and tipped her head to one side, studying his sculpted physique, watching as he preened under her gaze. Theatrically, she covered her mouth with her fingers. "Oh! I've been so busy recently. Captain, did I miss the wedding announcement? Is that the change I'm seeing? Is there a Mrs. Captain now? And little Caplings on the way?" She smiled at his blush. "Congratulations, Captain. I really am surprised that you've settled down with one girl. She must be really something else. Now, should I start knitting booties?"

He opened his mouth, stopped, then looked at her curiously. "You knit? That... doesn't seem like a very Doctor Libertine thing to do."

"Oh, I know," she answered. "It doesn't fit the recreational anarchist persona, does it? But I enjoy it, and really, it's just applied mathematics. I'm rather busy at the moment, but I'll make an exception for you, in light of how long we've known each other." She grinned. "Was that an answer, by the way? I rather like mint green for babies, don't you? Or would you prefer lavender? It's such a pretty color."

"No, that was not an answer!" Now he sounded indignant. Oh, good. Indignant was one short step away from postulating. "I'm not here to discuss my personal life, Doctor Libertine. Which, by the way, is none of your business. I'm here to put an end to your evil plans!"

She held up one finger. "Which evil plans? You're going to have to be specific. I've got several irons in the fire at the moment."

He folded his arms over his massive chest. "Yes, and they're all evil. So, does it really matter why I'm here?"

"Well, it helps to know for the future which ones caught your attention, and which aren't worth the follow-through." She leaned back in her chair and crossed her legs, watching his eyes as they followed the movement. His gaze lingered just a little too long, no doubt because her tight red skirt rode up and revealed the top of her stocking and a bit of thigh. Tight skirts, thigh-highs and heels were so impractical in the lab... unless she was expecting a caller. Unless she was expecting *this* caller. "I mean, if it's not going to catch your attention, it's definitely not worth my time."

His eyes narrowed. "You're not seriously telling me you're doing all this for my benefit?"

"Oh, I do nothing for *your* benefit," she answered. "Why should I? You're rich beyond the dreams of Croesus, thanks to your corporate overlords. How many are there now? Last time I checked, there were four pharmaceutical companies, that fake mega-church, five different Senators, that poison peddler that calls itself a biotech company, and not just one but two major oil companies. Have I got them all? How did you fit them all on the suit?" She smiled and gestured to him. "And really, look at you. You're blond, gorgeous, and your new wife would be able to wash baby clothes on those abs of yours. You are the very epitome of the so-called master race. Oh, and you're male. No, you already have every benefit society has to offer. What could I possibly add? I work for the benefit of mankind." She stopped. Frowned. Then shook her head. "No, I work for the benefit of womankind."

He scoffed. Of course. He *would* scoff. "Really?"

"Really," she answered. "So, which plan was it now? It can't have been the one to try and stem global warming. I haven't perfected that one yet, and I'm starting to think it's far too ambitious for just a single super genius recreational anarchist. I'm going to have to find somebody to help. My plan to regreen the Sahara failed. Twice. I need to revisit that one once I work out the bugs." She frowned. "Bugs. That... that might be it. Wait a minute, let me make a note." She picked up a notepad and scrawled the words *Bugs. Genetic modification to enrich soil. Cross reference with preservation of honeybees. How?* She set the pad down and shook her head. "Now, I do have high hopes for protecting the Amazon from deforestation. Did you ever see the movie *Swamp Thing*, Captain? It's inspirational—"

He rolled his eyes. "The plan where you were going to release toxic chemicals into the air—"

She looked up. "Really? Out of everything I'm working on, you picked *that* one? Please, contraceptives are hardly toxic," she countered. "The compounds are perfectly safe in 99% of cases, they only cause mild nausea in that remaining one percent, and they can be countered with a simple, harmless tablet that I'm making widely available to women's health organizations world-wide. Once this is done, no woman will be forced to carry a child if she doesn't wish to do so." She gestured to her computers. "I've checked and double-checked the research, Captain. The compound self-replicates in the atmosphere, so it will be a one-time application, and then women will be freed forever from the chains of unwanted pregnancy. So, tell me, what's so nefarious about this plan?"

He scowled. Then he held up one hand and started ticking off on his fingers. As he did, she reached over to the desk and grabbed the notepad and a pencil, turning a fresh page and sketching quickly.

"One, it's murder—"

"Wrong. Contraception is not taking a life. It's preventing a life," she interrupted. "Not murder by any legal definition. Try again."

His scowl deepened, and he continued as if she hadn't said anything, "Two, it's a violation of the rights of the father. Three, it violates medical ethics. Four, it's a violation of consent—"

That one startled her. "When did *you* start worrying about consent, Captain?" she asked. "Or do you think I've forgotten about all those complaints that suddenly went silent?"

He turned red. "They went silent because they were all lying," he growled.

"Fifteen women? Last year alone?" She sniffed and got up from her chair, setting aside the half-finished BINGO card she'd doodled on the pad. "What was that? Once a month, with two for one specials on Christmas and your birthday?" She frowned. "I'm missing one. Arbor Day? No, knowing you, it was the Fourth of July."

"There was nothing to any of those complaints. They were all attention-whores. All they wanted was to be famous. They came on to me, and after it was all over and done, they went crying to the press, trying to ruin my good name—"

"What were their names?" she interrupted.

He blinked, caught off guard by the question. "What?"

"Their names," she repeated. "What were their names?"

He frowned, then burst out laughing. "I don't remember! Why should I?"

She sniffed. "So much for becoming famous,

81

then? Two of them committed suicide, Captain. Did you know that? And four others aborted pregnancies." She walked over to the Captain and tapped him on the chest with one finger. "Which you paid for. You know, you really do need to pick a better password."

His eyes widened, and his jaw dropped. She winked at him, and turned away, heading toward the tiny kitchenette in the corner of her lab/studio apartment/villainous lair. "You're too easy, Captain. No, I didn't hack your computer. That's not my field. But you've confirmed my suspicions, so for that I do thank you." She looked back over her shoulder. "So, who really sent you? I know you don't go anywhere unless there are dollar signs attached. Who's paying for tonight's little call? The evangelical Senator from Alabama, the company that makes contraceptives, or that pompous idiot who calls himself a bishop, and who thinks that all women should sit down and shut their pretty little mouths?"

"He's right," the Captain growled. "You should sit down and shut your mouth."

Libertine shook her head. "No. Not going to happen. You and your masters are out to destroy the world for the good of your pockets. I'm not letting that happen. Drink?"

He stepped forward, then stopped and blinked. "What?"

"Do you want a drink?" she asked. She opened the tiny cube fridge and took out a bottle of water. "Just spring water. I don't drink soda, it's too late in the day for coffee, and my electric kettle broke, so I can't make tea." She held up a second bottle. "I just bought them this morning. They're sealed." She set the bottle on the counter, and when he came forward to take it, scooted up to sit on the counter and crossed her legs. "I don't understand you, John."

His face went ashen under his tan. "What did you call me?" he demanded.

She laughed. "Do you really think that after all the years we've been fencing that I haven't figured out your real name? John Faraday, heir to Faraday Enterprises. You're one of the richest men on the planet. I really never understood why you needed the sponsorships. And I really, really never understood why you aren't out there doing some good. John, you could do so much to help so many people." She opened her bottle and took a sip, then looked at it. "Something like this, for example. Water. We take it for granted. It's a luxury in some countries, John. Why aren't you helping those people?"

He looked thoughtful, then a crafty look passed over his face. "You know, you have me at a disadvantage," he said in a low voice.

She grinned at him. "I usually do."

"I don't know your name," he continued and smiled. He was so blasted handsome when he smiled. And so, so charming. "It doesn't make sense for me to keep calling you Doctor Libertine." He stepped closer, leaning on the counter next to her. "So what do I call you?"

"Oh, you can keep calling me Doctor," Libertine said. "I worked hard for my degree, and I still have the loans to prove it. But as for my real name? You haven't earned that yet."

He chuckled. "I have to earn it?" he said. He reached out and ran one finger up her stocking-covered leg, rested his hand on her thigh. "How do I do that?"

"By not trying to seduce me, first," she answered, reaching down and taking his hand off her leg. "And by actually doing something with your life. It's time to stop playing games, John." She took another sip of water. "Does Kelly know about those women, John? That's your wife's name, isn't it? I saw something in the papers of John Farraday getting married. She's a news reporter, isn't she? So she should know about them. The ones you used and threw away?"

He drew himself up and towered over her–even with her sitting on the counter, he was still taller than she was. "They were nothing. They just wanted a piece of me. I gave them what they wanted."

She looked up at him, met his piercing blue eyes. "Did you?" she asked. "Or did you just take what you wanted?" She slid along the counter and jumped down. "Really, John. Why? You're so talented. You could do so much good."

"I do good!" he protested, following her. "I do a lot of good. You know so much about me. You have to have seen all the news coverage. I do a lot of good."

Doctor Libertine set her bottle down and folded her arms over her breasts. "Cui bono, John?"

He looked at her, his eyes narrowed. "I... don't speak Italian."

"Close. It's Latin," she said. "To whom is it a benefit? Who benefits from the so-called good you do, John?" She shook her head. "Not the little guy. Not the regular Joe on the corner, trying to make ends meet. The only people who benefit from your heroics are the people who pay you to do them. You go out and shut down the women's clinics to save the unborn, but God help the single mother trying to make ends meet

84

because she shouldn't have opened her legs to start with. You champion the rights of gun owners everywhere, but you don't say a damned thing when it's a fanatic with a semi-automatic shooting up a mosque or a synagogue, or a school. You're all for life, liberty, and the pursuit of the all-mighty dollar, so long as you make two dollars on the deal."

She sniffed and slipped her hands onto her lab coat pockets. She was monologuing. She *hated* mono-loguing. "Do you know why you're the good guy and I'm the evil genius? Optics. That's all. I'm working for the good of society, but because you and your corporate overlords don't like that, I'm an evil whore, and I need to be stopped at all costs. Never mind that the products of my work feed the hungry and heal the sick. Never mind that my work helps everyone."

"You could work with me, you know," Captain Courage said. "You could change sides. Get yourself into a real lab, with real funding. If your work is that good, you could pay off those loans in no time."

For a moment, she was tempted. What could she do with real backing? Real funding. A real lab? Then she shook her head. "*All this I will give you, if you will bow down and worship me,*" she murmured. "No. No, money isn't the point, John. But you don't understand that, do you?"

He took a deep breath, and she watched idly as the spandex stretched over his chest. "No," he admitted. "No, I don't understand that. I don't understand why you bother. What's the point of doing anything if there's no return on investment?"

She walked away from the kitchenette, back to the bank of computers that dominated the room. "So, because you can't figure out how to make money off my work, you're going to stop me?" she asked. "Why? I mean, I haven't exactly done anything illegal. Not this time. Well, not yet, anyway. It's all plans. All ideas." She turned and caught him staring at her. "What?"

"You are a remarkably beautiful woman, Doctor," he said. For some reason, he sounded completely sincere. A little regretful. It was the regret that set her internal alarms blaring.

"They paid you to kill me, didn't they?" she whispered. "That's why you're here?"

"Make it look like a lab accident," he said. "Or suicide. They didn't have a preference. She's evil, after all. It's what I do. I stop evil." He frowned. "But… you're not. Are you?"

"It's all optics, John," she said. "The people I help think I'm wonderful. They think you're a clown in a costume."

He grimaced. "I never liked clowns," he admitted. "Do you like clowns?"

"No," she answered. "They scare me. But that probably has more to do with one stealing my popcorn at the circus when I was five."

His laugh was the delighted one of someone who had discovered a kindred spirit. "Me, too! The scary part, not the popcorn. Doctor… hey, since I don't know your name, may I call you Libby?"

"Libby?" she repeated. "Short for Libertine, I presume? Sure. Why not?"

He nodded. "Look, Libby. There's got to be some way we can both benefit from this. That we can both come out of this ahead. You're the big brain. How?"

She leaned against her desk, crossing her legs at

the ankle. "Considering that you came here to kill me? I can't think of any. Your plans hinged on you walking out of here with a convenient body left behind. Which is awfully dirty work for you, Boy Scout."

He rolled his eyes. "I know. But... yeah, you... you weren't far off with the money thing." He reached up and scratched the back of his neck. "This is my last job. This is the price for me getting out of the hero business. In order for me to get out, I need—"

"To kill me," Libertine finished. "Honestly, John. Can't you just say no? You're Captain Courage! Grow a pair!"

He stalked toward her. "It's not that easy!"

She met his eyes. "Yes, it is. No, I am not going to lie down and die for you. I have work to do." She turned back to her computers. "You owe me a new door. And really, don't you think that it'll be just a touch suspicious? The door exploded inwards, not outward."

"No one will be able to tell that when they comb the ashes." His breath ruffled her hair, and she could feel the heat from his body through her coat. "I'll make a good show of trying to save you."

"You should worry about saving yourself," Libertine murmured. She saw the movement from the corner of her eye, saw the red-haired woman step out from behind a screen and move into view. She had a special pistol raised. A very special pistol, and one that Libertine had hoped she wouldn't have to use.

There was a gasp from behind Libertine. "*Kelly?*"

Libertine dropped, and as she hit the floor, she heard the pistol shot ring through the apartment. Blood splattered, and Captain Courage staggered backwards, shock and pain warring for dominance on his face.

"What… what are you doing?" he wheezed. "What... what is this?" He looked down at the red ruin of his chest. "This… guns aren't supposed to hurt me! You can't kill *me*!"

Libertine got back to her feet and went to stand with Kelly. "You have this nasty habit of leaving DNA samples around, John," she said. "It wasn't hard to engineer a boutique weapon. Not with all that ammunition laying around." She looked at Kelly. "Did you hear enough?"

"Too much," Kelly answered, her voice thick. "I can't believe… I was so stupid!"

"Kelly." Captain Courage stepped forward. "I didn't… it's all a lie! All of it!"

"Even the things you said? Everything I heard tonight? The fact that you were going to kill Alex?"

He frowned, then looked at Libertine. "Alex? Your name is Alex?"

Libertine smiled. "Alexandra DiMarco. Doctor Alexandra DiMarco." She glanced at Kelly. "I think you might need to get him again. I don't think I made it strong enough. Or I can do it?"

"No." Kelly raised the pistol again. "Honey? I want a divorce."

She fired. This time, when the blast hit Captain Courage, he screamed. His body spasmed, then dissolved into dust. Kelly looked at the pile, her eyes wide.

"What was in this thing?" she demanded.

Alex reached up and pulled pins out of her hair, shaking long, brown curls free from the French twist. "Do you want the long answer with all the math, or the short answer?"

Kelly set the pistol down on the table. "The short answer. I hate math, Alex. You know that. I wouldn't have gotten through college without you."

Alexa smiled. "I remember. Kelly, I wish it didn't have to be like this. You were so happy—"

"How long would I have been happy with him?" Kelly asked. She wrapped her arms around herself. "What do I do now?"

"Now? Well, tomorrow you'll go to the police and tell them that John didn't come home, and that he isn't answering his calls. There's nothing that ties you to this place or to me. And I'll disappear—" She took off her lab coat and folded it over her arm. "No one knows what Doctor Libertine looks like. Not with Courage gone. I can set up anywhere. Have laptop, will create mayhem."

Kelly nodded, and followed Alex as she walked toward the area where Kelly had been hiding, which was separated from the rest of the room by screens. Behind the screens were a bed and a dresser. Alex kicked off her shoes and sat down on the bed, starting to roll down her stockings.

"What if I don't want you to disappear?" Kelly asked softly.

Alex looked up. "It can't be helped, Kell. I need to move. He was a corporate dog, and someone set him to hunt. I need to get ahead of them and find out who, so I can get them before they get me."

Kelly nodded. "I understand that. But... Alex, I don't want you to go. I just found you again."

Alex leaned back on the bed and smiled. "You made me start watching the news again, you know," she said. "When you got that evening show? I cheered. You deserve that, Kell. You're a fantastic reporter."

Kelly blushed slightly. "Part of that is you, you know. You're the one who started me paying attention to social justice and social change."

"Keep doing it. Make my job easier," Alex said. "I need to change. I need to pack. I don't need much—"

"How about a sidekick?"

Alex stared at Kelly. "What?"

"Or would it be minion?" Kelly continued. "Since we're evil and all?"

"You're about as evil as the kitten I don't own!" Alex protested. Kelly laughed and moved to sit down next to Alex.

"I just killed a superhero," she pointed out. "I think that makes me evil. And I think that should earn me an audition for sidekick."

"An audition," Alex repeated. "All right. Assuming I have a position open for a sidekick, what makes you think you're qualified?"

Kelly leaned closer, reaching out and running her fingers through Alex's hair. "I'm an investigative reporter. I know how to find things that people don't want to be found. I know how to research, and I know who to talk to and how to talk to them. I may not science the way you do, Alex, but I was always better at plain research."

Alex shivered as Kelly's fingers brushed her neck. "There's more to what I do than research."

"I know how to write grant proposals, too," Kelly added. "And..." she leaned forward and kissed Alex lightly on the nose. "I know 17 ways to send a certain recreational anarchist in to low earth orbit."

Alex's eyes flew open. "Seventeen?" she squeaked.

Kelly smiled brightly. "I told you. I'm really good at research."

Alex licked her lips. "I'd be interested in your findings."

"I bet you would," Kelly said with a laugh. She stood up and held her hand out. "Sidekick?"

"Oh, hell, no!" Alex protested. She stood up and rested her hands-on Kelly's waist. "There are no sidekicks here. I have an opening for partner. If you're interested? The benefits aren't all that good. Lots of travel. Lots of late nights."

Kelly chuckled and moved closer, her body pressing against Alex's. "Yay. Late nights," she murmured, catching Alex's mouth in a deep, possessive kiss. Alex pulled her closer, running her hands over Kelly's hips.

"You were such a beautiful bride," she whispered. "I saved the picture that ran in the papers. I cut him out, though."

"So did I," Kelly answered. "And we'll both be beautiful brides. In seven years. Once my not-so-lamented missing husband is declared legally dead." She looked around. "Is there anything you really want here?"

"My laptop. My external drives."

"Go get them," Kelly said. "Then we're getting out of here. An old college friend is coming over to help me in my time of need."

Alex blinked. Then she smiled. "A cover story?"

"I'm really good at cover stories, Alex," Kelly said. "Now, come on. I think we're going to pull an all-nighter tonight."

"I thought I was the evil genius here?" Alex protested.

Kelly just smiled. "I'm in training."

No Words Needed
By David T. Valentin

When the comet hurtled past the Earth, trailing red and purple streaks across the sky, I never imagined how it would change my life. It could be seen wherever you were, a once in a lifetime spectacle. After the first week, NASA told us it wasn't anything to worry about, described it as a scientific phenomenon, albeit a very strange one, and said that it'd vanish by the second week.

They were right—sort of. After the second week, the comet vanished, but the dust in our atmosphere remained. After the fourth week with the public growing afraid of lingering after effects, along with the usual skepticism and fanatic conspiracies taking over every news channel, NASA came out with an official, scientific statement and claimed the dust would burn up in our atmosphere fairly soon, like most tiny bits that broke off from comets.

Easy peasy, right? Well, not quite.

By the sixth week the meta-virus started, and global panic ensued. NASA released *another* statement to all world leaders to prepare for catastrophic biohazards. People pointed fingers at politicians, politicians pointed fingers at each other, and world leaders pointed fingers at their enemies.

After all the finger pointing, and the fear of mutually assured destruction, the world came to its senses and locked down. To avoid contracting the virus, people quarantined, curfews were enforced, and everyone was forced to wear hazmat suits 24/7. For almost two months, a yellow fog covered the planet and then as quickly as it arrived, it vanished. The quarantine was lifted after substantial amounts of testing and research. Life went back to some weird version of normal.

But then the unthinkable happened. Patient Zero, the first victim of the meta-virus, developed the ability to shoot fireballs from her hands. Apparently, she discovered it after she caught her boyfriend cheating and that went about as well as you'd expect. After tests, scientists discovered her DNA had changed, producing some strange chemicals in her body that created her abilities.

Then came Patient One, a power lifter who insisted on squatting a substantial amount of weight after a horrible back injury a couple of months prior and discovered he could turn his skin into diamonds when the squat bar had fallen on him. Patient Two, had healing spit. Patient Three developed a way to shapeshift his body. For weeks we heard about new telepaths, more shapeshifters, and a few people shooting things from their hands before everyone got bored and went back to their usual routines. Superpowers and superheroes popping up became as normal as puberty, and even in my small hometown I got the opportunity to know a few meta-humans.

Like my best friend, Rachel, who gained the ability to communicate through televisions and phones and stuff. They called it technopathy. Great fun until an incident with her girlfriend. Apparently, she lost control of her powers in the heat of passion. She accidentally projected them on every phone in the house. And yes, her parents were home. Luckily, they were comfortable with her choices.

Rachel's girlfriend, Sydney, discovered she could commune with the dead. Pretty cool, too, until she spoke to her deceased grandmother, her father's mother, who told her that her mother was cheating on her father. Sydney never told her parents, which was probably wise.

And me? What kind of superpowers did *I* get that completely changed *my* life? What spectacular thing can *I* do? Unless you can consider having a 99.99% chance of success rate with my gaydar whenever I have a day in the city of Oaksdale, I got the superpower of… well, absolutely nothing.

I'm just still the same old Theo Griffin, second in my college class and chemistry geek who crushes on hot guys on sports teams and one guy in my classes. No power, no relationship, not much of a life outside school. Which was okay because I couldn't tell you what I wanted beyond this coming weekend. Sure, there were times when I wished I had some meta-ability, but it wasn't meant to be.

I still spend a lot of time with Rachel, even though she went to a different college. Tonight, there was a huge frat party a few blocks down the road so that was the move for nearly everyone. The party started at 10:00, but Rachel and I did some drinking beforehand. We went over at 11:00 when the party was in full swing and we were starting to feel relaxed.

The house was typically plain—a two-story house, divided into two small apartments. You know, the studio ones where the living room and the kitchen were merged but the bedrooms were down some narrow hallways and stuffed with about three or four frat boys in them.

Like most nights, the house was completely trashed. Not that there was much to trash. These apartments consisted of nothing but hand-me-down couches and chairs, along with cheap folding tables for beer pong and crushing come the end of the night. The house was packed to the brim, not just with frat guys and friends of frat guys, but friends of friends and a few of their friends. From the front porch we could see fire swirl out and up into the air, disappearing into the night sky, and that's where we had to go.

Rachel and I went through the house and into the backyard where we spotted Charlie Lee, president of the frat and owner of the house. The type of guy who insisted on wearing button up shirts, chest out, in a clear statement of trying to be presentable, not messy, but come the end of the night, if there was an end, he'd be splattered in beer or wine spots from head to toe. Charlie was standing at the edge of a gathering circle. In the center came the torches of fire, hurtling into the air from none other than Jason Lee, Charlie's twin brother.

We reached the circle and took a spot next to Charlie.

"Aren't you going to at least pretend to be a little afraid of the cops showing up?" Rachel asked Charlie, taking him by surprise.

He turned toward us, his icy blue eyes standing out from a pattern of deep blue veins on his skin letting anyone who met him know that freezing things was his specialty. His face lit up. "What?" he asked. "I think we're keeping the noise pretty low, no?"

Rachel rolled her eyes. "The fire, you dingus."

Rachel had become a favored guest at these sorts of parties due to her ability to out drink most, if not every, guy in the frat. They'd also taken a liking to the untraceable prank calls they'd do together when she'd come over. It's the little things in life that counts.

"No," Charlie said. "Not really. Cops barely have their shit together to deal with normal people, let alone folks who can shoot fire from their fingertips. Anyway, enough of this boring talk. I got a little something for you two." He beckoned us to follow, and we did.

We maneuvered through the house as best we could, stepping around stumbling students and finally making it to his room.

"So, here is your little treat." Charlie said as he reached from under his bed and pulled out a bottle of tequila.

"Tequila?" Rachel raised a brow. "Shit's nasty."

Charlie chuckled. "Oh, not just any tequila. A new kind of tequila fused with a little c-19 dust collected straight from the comet. Ingesting it heightens your senses to their limits, making you perceive everything around you in a new way. It's a different experience for everyone apparently."

He poured the electric blue liquid into three shot glasses. I could already tell it was going to burn going down.

Rachel took the bottle and examined it. "Where the fuck did you get this?"

"My father," Charlie said nonchalantly. "Got it

from one of his bosses, who apparently got it off some truck... somewhere. Here." He handed us each a shot glass.

I raised the glass to my eyes, examining the blue electric liquid inside. "Is it safe?" I asked.

Charlie cocked his head. "I'm still standing, aren't I?"

Rachel and I glanced at each other for a moment, wondering exactly where this night was going to take us. "I say... cheers?" I held up my glass to the air, faking a smile. I wasn't sure, but it was worth a try.

A wicked smile split across Charlie's face. He and Rachel held up their glasses. "Cheers! To a good night!" And with that, Charlie took in a deep breath, exhaled an icy blast on to our shots, chilling our drinks and took the drink.

Rachel and I followed.

The first hour or so after was a lucid blur as Rachel and I drifted from room to room, talking to everybody. At one point, Charlie and a few guys busted out some karaoke, using their hand-me-down couch as a stage. Charlie insisted we join in, but I wasn't feeling it. Not yet, at least. I took another shot of Charlie's tequila. Charlie cheered me on, but Rachel sent me a concerned look.

After the second shot everything immediately started swirling. I could feel the drink burning in my stomach. People's faces became mismatched, stretching disproportionally like they were morphing blobs. Voices grew louder and yet distant. Like an echo but not quite. I found myself outside in the backyard with Jason. He was still showing off to an audience, shaping fire into different patterns. I busted through the crowd to the center, shouting. Even my own voice was distant and muffled.

As I stood in the center with the fire around me, I had tunnel vision. The circle of people was just a blob of black and the only thing I could make out was Jason's face. I shouted something at him, something about a dog, I think, because a few moments later he was twirling fire in between his hands and out came what looked like a huge, cuddly golden retriever.

An urge took hold of me, and I ran forward with my hand out to pet the dog. Someone grabbed me, before my hand made contact with the flames, and pulled me back. The dog disappeared.

I turned around and spotted Rachel. She was holding me by my arms, shouting words I couldn't hear. I squinted, focusing on her lips so I could make out what she was saying.

"Be careful," she was shouting. Then she took me by the hand and led me to the living room where the karaoke was still kicking it full swing. "Come on," she said, handing me a microphone. I made a face. "Let's try something a little safer for you. *How's Holding Out for a Hero?*"

I nodded and climbed up on the couch with her. The rest was a horrid blur. I was belting lyrics from the top of my lungs. My hips were swinging, my body swaying and gathering a crowd. Almost everyone from the party surrounded the stage. Rachel and I were living it up. I heard my name, like a clap of thunder from the crowd. They were cheering me. Me—Theo fucking Griffin, chemistry nobody. The attention was all on me, and I was loving it.

Feeling the finale coming closer, I handed the mic

to Rachel. She gave me a puzzled look, but I reassured her with a quick wink. Then I committed. I squatted down and placed my hands firmly down on the couch. Then, in one quick motion, I hoisted my feet up against the wall. And in a moment of impossibilities I started working my hips.

The crowd roared. I caught a glimpse of Rachel, standing there with a big grin as her jaw dropped. Dollar bills fluttered my way, and the song came to an end, I propped myself upright and snagged a few of the bills being thrown my way. The world was swirling around me, but I felt alive for tonight.

I looked out at the crowd, their faces bathed in flashing neon lights. There, as if a spotlight hit him, was Robert Hernandez. He was a chemistry major like me and in most of the same classes. One semester in organic chemistry lab we were paired together as lab partners. We got talking, became acquaintances, and were comfortable with each other. But our friendship never grew beyond that, and I don't think he ever knew I was silently eyeing his bulging biceps and tabletop chest every time he wore his thin cotton polo shirts, which he was wearing now. He always undid the top two buttons, letting a bush of brown chest hair peek out.

Our eyes locked on one another, and I had to do something. I hopped off the couch and made my way through the crowd. Our friendship was always casual and kept to the confines of the classroom. But tonight, was different. *I* felt different and since he was there, I wasn't going to let the opportunity pass.

Finally, we were face to face and while normally I'd bite my tongue, confess to a loss of words, and

100

leave, I didn't this time. I had too much to say and I wanted to say it all.

"Hi," I said, lamely. *Hmmm… that wasn't exactly what I wanted to say.*

He smiled. "Hi. Impressive performance."

"Oh, that?" I said, pointing to the couch. "That was nothing. You should see me at the Salsa club a few blocks from here. Fun stuff."

"I've enjoyed my fair share of Latino music." Robert gave a little wiggle of his hips and a one, two, three step with his feet. Then he took a swig of his beer and nodded.

I squealed and clapped my hands, like an excited little kid in a candy shop. I certainly had plenty of candy to gawk at, after all. "That was good! Maybe next time Rachel and I head down there you should come. Show me a few moves?"

"Maybe." He took another sip of his beer and glanced around for a moment.

Was he losing interest? Was I boring? Maybe I was beating around the bush just a little too much? Taking too long loading the gun when I should have just been taking my shot? No more waiting. "Hey," I said. "Can I ask you something?"

He raised his eyebrows and nodded. "Shoot."

"How come we don't ever hangout outside of class?"

"You know, I'm not really sure."

"Because we've been in the same classes for the last three years now. We talk. We're lab partners and all…"

"Then maybe we can change that?" he said with a gentle shrug.

101

"I was kind of hoping you'd say that," I said, scooting closer to him.

"Did you now?" he leaned his head forward.

"Yeah," I started, then stopped. Then started again. "Yeah, because... because I think you're kind of cute." I paused, taking a moment to catch my breath. I gave him a poke in the bicep, thick and firm to the touch like I knew it would be. There was a shock between the two of us, but I didn't flinch. "You know and it's not... it's not the... tequila—"

Just before I could get the full word out, the world spun around in a violent rainbow swirl and everything faded to black. In the distance I heard Robert saying something, and then there was Rachel's voice.

When I opened my eyes again Robert had taken his shirt off and was wearing only a tight, white tank top. Nice, I thought. Rachel mumbled something to me, something about needing to leave. I bobbed my head, nodding.

Someone tucked their arms under me, and then someone else tucked their arm on the other side of me. I felt my body moving, but it was more like moving under water. Next thing I knew I was feeling the chill of a cool spring night. We were outside.

I looked to see Rachel on my left side, Robert on my right. They were both carrying me along as my feet stumbled over one another.

"Where are we going?" I slurred.

"Back to your apartment, buddy." Robert said.

"I'm your buddy?" I asked.

"Sure," he said. "Sure, you are."

"Hey," I said as part of my memory gave a flash.

"What?" Robert asked.

"I'm sorry I think I threw up on your shirt."

He smiled and shook his head. "Oh, no worries. I have plenty."

"Oh, cool."

The world swirled and faded again. When I could focus again I heard Rachel and Robert mumbling something, then the voices vanished. Then next thing I remembered, Rachel was gone, and I was alone with Robert. At least this time I recognized the place. We were in the elevator of my apartment.

"Where'd… Where'd Rachel go?" I asked. The door to the apartment elevator opened and we stepped out.

"She said she had to go back home. Called an uber and headed out," Robert said. "I'm just helping you to your bed and then I have to go too. Do you have your key?"

I reached into my pocket and yanked my apartment key out, all while using my free hand to hold myself up on Robert's shoulder, which was bulky and solid. It made me feel safe.

He took the key from my hand and unlocked the door, all while he held his arm under me and kept his arm around my back. Once inside he helped me through my small apartment to my bed, where I flopped down and sighed.

"Alright, time to a sleep, buddy." Robert took hold of my shoes and tugged them off, tossing them to the floor.

"Hey, Robert?" I called, pulling the sheets over me, all the way up to my face. "I'm sorry if I weirded you out by calling you cute."

"Nah," he said with a big smile. "It's no biggy. I promise."

"No, it kind of is." I propped myself up on the bed as best I could. Immediately I felt my vision blur. My stomach lurched, but I held it in. "I don't even know if you like guys that way, and it's not cool to assume."

"Theo, it was just a compliment," he said. "Didn't mean it had to be anything more, right?"

I paused to think for a moment. That was the issue, wasn't it? Was it just a passing comment or something more? I knew my answer. And although he said it didn't have to mean anything more, something about the look on his face told me he was thinking it might be.

"Yeah," I finally said. "Yeah, you're right."

He nodded and sighed. "Alright, get some rest, buddy." Robert reached his hand out and gently poked his finger to my forehead. In my head I heard Robert say *sleep tight, Theo* as if from a distance. And yet I didn't see his lips move.

There was that shock again, only this time it spread from my finger and rippled through my whole body. Then everything went white.

I was seeing people, a large family of seven in a small house somewhere in the suburbs. There were three women and four younger boys who looked like little s. The boys were scurrying about as the women sat at the table. Dinner was served. There was laughter in that moment, happiness. But I felt a sadness, too, and a sense of shame. I looked down at my hands and they were tanned. This... this was Robert's memory. And he wanted to talk about something personal. What was it? I searched in my... well, 's head and I found my answer. He wanted to tell them something that

104

would change the way they saw him, the way they felt about him. He wanted to tell them he was gay. A pervading sense of stress overwhelmed me. Everything went black.

* * *

I woke up the next morning, my whole body aching from head to toe. The night was a blur, but I remembered Robert helping me home and a bit about what happened after. I leapt up from my bed, spotted my phone and picked it up. A message from Rachel *Hey love, hope you're feeling better!*

I immediately texted her back, frantically texting a quick *we need to talk. NOW.*

Minutes later I was on the subway, heading into the city downtown. As the train shook and rattled my head, it made my headache even worse. My phone buzzed.

A text from Robert. I felt a feeling of nervousness, but also giddiness. Was I feeling my own feelings or his? Or perhaps both. I smiled at the phone, locked it and stuffed it back into my pocket.

As I walked into the tiny ramen shop, a small little place stuffed between two huge apartment buildings, I spotted Rachel already sitting at a booth, waving me over. I took the seat across from her.

"So, talk to me," she said. "What's going on?"

"I don't remember much about last night, but…"

"Yeah, that kind of happens when you drink as much as you did."

"You're never going to believe this. Robert took me up into my apartment, everything was still spinning then he told me to go to sleep. Then he touched me and the next moment his memories were whirling and spinning in front of me. And the weirdest part was, I could *feel* his memories, almost like they were happening to me. Like it was happening to me."

The waiter came and put two large bowls down in front of us and then hurried away.

"So, what are you trying to say?" Rachel said, slurping up a chunk of noodles into her mouth. I told her about his coming out memory. "This is a good thing, isn't it?"

"Why would it be?"

"Because you like him."

I felt the heat flush into my face. "And how would you know that?"

"Theo, you don't stop talking about him on the days you have class together, and you were *all* over him last night."

"What?" I said. "What the hell happened last night?"

"Well," Rachel sighed and put her chopsticks down to think. "You took one too many shots, twerked up against the wall, proceeded to talk to Robert, and threw up on his shirt. Then we took you home and I bounced."

"And why didn't you stop me?" I groaned.

"Stop you from what? You were talking to a cute boy for once," she said with a shrug. "I thought, why not let him take his shot?"

"Rachel, he's a Division One athlete with perfect grades and involved with student government. I could barely handle one club with my major. I'm a mess compared to him. Let's face it—I ain't got no shot!"

"Theo, that's not the point. You like him, right?"

"Yeah, so?"

"Then you need to figure out if he likes you and it's a date. We also need to figure out how you did your weird memory transference thing and get you to do it again. Then you can live happily ever after. Let's get started."

She could be right. I hoped she was. "It happened after we made contact, when he put his hand on my forehead."

Rachel stuck out her hands, palms pressed down. "Let's do something a little like palm readings. I'll let you search my memories. Find something I haven't told you."

I pressed my fingertips to her palms. "How do I do this?"

"I don't know. It's your power. What happened last night?"

"My eyes were closed, I was thinking of him, saying good night and then I heard his voice in my head."

Like this?

Rachel's voice was clear. I took that as a good sign. I closed my eyes and reached for a memory of her, something we shared. Between our fingers and the palms of her hand I felt a shock ripple through me and into my head. It was a tingly feeling, like remembering an airy childhood memory. And then I saw the day Rachel and I met. We were sitting in our middle school cafeteria, and I was alone. She came up to me, asked if she could sit with me, and I agreed.

I searched farther, past the memory. A place I hadn't been, a thing Rachel hadn't told me. I felt a pinch in my head, a worse headache coming along. Then I saw something I wasn't a part of, a memory of Rachel's with her in Charlie's room. They were pressed against one another, his arm wrapped around her leg and their lips locked on one another. There was breathlessness. There was heat.

"You hooked up with Charlie?" I opened my eyes, tugged my fingers away and stuffed them into my lap. "And you didn't tell me?"

"Made out." she said with a sly smile. "It was before Sydney. Freshman year. I forgot about it until you just mentioned it, honestly."

I raised a curious eyebrow.

"Anyway," she said, putting up her hands up defensively, "this is so cool. You have a power, and now that we know how it works, let's give it another go."

"No, not today," I said. It was all a little too much. I stood up to leave. "My head is killing me. I think I'll head back to my apartment."

"Hey, Theo."

"Yeah?"

"Everything's going to be fine. This is a good thing."

I nodded and left, not sure if I agreed with her.

On the train heading back to school I looked at my phone and at the text message from Robert. *Hey, buddy. Hope you're doing better and slept well.*

I remembered his memory, the feelings he was so afraid of. Then I remembered he'd been with Rachel. Maybe he didn't want to be out at college. If I told him my feelings, it might scare him away. And with my new powers I didn't know how he'd react when he found out how I learned his secret. I'm not sure he'd be okay with me probing his memories, even if it was an accident.

The train came to a stop. The doors opened. I glanced outside. Two more stops. As I turned my head back to my phone, I spotted Robert stepping on to the train. He looked around, scouting for a seat. We made eye contact. He smiled at me, waved, and walked over, holding on to the handrails above and to the side of him as the train pulled away.

"Hey, buddy. Mind if I sit with you?"

I shook my head. "No, I don't mind at all."

He slid into the seat and turned to me with a big smile. "So, how are you feeling?"

I pulled my body away from him, making sure our skin wouldn't touch in case that triggered my power, and trying not to make it obvious. I wasn't quite sure how the technicalities worked. I had to play it safe, play it cool.

"A little shaken really. Head's killing me," I said. "But I guess that's what I get for drinking so much."

"Hey, a little fun from time to time isn't a bad thing. Sometimes you gotta do a little singing and drinking and twerking to get your energy out."

I didn't dare tell him I got that drunk almost every weekend. He'd think I'm an alcoholic. Then again, which college student wasn't to some degree? "Yeah, Rachel told me about my performance. Was I any good?"

"Oh, yeah," Robert said with a chuckle in his voice. "You don't remember?"

I shook my head. "Not much. To be honest the only thing that's clear is you taking me to my room and putting me to bed." That wasn't quite true, since I remembered his voice and the memory, but I wasn't about to tell him that.

His smile slipped and his gaze drifted away. "Oh, okay."

"Thank you for that, by the way."

His smile returned. "Of course, no problem."

The train came to a halt. We both looked up to see we were at our stop. We left the train and made our way down the stairs from the train station, neither of us saying a word. I made sure to keep my space.

When we were out on sidewalk and turned to one another, he said, "Well, my apartment is back that way," Robert said, pointing his thumb behind him. "See you after spring break?"

I nodded. "See ya."

Robert turned on his heels and started walking away. As I turned, I noticed a nagging feeling in my head and an almost electrical shock buzzing me at the back of my neck. I had the sense that if I didn't act now, if I didn't say something, we'd go back to where we were before, when I was just his lab partner and a passing friend. We'd never get past simple hellos and goodbyes. And would I regret it? Hell yeah.

In that moment I decided that I couldn't let him be the chance I never took

"Robert!" I called. He turned. "Want to get some ice cream?"

I watched as he thought for a moment, his eyes moving around as if he were searching for an answer somewhere. Then he looked at me, smiled and said, "Sure."

We walked a few blocks to the Ice Cream Gardens. The minute we walked in he said it was one of his favorite places in the area and asked me how I knew. I shrugged and said lucky guess. We took our cones—his, a cherry scoop fashioned in the shape of a rose—to a park looking over the west harbor where the sun was beginning to set.

"You know," Robert said, keeping his eyes on his cone. "Who would've thought to spin ice cream into beautiful roses? Something that tastes amazing and looks gorgeous." Robert took a small lick of his ice cream, and I could tell he was trying not to ruin the design while still trying to get a good taste.

"I guess that's really the beauty of the city," I said. "So many choices. So many decisions."

"Where I'm from you get one choice, a small mom and pop shop called Sunshine Scoops with only about eight flavors and, if you're lucky, two specials each week."

"Sounds a bit boring."

Robert shook his head. "Not really. I actually appreciate the simplicity. And honestly? After three years of living in the city, I kind of miss it. Everyone here is in some kind of rush or whatever. But me? I'm just looking to slow down. Five or six years with a job out here and then I'm moving back home. What about you?"

"Me?"

"Yeah, where do you come from?"

"A small town out Midwest. My parents actually came from here, but, like you, the city was more than they wanted. They left and settled down there for a quieter life. Figures they'd have a son looking to rush out of there. But I love the city and all the people. So many stories, so many different lives in one place." I paused and turned to Robert. He was looking at me with one eyebrow raised. Curious. "Sorry. Just rambling."

"No," Robert said. "I think it's kind of poetic. And cute."

I bit my lip. "Thanks." I looked over to sun setting across the harbor. The truth was I didn't know what I wanted beyond college. I figured I'd find a job where I could use my degree and that was it. But with my newfound powers I had other things to consider. Maybe I could use them to help. I could work with the cops if a suspect didn't want to tell them the truth. There was a chance Robert wouldn't want to be a part of that, but I was pretty sure I didn't want to ignore this new part of myself. After all of this time, I had a gift and I wanted to figure out how use it. I shivered at my thoughts and took a bite out of my ice cream cone.

"Hey. Can I ask you something? About something you said last night?"

Oh, god. "Of course."

"At the party you called me cute," he said, plainly.

I pressed my palms to my pants and rubbed my legs. "Oh, I'm sorry."

"No," Robert said, leaning his head closer towards me. "I... I think you're kind of cute, too. And I think I want to get to know you better."

I moved my hand in closer, just as he did. This is what I wanted, didn't I? But at the last moment I pulled away and stood up.

"No," I said. "No, I'm not what you want. I'm not who you think I am, and this isn't what you want. *I'm* not what you want."

"What do you mean?" he asked. "Come on, talk to me."

I sighed and it all spilled out. "I have these powers. It just happened last night. Probably that laced tequila. When I touch someone, I can see their memories and feel them, too. Last night when you were in my apartment, we touched, and I saw you trying to come out to your family, but you were scared." I shook my head. "I know. It's wrong. That wasn't for me to see. I'm sorry."

Robert smiled. "Take my hand. Look into my memories."

He trusted me, so I decided to trust him. I put my fingers into his palms and searched his memories, like I did with Rachel. This time I recognized the tingly feeling in my palms that extended to an aching feeling in my heart. I saw the memory from last night, only it went on past the black. His family sat around their dining room table, and I felt his fear and then he told them he was gay. There was a moment of silence and then smiles all around. They stood up from their seats and hugged Robert. The memory faded away, and I was back with Robert at the park.

"I told my family," said Robert. "And although they were unsure at first, they love me all the same. A little too much, sometimes."

I shook my head and looked down. "When you talked about your life back home, I thought, wow, this guy knows what he wants and he's confident about it. But me? I don't know what want. I always feel like I'm chasing something. Like this new power. I've wanted one, but now that I've got it—I have no idea what to do."

Robert laughed. "Are you crazy?"

"What do you mean?" I asked.

113

"That's not how I see you. In class you're always so self-assured, Theo."

"Chemistry is the one place where I know my stuff."

"I admire you for that. And if this new power brings some adventure to our relationship and our lives, then so be it. We'll deal with it together."

"Together? Relationship?" I said out loud. The words sounded weird to me. Other than my friendship with Rachel, I typically did things on my own. Like my new power, it would take some getting used to, but I didn't want it any other way. I smiled. "Together. I like that."

Robert nodded and took my hand. "Just promise me we'll talk things out when stuff comes up. No need to keep everything bottled in that big head of yours."

"I promise," I said, and decided that being with him could be even better than a power.

Swiftly in Love
By Stella B. James

"Portia is the absolute bomb! She took down MegaMuscle in no time!"

Parker rolled his eyes and chugged half of his old fashioned down before he said something stupid. The bar was full of its usual sports fans, and he thought coming here would grant him one moment of peace without *her* coming up.

But, of course, she would dominate the conversation even in a bar full of avid football fans. The highlight reel of her latest capture played a constant loop on the only television screen in the entire bar that kept the news on. That one screen attracted the majority of the bar patrons during the commercial breaks, and even with the game, some of them still kept half their attention on Portia appearing out of literally fucking nowhere to surprise attack MegaMuscle.

There was no way that she was faster than Swiftfoot. No one was faster than him. *No one.* Not to mention that Swiftfoot had been Dorville City's resident superhero for the past three years. How could Portia think that Swiftfoot was replaceable? Better yet, how dare she try to replace him in the first place!

115

"That Portia sure is giving Swiftfoot a run for his money," the man next to Parker chuckled.

Oh, fuck this.

Parker finished his drink and slammed it down on the wooden bar top. The men around him threw him a questioning look, one of them chuckling that he needed to get some, but overall, they ignored him. Too bad Parker's blood had reached its maximum boiling point. If his heart were a volcano, it would be rumbling and spewing out lava.

Tapping the guy chuckling on about how much better Portia was for the city than Swiftfoot, Parker didn't think twice as he swung his fist into the guy's crooked smiling face. He went down like a sack of potatoes, and Parker found himself surrounded by an angry group of what he supposed were the guy's friends. Or maybe just comrades in their sports watching, Swiftfoot-trashing hang outs.

"Outside, boys," the bartender drawled, narrowing her heavily lined eyes on Parker. "And don't go easy on him."

Parker rolled his eyes, further aggravated that Portia had made him seem like a sexist pig. It had nothing to do with her being a woman. It was just... where did this city's sense of loyalty go?

Not fearing for his safety for a minute, Parker stepped out of the group and led them outside. This would be over fast. He had taken down bigger threats. Deadlier too.

"You got a problem with our friend in there?" one of the men sneered as the door to the bar slammed shut. Parker sighed, shrugging off his jacket and throwing it off to the side.

"No. Just sick of people forgetting that Swiftfoot has protected this city, has saved this city, for much longer than Portia has. Your friend ran his mouth, and I shut it up for him." The men gawked at Parker for a moment before sharing a knowing look.

Parker jumped into a fight stance the moment they huddled together, but relaxed when he saw they weren't strategizing against him, but laughing at him. They leaned on each other for support as they bowed over and laughed until they were red in the face. Parker took the time to assess them.

Five men, all wearing their red jerseys with pride, a lot of them favoring number 11. Figured they'd be a bunch of sheep. Probably why they liked Portia. They were mostly on the shorter side, stocky build, and Parker took a guess that they were failed sports heroes, living their dreams through the players who made millions on the screens they'd been glued to inside. This would be over quick, and maybe he could grab a burger on the way home.

The whiskey settling in his belly reminded him that he needed to eat if he wanted to make it to work without a slight hangover in the morning. The men straightened, forming a half circle around Parker, and his daydreaming of a big juicy cheeseburger quickly disappeared.

Right, kick their ass, then burger time.

"We get it now, pretty boy," the bald one of the group sneered, cracking his knuckles. "You got a hard on for Swiftfoot or something?"

Parker started at that. Well, he guessed his overdefensive nature for Swiftfoot could easily be mistaken for a crush. But it wasn't that. More of a sense of pride than anything.

"Whatever, guys. Let's just have at it," he sniffed, waiting for one of them to make their move.

"With pleasure." Baldy chuckled, the sound not at all reassuring, and Parker huffed in his impatience. This guy would make an excellent villain with his little snarky smack talk before the actual action began. At least Parker felt right at home with this fight.

The first punch never landed. Neither did the second. Or the kick that another guy threw out. Parker smirked at their bewildered expressions, as he stood before them unscathed in the same exact spot they had attempted to jump him.

"If he didn't move, then how..." The voice trailed off as the five men looked at each other and then back at Parker.

"I've got all night, fellas," he said, crossing his arms. This was almost fun. His anger had dissipated, and aside from wanting to eat, fucking with them seemed like a much better idea. He hadn't gotten to do this in a while. Stupid Portia.

The five men, as if reading each other's minds, all nodded at once before closing in on Parker. Before he could deliver his signature move, *she* appeared. Portia, Dorville City's newest superhero, in the flesh, taking a protective stance in front of Parker.

"Wow, she's even hotter in person," the shortest guy said, his hand reaching out as if he was going to touch her and test if she were real. Parker reached around and smacked his hand away. The man scowled but backed up a step.

"You boys think it's okay to gang up on some-one?" Portia asked in her enchanting raspy voice, her hands fisted on her hips. Parker snorted behind her.

Amateur. Show off. Sticking her nose where it didn't belong.

"Hey! He was talking shit about you! We're your biggest fans."

Portia tensed for a minute and turned an amused glance back at Parker. He raised an eyebrow at her, never one to take back his words. Yeah, he didn't like her. What was she going to do about it? Portia gave a half shrug and turned back to the group.

"Not everyone has to like me. While I appreciate your valiant attempt to protect my honor, I do wish you would put your efforts to better use. We have enough villains causing trouble without me having to come and break up petty fights."

"No one asked you to come," Parker muttered under his breath. Portia didn't seem to hear him, and if she did, she chose to ignore it.

"Go on inside, and I'll have a little talk with my latest troll." The guys all snickered at that, and with a shy wave towards Portia, they sauntered back into the bar.

"I see your precious Swiftfoot didn't come to the rescue! Guess your little crush doesn't give a damn about the few fans he has left," Baldy hollered over his shoulder.

"Fuck you!" Parker yelled back. The door closed before he could yell anything else, but he wasn't at max mental capacity to come up with anything soul splitting.

Parker's stomach rumbled, reminding him of other pressing needs, and he turned around, eyeing the buildings around them. The burger joint he craved was a few blocks away, if he remembered correctly, and it should be... he turned towards the right and started walking. Yeah, this looked about right.

"Hey, wait a minute!" Portia's voice called from behind him. Now what the hell did she want? Parker turned towards her, watching with mild fascination as she stomped up to him.

Her outfit was completely unfair. The tight blue spandex hugging her in all the right places, the sweetheart neckline enhancing her cleavage just so. Did the villains slip in their drool before she took them down? And her eyes! Those clear blue eyes, shit they were almost gray they were so light, and they just electrified him, sending sparks of recognition all through him.

His body reacted without his permission, but he was wearing loose jeans in her presence for once. If she ever found out what she really did to him, ugh, that would make things 10 times worse. He felt the heat of her body radiating against his before his brain caught up with the fact that she was right in front of him. His eyes crossed a second before finally focusing on her.

"What?" he slurred. Because of the alcohol. The whiskey and the lack of food. Not because of Portia, and damn, she smelled like cinnamon. He suddenly wanted churros. Did burger places sell churros?

"Not even a thank you?" she demanded, her finger hooking into the collar of his cotton shirt to shift his attention back to her teasing smile. "I just saved you from a beating that would've left you with a nastier headache than your hangover will."

Parker grunted, and pulled away from her, hands running over his shirt to smooth out the collar she probably stretched out. He tried to glare down at her, but for some reason, his hands betrayed him and the smooth texture of her spandex under his fingertips sent a blaze of heat straight through his veins. His hands were on her hips, to steady himself, right? Had he even been in danger of tipping over?

He was making an idiot of himself, as usual, but he couldn't help it. Portia did things to his body and, as much as he absolutely hated her, his hormones were not in agreement. He shook his head, trying to gain his bearings, but his hands moved up to grasp at her waist.

"And I said," he drawled, pushing her away from him a step, "that I didn't need your help." He felt lightheaded and dizzy, but he didn't drink that much. Enough to need food, but not enough to stumble and slur on his words. Shit, he was getting drunk off of her. Portia disoriented him somehow. He had to get away from her, but the throbbing in his jeans argued that he needed to pull her in closer.

"You seem a little handsy for not liking me." The tease was lost on her soft pants, and alarmed, Parker got a better look at her. Her chest rose and fell with each soft, rapid breath she took and a light dusting of pink across her cheeks gave her away. Parker flustered her. Well, then.

"And you're letting me," he murmured, leaning in for one last whiff of her. "Is this how you best Swiftfoot? You seduce your bad guys before he can get there?"

Portia tensed up and wrenched out of Parker's grasp. Her lips formed a thin line and she was back to her professional, fists on hips, superhero stance. "I *am* faster than Swiftfoot, and I took those guys down with my skills. I can kick your ass if you need a demonstration."

121

Parker gritted his teeth and crossed his arms. "Swiftfoot has been protecting this city for longer than you can imagine. I doubt you'll last long, and guess who will be there to pick up the devastation you'll leave?" A look of realization crossed Portia's features, and she stepped right up into Parker's space again.

Parker winced as she raised her hand, and he closed his eyes, preparing himself for a slap, but none came. Opening his eyes, he was met with the inside of her gloved hand. His face fell in confusion, wondering why she would take the time to cover his eyes. Portia was a strange one, that's for sure.

"I thought so," she whispered, before backing away with a silly smile. None of it made sense and Parker's stomach rumbled again.

"Are we done here?" he asked, suddenly remembering the jacket he had tossed aside.

His eyes swept across the pavement and he spotted it, crumpled on top of a car's hood. Not caring for whatever else Portia wanted to say to him in that moment, he scooped up the jacket and shrugged it on, fisting his hands in the pocket.

"Until next time, Swiftfoot," Portia's voice rang out. Parker paused, whipping his head back towards her, but she was already gone. So, she had recognized him.

Well, didn't that just ruin everything. Once again, Portia had bested Swiftfoot at something. Parker reached down to adjust himself and mentally cursed Portia for all of his problems, some more pressing at the moment than others.

* * *

122

Parker had been birthed with super speed, but it was a power that developed with him. When he was younger, he was faster than most of the kids in his school, but it was nothing noteworthy. Just enough speed to have parents and teachers joke that they had a future Olympian on their hands.

As Parker grew older, though, his speed grew faster, and in a moment of panic his super speed sprouted. His dad's workshop had caught fire with his little brother inside. It was almost uncanny how quickly the inferno occurred. Parker's dad had been giving him driving lessons when they saw it go up in flames, and as they rushed out of the car, they could hear his mom screaming for Nelson.

Parker would never forget the surge of electricity that hit him. All he knew was that one moment, he was in the driveway, and the next, he had Nelson in his arms in the upstairs bathroom. He had saved Nelson's life that day, and it felt good.

When more buildings suddenly combusted into flames, Parker searched for the cause, running into his first villain: Scorcher. That was the day he became Swiftfoot and used his super speed for good.

But what good did it do him when Portia gallivanted around, showing him up at every turn?

Parker had not left his hometown and adopted this one as his own so that some sexy little number could try to outdo him. What he couldn't understand was how she could possibly be faster than him. At 23, Parker was certain that he was fully grown, his superspeed had reached maturity. His powers were so versatile he never worried for his own safety. What in the hell did she have that he didn't?

123

It wouldn't matter tonight. Dr. V had escaped once again, and Swiftfoot would be the one to take him down. No one knew Dr. V's mastermind the way that Swiftfoot did, and, for once, Parker felt hopeful. Tonight would show the city that Swiftfoot wasn't ready to surrender his title as the city's hero just yet.

"Ah, Swiftfoot. So good to see you made it."

What in the actual fuck? There, before his very eyes, was a handcuffed Dr. V, and an annoyingly smug Portia shaking the commissioner's hand.

"While she's more fun to look at, she is definitely less fun than you," Dr. V grumbled as he passed Swiftfoot and ducked into the back of the police car. Swiftfoot almost responded in kind, but he couldn't exactly side with a villain at a time like this, could he? Wasn't there a code or something superheroes lived by?

Swiftfoot watched on in disbelief as the scene cleared, unable to keep his glower from Portia, who looked way too giddy in the moment. He used to feel like that after taking the enemy down. He thought he'd get it back tonight.

"Oh, stop pouting! I swear, you look like someone rolled over your puppy." There she was, in his space again. She did that a lot lately.

Swiftfoot balled his hands by his sides, more to keep himself from groping her like the last time they had been in each other's presence. Her cinnamon signature scent teased his nose, and he closed his eyes, trying his best to keep his body under control. He was in his suit this time, and a noticeable bulge would not help his case.

"Alright, I've had it!" Swiftfoot took a step closer, ignoring the way her chest pressed against his. Leaning his face in, he tried to look as menacing as possible as he uttered his next challenge. "You and me, across the rooftops. It's time to settle who's faster."

Portia stepped up onto her tiptoes, forcing his head back an inch and their noses brushed before he moved back a step. "I think it's pretty obvious who will win. I would hate for your inflated ego to take any more hits."

"My inflated ego isn't what's been bothering me all these months," he ground out, and immediately felt himself flush. He hadn't meant to say it out loud, had been merely thinking it as her hips flushed his. It took everything he had not to grind into her.

But it wasn't what they were doing right now, or was it and he just couldn't read the signs? No, he was taking her down. Tonight. Maybe not in the way his body wanted, but for his sake, for his reputation, he had something to prove.

"Hmm, maybe I'd be willing to help out your little problem," she smirked up at him as she ran her palms up his heaving chest, "if you can catch me that is."

Swiftfoot made a grab for her before she turned around, and he sped up the side of a building with her in tow, just in case she attempted to cheat, he assured himself. He set her down next to him, facing her in the direction he wanted them to go.

"I'm looking to beat you, not catch you." He pointed off in the distance, waiting for her to follow the line of his hand. "You see that clearing? And the warehouse just sitting there?"

"Barely, but yes. You sure you can run that far?" He chuckled at her insinuation and nodded his head.

"No one has complained about my stamina before." She shot him an unamused looked, but he nodded down at the street, redirecting her attention to the traffic light down below. "When the light turns red, we go."

The two stood side-by-side, eyes trained on the traffic light. Swiftfoot tried to focus, he truly did, but something about Portia intoxicated him more than he wanted to admit. He shook his head, eyes waiting for the red. He could deal with his confusing attraction to her later.

The light switched to yellow. Swiftfoot tensed, his body already vibrating with the electric speed ready to set loose. The cars slowed, and at the red, everything else sped up. The world blurred around him as he sped forward, darting across rooftops. But out of the corner of his eye, there was no Portia beside him, nor was she a little behind or in front of him. Her blue outfit was nowhere to be found.

She couldn't already have gotten there. He would have seen her blur by him, would have felt the wind of her rushing past. Where the hell was she? And then, just there, on the next rooftop, he saw a blip of blue before it disappeared. The fuck?

He pushed himself harder, surprised when a burst of energy jolted through him and sent him to a speed he didn't think was possible. He saw her again, a few feet ahead, leaning against the ledge. With a smile, she disappeared again and reappeared two rooftops down.

The realization hit him like a ton of bricks. Portia was a damn teleporter. She wasn't faster than him, just had a different kind of power. A power that got her places before he could even imagine getting there. And

126

she was teasing him with it right now, playing with him. She knew all along.

He didn't give up. He still wanted at her, in more ways than one. The adrenaline had taken him too far, and now, well now he just needed something to do with it. She couldn't take the city from him. He wouldn't let her. This was his city. Without that, what else did he have? He was nothing without Swiftfoot. The superhero thing was his destiny, something he was born for.

By the time he reached the warehouse, Portia was leaned up against the brick, tapping her foot in a playful way. Those electrifying eyes blazed him to his core, but he didn't stop marching up to her.

"Well, it's about—" the rest of her sentence was swallowed up by Swiftfoot's mouth as he claimed her lips in a searing kiss.

He wasn't sure why he did it. He planned on fighting her and telling her to get lost, but something… dammit, there was just something else he had to do first.

Luckily, Portia was receptive to his sudden onslaught of kisses. Her fingers threaded through his hair, pulling him in as she opened her mouth against his and let him slide his tongue against hers. He groaned into the kiss, his hands roaming over her curves as his body pressed her firmly against the wall. She didn't taste like the cinnamon he was so used to smelling on her, but she tasted divine either way.

Divine, really? What did this girl do to him?

Portia's hands did her own roaming, and he grunted into their kiss when he felt her hands squeeze his ass, grinding his hardness into her. Without a second thought, he ran his hands to the backs of her thighs, picking her up as she got the message and wrapped her legs around him. They moved against each other, their skintight suits providing very little between them. Fuck, but why couldn't these things grant easier access.

He wanted more, and by her frantic movements against him, so did she. Where could he take her, or better yet, where could she take them? How did her teleportation powers even work? Swiftfoot felt like he couldn't breathe, his mind was on a whole other plane of pleasure, his body thrumming with the smell and rhythm of hers. Portia had reduced him back to his virgin high school days, playing seven minutes in heaven in a stuffy closet, trying his damnedest to make those seven minutes count for something.

A sound of something falling inside the warehouse startled them, and she broke away from him with a gasp. They stared at each other, their uneven breaths mingling in the coldness between them, and Swiftfoot leaned in for one more chaste kiss before setting her down and backing away.

"Sorry, I, uh, don't know…" Swiftfoot stumbled over his words, not able to formulate anything beyond wanting to kiss her again.

"I thought you hated me," Portia breathed out, her hands grasping his biceps.

"I do." At her look of betrayal, Swiftfoot clung to her before she could leave him. "Or I did. I'm really not sure anymore."

Swiftfoot closed his eyes as her fingers outlined his jaw, before creeping up to the edge of his mask. Her fingertips slipped underneath, and she paused a moment, maybe allowing him time to stop her, before peeling the mask away from his eyes. It didn't matter now, not really when she already knew what he looked like.

But he still didn't know what she looked like, and that intrigued him. With just as slow movements to match hers, Parker caressed her smooth skin, bringing both hands to cup her face before grasping at the edge of her mask and lifting it on top of her head.

"Hey," he whispered in awe. She was absolutely breathtaking to him. Her cheeks flushed and she bit her lip, looking down at the little space left between them before meeting his gaze again.

"So why don't you like me?" The uncertainty in her voice, so different from her cheeky confidence, caught him off guard and he felt himself backpedaling.

"It's not you. It's just, why do you have to be a hero here? Why are you trying to take my city away from me?"

Her mouth dropped open in shock and her eyes lit with understanding. "That's not what I'm trying to do. I thought if I showed you how good I was, how useful I could be, that maybe you would want to team up."

Portia wanted to team up? With him? This wasn't comic book life. But if you were going to put any stock into comic books, they proved that dynamic duos never worked well. One always felt inferior, or one would get used against the other. Swiftfoot couldn't be tied down to Portia all the time, constantly compared to her, sharing the spotlight. He started this thing alone and he was going to end it that way.

"I worked hard to establish my legacy here. If I wanted a sidekick, I would have had one by now. I work alone." He turned away from her, staring up at the starry sky and sighed. "Why don't you go fight bad guys in a different city and become their hero?"

Portia appeared before his eyes faster than he could blink, and her hand connected with his cheek faster than he could duck out of the way. It didn't hurt, well it did, but he had suffered worse hits to the face. It was the fact that she had slapped him, he almost felt betrayed though they had nothing more between them than a pissing contest and a hot make out session.

"I know you aren't from here," she hissed out between her teeth, glaring up at him in disdain, "because I'm from here. I grew up in this city, I watched someone like you come in and show off your abilities, and you know how that felt?" Tears welled up in her stormy eyes, and all Parker could do was shake his head.

"I felt relieved that there was someone like me. That I wasn't such a freak, and I wasn't alone where I lived. I had this vision of us running across the rooftops, taking out bad guys, and maybe grabbing a beer after because I could know who you were, and you would know who I was.

"And we would have at least one person who knew all of us and it would be nice. I never would have pegged you for a chauvinistic pig, and I can't believe I considered hooking up with you!"

Parker grabbed her wrist, keeping her in place before she popped out. She had him all wrong. He didn't care that she was a girl, he actually preferred it. If she had been a guy, he would've just kicked her ass. But she was a girl, a stunning, feisty, amazing girl with amazing powers.

"It's not like that. I don't care that you're a superhero, just go be one somewhere else." His eyes softened as he reached up to smooth her hair away from her face. His face fell once she slapped his hand away.

"I refuse to leave. This is rightfully *my* city. You leave."

"No way!"

With a stubborn set to her jaw, Portia squared her shoulders and managed to look down her nose at Parker though she was about a foot shorter than him. "Well, I'm staying."

"You stay and I'll consider you my enemy." His face lowered to her level so she could feel the full malice of his next threat. "And I take down *all* my enemies. I don't want to do that to you, but this hero gig is all I've got."

Her lips took his by surprise, and he squeezed her to him, relieved she finally understood. If she chose to pursue her hero dreams elsewhere, he'd miss her. He could admit that much now. Maybe if she chose a civilian life, he could track her down, and they could date or something.

She pulled away from him, yanking her mask over her eyes, but he could still make out the wetness on her face. He made her cry. Well, shit, there went any future possibilities for them.

"Well, you could've had more."

Parker reached out to tug her back into him, to show her how much more he was willing to give her, but his fingers swished through the night air, catching on to the emptiness she left behind.

Fine then. It was her call now.

* * *

Portia stayed out of the news and off the rooftops after their last fight. Swiftfoot once again regained the glory and respect of his city. Sure, the people missed the incredible Portia, but they were happy to be protected. No one missed Portia more than Parker.

He checked the internet and national news more times than he could count, hoping she would show up in another city. He just wanted to know that she was okay. And where she was so that he could find her and apologize. He had been an ass. Now that he had the city back to himself, it felt empty without her.

He felt empty without her.

Two weeks of her disappearance did not stop the threat of villains, old and new. His latest call was at a bakery, some kind of fire villain. Those were the worst sometimes, but why a bakery of all places? Did the guy have something against gluten?

Once Swiftfoot rushed inside, he sighed in relief at the familiar figure. "Thomas, buddy, someone piss you off again?"

The flaming fireball, known as Thomas in human form, growled at him and roared in his direction. Thomas was always a complicated capture, mainly because he wasn't truly a villain. Just a regular guy with anger issues and a dangerous side effect of those issues.

Customers cowered under tables, too afraid to move and set off the flaming man before them. Swiftfoot noticed a melted chair by the door, and figured at least one person had gotten away, leaving everyone else with a taste of how volatile Thomas could become at any sudden movements.

Well, Swiftfoot was all about sudden movements, but in this case, his speed did him no good. Fire and a breeze weren't exactly a good combination in an enclosed space such as this one. With slow, measured steps, Swiftfoot made his way to the counter where someone crouched, frozen behind the pastry case.

His heart dropped to his stomach, and his blood heated, rushing south. Only Portia had that crazy effect on his body, and there she was, looking up at him in a mixture of disbelief and resentment. It made him want to scoop her up and drown her in apologies and kisses.

Unfortunately, there was no time for that, and with the way she was looking at him, she wouldn't be up for it either. Still, she was here, though as a civilian, and he actually needed her help. She was perfect for what he needed to accomplish.

"Hey," he murmured, approaching her so that only she could hear him, "where is your outfit? Why aren't you fighting him?"

"I work here. I was just clocking out when he suddenly burst into flames." Huh, well that explained her cinnamon smell.

"What happened right before he burst into flames?"

"I don't know... he was standing in line, checking his phone like everyone else waiting." Okay, so maybe Thomas got a bad email or text message. Poor guy tried his best not to get angry, especially in public. Must have gotten some really bad news.

"Okay listen, I need to knock out Thomas..."

"Thomas? His villain name is *Thomas*?"

"What? No! He's not a villain, just has some screwed-up powers." Portia looked at him skeptically, and Swiftfoot's shoulders sagged. "The media calls him Fireball when he gets like this. Anyway, do you guys have a fire extinguisher?"

"Of course. It's a bakery." Damn, he wanted to kiss the sarcasm right out of her. Her saucy temperament did things to him that he couldn't exactly act on right now.

"Portia, I need your help. While I distract him, I need you to extinguish the fire on his head and knock him out. When he's unconscious, the flames die out."

"I can't do that." Her timid voice surprised him, and he hated the look of uncertainty in her eyes.

"Look, I was wrong before. So wrong. I don't want you in another city. I want you in this one. And I need you right now, so go get it…"

"No, like, I really can't. I'm from here, remember? These people know me. I can't teleport in front of them and fight off a fire guy." He watched her as she stooped down behind the counter and retrieved a fire extinguisher, thrusting it in his hands. "You're on your own."

"No, I can't do this without you. I need you."

Swiftfoot glanced at Thomas, relieved to see that he was still in the growling and occasional flare up stage of his anger. Soon, if allowed to continue in this phase, fire would start shooting from his body, and that always made things 10 times more difficult.

"I'm sorry, I can't…" Swiftfoot cupped her face, pressing his thumb against her lips, and waited for her to focus on him.

"Can you teleport things?" She shrugged at his question, like it was no big deal, and sighed.

"Well, sure, I can bring all kinds of things with me, but once again, I can't do it in front of these people."

"Could you teleport me? Like if I hung on to you or something?" A doubtful expression crossed her face and Swiftfoot pressed on. "If you could just make us pop up behind him, I'd have a better chance at this thing."

"I can't... no, I won't! I've never done anything like that before, and what if it," she paused, as if trying to find the words as her hands flailed out in an exasperated manner in his general direction. "What if it like, messes up your molecules or something crazy?"

Swiftfoot chuckled, catching her hand in his as he cradled the fire extinguisher against his chest. "I trust you." She looked like she wanted to cry or punch him, he really didn't have time for either option. He drew his arm around her, squeezing her to him. "Now!"

It felt weird, and a bit discombobulating. One second, he was behind the counter with Portia in his arms, and the next, he felt like all the oxygen had been sucked from his lungs. He felt the heat of Thomas before he opened his eyes to meet the blaring inferno before him, and he sucked in a ragged breath, crouching to gain his bearings.

Luckily, Portia was prepared for his moment of unsteadiness, and she grabbed the fire extinguisher from his arm, pointing it towards Thomas's head. The white foam came shooting out, covering him from head to shoulders. Portia looked pleased with herself, but Swiftfoot knew the foam would last only so long for someone like Thomas.

In another 10 seconds, the foam would disintegrate, and the flames would combust to disastrous proportions. Grabbing for the extinguisher, Swiftfoot moved fast and swung it into Thomas's head. The guy crumpled to the floor, and the flames all but fizzled out. Swiftfoot stooped down, wiping away the leftover foam from Thomas's face, and Portia ushered the rest of the customers safely outside while the police cautiously stepped inside.

"Ah, poor Thomas. Must have had a bad day, huh?" Swiftfoot nodded at the officer's response, clapping him on the shoulder as the stretcher came in to retrieve the unconscious man. "Good work, as usual, Swiftfoot."

"Thanks, but I had a little help." Swiftfoot smiled, nodding over to Portia, who stood in all her civilian glory by his side.

"Damn, that's some help." The officer coughed in embarrassment and offered an apologetic smile. "Thank you, miss. See ya next time, Swifty."

"Don't start that again, Jamal!" Portia's giggle caught him off guard, and he pulled her against him, pleased that she didn't disappear on him. "Hi."

"Hi." She looked around them in an obvious way, and then met his gaze full on with a beaming smile. "All in a day's work, huh?"

"We make a good team." The breath hitched in her throat, and her hopeful eyes melted his heart. "If you're still interested."

"Really?" she asked in earnest, her fingers dancing along his chest before cupping the back of his neck.

"Sure. I really missed you out there." He pressed his forehead against hers, and whispered, "And maybe, we could go out sometime? As us?"

"We could do lunch now if you want. I was about to leave work."

Swiftfoot looked down at himself and shook his

head. "Can't exactly go to a restaurant looking like this. I'd need to go back home and change."

"Do you live far from here?" He didn't miss the mischievous glint in her eye, but decided he rather liked it, and he opened his mouth to answer her when that whole breath sucked out of his lungs feeling attacked him again.

"And here's my room," he said in disbelief, ripping his mask off to make sure he wasn't seeing things. "How... how did you do that?"

Portia giggled, seeming giddy all of a sudden, as she also took a look around. "I didn't know I could. I just thought that if I can teleport with people, and if that other person knew where to go, I could just channel my powers into them and voila. It worked!"

"You're incredible, you know that... what do I even call you? When you aren't Portia?"

"Oh, right. I guess we never have covered that, have we?" She stuck her hand out then, and he took it, liking the feel of how tiny it felt in his bigger one. "I'm Alice."

"Alice, really? Okay."

"Is there something wrong with Alice?"

"No, it's just... it seems too innocent for you, especially with a hero name like Portia. I don't know what I expected. No, I like it. Alice." The more he said it, the more it seemed to fit. It was a different name, and she was definitely a different girl. Her blue eyes looked up at him expectantly, their hands still locked in a handshake, and Parker almost choked in embarrassment.

"Oh, right. Parker," he pointed to himself with his free hand as if his words would confuse her, "I'm Parker."

"Hmm, I like it. It's got that boyish charm, like

you do." He rolled his eyes at her obvious teasing and shifted on his feet.

"So, I guess I'll change out of this suit and we can head out. If you want, you can make yourself at home, and…" The words died in his throat as she pressed her body into his, her lips tracing over his exposed collar bone.

"You don't want any help out of this?" As innocently as she posed the question, he knew what she was trying to do to him, and he'd be damned if he didn't take advantage of a golden opportunity.

Bringing his finger under her chin, he forced her lips away from his skin and kissed her with every intention he had. He parted from her just enough that their lips still touched, and her panted breath ghosted along his lips.

"If you help me out of this suit, there won't be any lunch for us for a long, long time." She moaned against his mouth, pulling him down for more heated kisses. Fuck yes, but she was perfect for him.

Pulling away, she took his hand and backed them up until her knees hit his bed, her body collapsing back onto his mattress. She scooted away as he crawled over, landing kisses on any part of her body within reach.

"Whoever said I was hungry for food?" she asked, and Parker all but ripped his suit from his body, using his speed to undress her as well.

Despite speed being his best attribute, Parker intended on taking is time acquainting himself with Alice's body. He wanted to savor every inch of her in the best ways possible.

Kissing up the slender column of her neck, he chuckled at her slight shiver. "I'm pretty hungry too, and I plan on making a five-course meal out of you."

138

SUPER HEAT STORIES

Supergay
By Julie Behrens

Spitfire approached the ship cautiously. She might be decked out in a suit of armor based off alien tech so advanced they barely understood what it did, but Vixen's tech wasn't too far behind, and this was a strange situation. Vixen's sleek battleship, the *Kitsune*, hovered above the museum, which had a neat hole through the roof and a cable running into it. This was an alarmingly obvious move for the super villain thief; usually she was at least a little subtle, opting for heists and cleverness over busting in with guns blazing. That was usually Spitfire's role.

She zoomed in on a spot of movement below the ship, and spotted Vixen rapidly ascending from the museum roof, her familiar orange braid swinging behind her. Spitfire sped towards the ship, watched Vixen disappear through the port, and gunned it to burst through the port doors before they shut.

Vixen shrieked and leaped away from her, scrambling away from Spitfire's blaster fire. "Spitfire?! Shit! I surrender!" Vixen yelped, holding up her hands. Her eyes showed white all around her irises, standing out in sharp contrast to her dark skin

Spitfire ceased fire. "What?" No fight?

"I surrender! I don't want to fight you, I want to talk. There is shit you gotta know!"

"Goddammit," Spitfire said. "That's not fair."

"Surrendering isn't fair? What's your basis for comparison?"

"Never mind. Just keep your hands visible." Spitfire circled to the side, keeping an eye on those hands. They didn't know how Vixen generated her power blasts, whether it was technology, a mutant ability, or something bestowed upon her some other way. They just knew hands were involved.

"Spit, let me show you."

"Fat chance."

"We're all going to die otherwise. All of us! So many people!"

Spitfire hesitated. Vixen looked genuinely frantic, and not in a just-got-caught kind of way. "I'm recording this, so if you spin me a story you at least have to keep the lies consistent."

Vixen huffed. "I'm not lying. I'll show you. Listen, there's aliens, right? You know that?"

How could she have missed it? The whole 'invasion of the Pentagon and subsequent destruction of several important cultural heritage sites thing that happened last year had convinced everyone pretty quickly. But she just stuck with "Yeah?"

"There's a fleet coming here because we have something of theirs. Well, I have it now. It's really bad. We need to turn it over to them. Spit, this isn't a supervillains vs. superheroes thing. This is bigger than that. I teamed up with you guys in the last invasion, right? There's precedent here."

Spitfire didn't want to admit she was thinking the

same thing. Vixen was a great liar, but what she was saying rang true. "How do you have all this info, anyway?"

"I know a guy."

Spitfire rolled her eyes, though behind the mask, it wasn't visible. "Sure you do."

"You wanna see it? It's in my bag. Here, I'll take it out, nice and slow." Vixen reached for her bag, undid the top flap, and slowly, slowly took a glowing yellow sphere out and set it on the ground. "I only got wind of it because they sent out a signal, and it... started up. A contact through the museum network..."

"You steal from museums! Why would they tell you anything?"

"Money! They need money! Desperately!"

Oh. Well, that tracked. "So this contact of yours..."

"Isn't at this museum. But word travels fast. And someone in NASA told me about the incoming signals they were getting from space..."

"You have a contact at NASA."

"Yes, shut up, I'm telling you way more than I ever intended to tell anyone. Why would I reveal all that if this wasn't dire, you levitating metal melonhead!" She escalated into a shriek. When Spitfire didn't have a comeback for that, Vixen regrouped and soldiered on. "Look, it's not that hard. We have a thing they want, and they're coming here to get it. And I am desperate enough to see this through that I'm telling you, my nemesis, all about it."

A warm feeling curled in her gut. "I'm your nemesis?" she said, perhaps more softly and reverently than she'd meant to.

Vixen closed her eyes, lips moving faintly. About

10 seconds later, she squared her shoulders and nodded. "Yes, you're my nemesis."

"I'm not sure how to respond to that. This is huge." A nemesis? She'd never had one before. She'd never been important enough, consistent enough, to have a nemesis. This was so exciting!

Vixen was the one with the focus, luckily. "We can address it later. Right now, we have a space thing. Bad space guys coming. Will you help me get it to them?"

"Um. Sure? Hey, where did we get it anyway?"

"Asteroid. Or... meteoroid. I forget which one is on Earth."

"Meteorite, I think, if it made it all the way down. I saw a documentary."

"Yeah one of those. Here, I'll show you everything."

Spitfire walked hesitantly into the *Kitsune's* cockpit. It may have been all chrome, bristling with firepower on the outside, but inside it was surprisingly posh. Much of the interior was padded leather and woodgrain, and the recessed lighting lent it a serene atmosphere that contrasted jarringly with the purpose and exterior of the ship.

She sat down in the co-pilot seat, which was comfortable and sturdy, nice lumbar support and buttery leather. The console was an organic mix of metal and wood that managed to be both functional and lovely. She wanted to take her gloves off and touch everything. "It's really nice in here."

"Don't act so surprised," Vixen grumped as she brought up the data on the Spaceball, as Spitfire had dubbed it.

"No, I just mean... I've never been in your ship, so I didn't know what to expect."

"Well, now you know. I have good taste. Here, read this."

She looked. She read. She cross-referenced. To her credit, Vixen let her take as much time as she needed, which was hours. She desperately wanted a coffee break, but she couldn't drink with the helmet on. Stupid suit. She also couldn't go to the bathroom. She could track her mood by how annoyed her suit made her.

Vixen answered her questions. The facts lined up, even, she had to admit, the reasons Vixen's contacts would go to her and not to the Squadron, which had rather a spectacularly bad track record with the aliens they'd met so far.

Finally, she turned off the screen. "Alright. I'm convinced. Take us up into a low orbit, and I'll help you defend the Earth from rudely possessive aliens."

"Can't you pilot? I mean, I'm happy to do so, but even though it's my ship, I'm kinda surprised you're okay with me driving."

"Pilot a ship like the *Kitsune*? No. I do well piloting my Prius through traffic."

Vixen laughed. "You have a Prius? Big guy like you?"

"Yeah, about that..."

Spitfire sighed. If they were going to spend a lot of time in close quarters over the coming days, Vixen was going to find out. Hell, the whole world was on the verge of finding out. She might as well have the revelation come about on her own terms, pick her moments. Besides, being in the armor this long was about to drive her mad. She really had to pee. She took off her helm and finger-combed her black chin-length hair.

Vixen gawked. Her hands froze over the controls. "You're a girl!"

"I haven't been a 'girl' in many years, thank you."

"A woman!"

"There we go."

Vixen left off the controls and swiveled her chair to stare at Spitfire, her slack-jawed stare morphing into an open-mouthed grin. "Oh my god, Spitfire, I had no idea. I'm so stupidly excited!"

Spitfire leaned forward and stripped off the bulk of her armor, making a mental note to thank Dr. Kettler for designing a suit easier to remove. See? Her mood was improving if she could think fondly of the armor at all. "I can't imagine why it would matter to you."

"Because I'm super gay!"

Spitfire leaned back in her chair and laughed. "Holy shit, woman, did this suddenly become a seduction because of the surprise boobies?"

"More like because of the surprise... gender fuckery."

"Your seduction sucks."

Vixen smiled, wide and toothy. "I'll work on it."

* * *

Spitfire was tired of waiting. She'd sent messages to the Squadron, the local superhero group, over an hour ago, and no one had responded yet. She'd divested herself of the rest of her armor, which allowed her to finally go to the bathroom. Feeling better, she regarded Vixen as the villain went through her stretching routine (yoga? Pilates? Katas? A mix? She couldn't tell). The woman was achingly beautiful, she admitted to herself, both graceful and strong, with a gorgeous head of hair she'd let down out of her braid. It spilled over her black and white and orange tactical jumpsuit and her umber skin. But weren't most people in their line of work either gobsmackingly beautiful or monstrous? Spitfire was one of the few who landed firmly in the "kind of ok" camp of attractiveness. Over six feet of muscle and scar tissue, an olive complexion that made a lot of rude ass people ask "what are you?" as if the parents who had dumped her at the orphanage were of any concern to her. The armor made up for a lot of her perceived short-comings. It was ok for a male to be big, to be over 35, to be just an average kind of pretty. To be kind of an asshole, if she was perfectly honest about it.

"See something you like?" Vixen was watching her over her shoulder and waggled her rear back and forth.

Spitfire started. "Sorry." She tried out a couple of explanations in her head—it was late, she was tired, she hadn't eaten dinner—and finally just repeated herself. "Sorry."

"Don't be. Look all you want, baby." She shifted poses, and Spitfire found something interesting to stare at on the ceiling. "I don't know much of your history. What got you into superheroing, anyway?"

Spitfire shrugged. She didn't particularly like this line of questioning. "Kind of fell into it. Dr. Kettler did

147

some work with the orphanage. When I aged out, he offered me a job. Essentially a test pilot sort of thing."

"He got kids to test his shit?"

"Like I said, I aged out. I was 18. I knew what I was doing."

Vixen rolled over, her copper hair splaying across the mat and stretched, the lean line of her body drawing Spitfire's eyes despite herself. "And what *were* you doing, darling?" She sat up on her elbows and dropped her voice. "Did you have a crush on Dr. Kettler?"

Spitfire burst out laughing. "Oh God, no! No, it wasn't like that at all."

Vixen looked at her from under long lashes. "So, what then? Self-sacrificing, trying to be useful? Clinging to whatever source of approval you could find? No, no, don't get mad!" She rolled up to kneeling, gesturing for Spitfire to sit back down, as if she could wave her back into the chair. "I'm sorry. I'm not making fun!"

Spitfire wasn't having it. "Oh sure! Because guessing how someone's trauma manifested is a great way to chat up new buddies!" Her gut twisted in anger and humiliation. This was bullshit.

Vixen was on her feet now, still making placating gestures. "I'm sorry! I fucked this up. Spit, I know what it feels like to not be wanted, to not have purpose! I know exactly, horribly, what it's like to hate to show yourself to people, not because of all the things they might say, but because you think they're right! Oh…" Vixen said, backing up, eyes wide. "That was the wrong direction to take this conversation."

"What the crap?! Is this negging or something?"

Spitfire advanced on her, boots clanging heavily on the floor of the ship in contrast to Vixen's silent bare feet. "You want to keep going? How about you next go into how I'm one of the longest running Squadron members, but I've never been in charge and never will be? You surely know what a popularity contest that is!"

Vixen stopped and looked confused. "Scott won the popularity contest this last go round?"

"You know what I mean!" She stopped. She had Vixen in a corner now. There was nowhere for her to go. "Let's delve into my romantic past while we're at it! That's a shit show! We can talk about the Sherad debacle, and the time Dr. Kettler was lost in a time warp, and the years it took for me to get out of the damn Crystal of Solace!" She caged Vixen in with her arms, her hands on the wall behind her, on either side of her. "Pick an issue! Let's go!"

Vixen was breathing hard, eyes wide. "Oh Spit. I'm so turned on right now."

She straightened and took a step back. "What?"

Which gave Vixen the room she needed to charge and launch a short power burst, right at Spitfire's stomach. She flew backwards and hit the opposite wall, leaving a nice sized dent in the locker she'd hit. She hit the ground next, barely catching herself on her arms so she didn't faceplant. She was dead. It would happen any minute now; she was sure of it. She'd seen people torn to pieces by those power bursts. She hadn't noticed Vixen was holding her hands behind her, and now she'd taken one directly to the stomach, without her armor. It would start hurting any second.

But she could feel her legs. She pushed up on her elbows. No blood beneath her. She touched her

149

abdomen; it was sore and would probably have a bruise colorful enough to be mistaken for a Monet in a day or two. But she was intact. Her shirt wasn't even torn.

She looked at Vixen. "You didn't kill me," she said, mystified.

"Oh, for fuck's sake," Vixen said, exasperation thick in her voice. "Spitfire. Why would I kill you? I need you to defeat Whosawhatsit out there. And when it comes down to it, I'd rather fight with you than get along with just about anyone else." She walked over and extended a hand. "Besides, there's a shortage of tall, hot women in the world. Waste not."

Spitfire considered Vixen carefully. Finally, she said, "You like fighting me?" They were nemeses, of course she likes fighting you, she thought, remembering the wonderful revelation from earlier.

Vixen threw up her hands. "*That's* what you heard out of all that. Yes, I know when I go up against you, I'm probably not going to die. Captured, plans foiled, yes, that might happen. And it's almost fun, because you're formidable, you're interesting, you do unexpected things. But if I took you out? The next person to fixate on thwarting me might just launch a grenade at my head. Trust me, I'd rather have you." She grinned. "And sometimes I win."

"You've never killed me, when you had the chance."

"Not for real, anyway."

Spitfire let out a breath. "Truce, then?"

Vixen took the outstretched hand. "Truce." She brought Spitfire's hand to her mouth and kissed the scarred knuckles. "More than truce?"

Spitfire politely disentangled her hand. "Definitely not. You are not invited into my pants. I'm going to go lay down for a while. I need to think." She stalked towards the alcove where the spare bunk was; a curtain would at least afford a little privacy while she thought. She pretended not to hear Vixen say, "We'll see."

* * *

Spitfire lay in her bunk that night, listening to Vixen snore above her. It was pretty impressive. The lady needed to get herself checked for sleep apnea. Spitfire couldn't sleep, but it wasn't about the snoring. She could sleep through any kind of noise. It was a talent cultivated through years of sleeping in the same room as lots of other kids. No, it was something else keeping Spitfire awake.

Vixen... understood. Sure, she'd been stupid and insensitive about it, but when had any of the other Squadron guessed at any of her issues? They'd never even tried. And Vixen just... spoke them out loud. Like it was a thing to talk about. Who *did* that?

She wondered what else Vixen would talk about if she let her. Yes, Vixen had said she was attractive. She hadn't missed it. She'd just chosen to panic and ignore it in the moment. Did she mean it? Or did she want something? What could she gain by a seduction? Maybe she was just bored. Bored and horny, waiting for aliens. They'd messaged the other Squadron members again and anyone they could think of who might help. So far, no dice.

Maybe Vixen would talk about what had happened to her, to make her steal artifacts from museums. Rumor

151

had it she returned them to their homelands. But maybe she sold them on the black market. And anyway, wouldn't a lot of that stuff just end up back in the hands of rich white folk anyway? It didn't seem like a sound strategy. Maybe there was more to it.

Maybe not. Maybe she saw an injustice in the artifacts being kept from their homelands and ran with it.

Maybe she was just cruel.

Maybe she was bored.

Vixen seemed like the kind of person who would do a lot of sketchy stuff to stave off boredom. Like seduce a member of the Squadron, she thought testily. Her body was really not being terribly helpful. She closed her eyes, turned on her side and hugged a pillow to her chest. Her imagination helpfully supplied a mental image of spooning up behind Vixen. She'd be warm and strong and would push back against Spitfire, making little noises, asking for... .

Ok, that was quite enough of that.

But her boobs were nice.

All boobs are nice, she told herself irritably, and rolled over. Besides, she'd never enjoyed casual sex. What could she and Vixen possibly have once this bizarre joint venture was over? Vixen was a thief.

Yes, but...

No, she shut down her train of thought. Not buts.

Vixen's butt.

She buried her face in the pillow and made a horrible noise of frustration and anger. Vixen broke the law. Dr. Kettler and the Squadron were perfectly clear: they followed the law. They enforced the law when the police and military couldn't, when the villains outclassed them. When there was no one else to do it.

Spitfire's mind whirled with the confusion of the past 24 hours, the past year, the past decade. Most of the time she was just a brick, certainly to the Squadron. They didn't believe Spitfire had much of a brain, but she did. She'd been thinking. She'd been reading. And thinking more. About police brutality, about the for-profit prison system, about civil rights and media narratives. About systems created specifically to perpetuate injustice.

About how they only had one life, and to spend that life restrained by a deliberately cruel and extortionate system that held you back from what you could be wasn't just wrong. It was tragic. Tragedy on a massive, invisible scale.

Vixen wasn't stealing from the vulnerable. She wasn't stealing people's lives. She was stealing artifacts that had themselves been stolen from their homelands. No telling how she gets the funding, Spitfire reminded herself, looking out of her bunk at the very nice ship. But if what she did ended up having a net positive good in the world…

No! This wasn't who she was! Vixen was a villain!

Do you actually know who you are, she asked herself? She'd gone from an orphanage to the Squadron, and they'd put her in weaponized armor. There she'd stayed, behind a mask, for so many years.

She curled up tighter and willed herself to sleep. These weren't questions to ask herself in a crisis. These were things to ponder at length. There would be no spontaneous actions, she promised herself. She could keep control of herself.

She could.

It would be ok.

153

* * *

"Spitfire. C'mere."

Spitfire rolled herself out of her bunk and came up behind Vixen in the cockpit. She looked at the display graphic and shook her head. "What am I looking at?"

Vixen tapped the screen. "This is us—no, don't zoom in, argh, this is a new interface, sorry—ok, this is us, and this is the incoming group of ships. I think we have about two hours before they get here. You need to do anything besides suit up?"

"Yeah," Spitfire said. There were so many dots. So many. "I need to call the Squadron."

Vixen rotated in her chair and fixed Spitfire with a strange look. "You already tried that."

"Well I need to try it again!"

"They're not going to like my involvement."

Spitfire gesticulated wildly at the screen. "Well I don't like dying!"

Vixen stood up and held her head high. "Fine. Call the Squadron as many times as you like. See where that gets you." She stalked past Spitfire to the back of the ship.

Fine, let Vixen be haughty about Spitfire still wanting her stupid teammates to join her on this stupid mission with a stupid Spaceball and stupid aliens. Fuck. She sat in the co-pilot chair and hailed the Squadron. Again. And again. Each of their individual comms. Nothing. She was about to give up when she got an answering blip. Yes! She put it through.

Blink's young face appeared on the screen, with Chasmos behind him. "Hey Spit," they said.

"Finally! Thank gods! Blink, can you get the others on the horn? There are alien ships incoming in about two hours and…"

"Spit, you gotta stop comming them."

She stopped. "Come again?"

Blink and Chasmos shared a strained look. "Listen, when you left with Vixen, Dr. Kettler said not to contact you. He said… you'd turned."

Every muscle in her body tensed. "What. Turned? Turned to what? That doesn't make any sense."

"He said you'd do anything to get to the rest of us, too. And… well he said a lot of stuff, I'm sorry, I could get in a lot of trouble for even talking to you, but… I don't really believe them. I think you just made a bad decision, and they should let you come home. But I don't exactly have a lot of pull." Chasmos made a similarly helpless shrug.

Spitfire waved frantically towards the window. "That also doesn't make any sense! Is this real life? It's not a lie! There's *bad stuff* coming, and people are going to die!"

"Are you sure? I mean, it's not like you can trust Vixen."

"Take a damn telescope outside. You should be able to see them by now!"

"I'm sorry, Spit," Blink said, and the comm died.

Spitfire sat for long moments in the chair, feeling like there were explosions going off inside her head. It didn't make any sense. Nothing made sense. She wanted things to stop spinning out of control and make sense. She was really stuck on that word, "make sense." When did the world go upside down, and how could she right it?

155

She felt a hand on her shoulder. "I'm sorry."

"You heard all that?"

"Kinda hard not to. It's a small ship, and you were yelling for part of it."

Spitfire stood up. If Dr. Kettler, and the entire Squadron, thought she'd turned on them, whatever that meant, what would they do? Why would they have believed with so little evidence, without even asking? Why was it so easy for them to write her off?

Vixen brushed a hand against her cheek, and Spitfire realized with a start she'd just been standing there, staring at nothing in her shock.

"Hey there sweetheart, you ok?"

Spitfire managed to meet her eyes. Beautiful black eyes with phenomenal lashes. They weren't even fake, she realized, because Vixen wasn't wearing any makeup. She was fresh out of the shower, her fox-orange hair still damp, her black tactical shirt clinging lightly to her skin.

"No," Spitfire said, and carefully added, "I don't think I've been ok for a while now."

Vixen pulled her down, and for a moment Spitfire thought she was going to kiss her, but she just touched their foreheads together and closed her eyes. "They don't know what they've got. You're incredible. Courageous and reflective and passionate and smart."

She chuckled. "I don't know about that last part."

"No, you are. Do they tell you you're not?"

Spitfire didn't answer. Compared to the rest of the Squadron she certainly wasn't the brightest bulb. It didn't seem worth arguing about. "They think I joined you."

Vixen's arms went over her shoulders. Around her neck. "You kinda did."

"Just for this mission! Because of what's at stake!"

Vixen opened her eyes. "You were willing to be gray, in a world of black and whites. That's going to paint you as the villain to a lot of people. I've been there."

"They don't want me to come back," Spitfire said, grief tightening her throat. "How is this real? How did I land in such bedlam?"

Vixen brushed her mouth against Spitfire's, ever so briefly, but it sent an almost electric shock all the way through her. "I want you here."

Spitfire grabbed that tiny spark like a life rope. She kissed, firm and needy at first, then relaxing enough to turn it into a caress. Vixen made a wonderful noise in the back of her throat and sank into the kiss. Her lips were so plush, so soft, and she was so small in Spitfire's muscle-thick arms. She was so beautiful. She was so... so...

Spitfire pulled back, breathless. "What are we doing," she gasped.

"Making out," Vixen said, and tried to pull her back in.

"No, I mean, this is still a temporary alignment, we're not together."

"For crying out loud, Spit, it's just kissing."

She swallowed. "Sorry. I'm just... not casual about this stuff."

"Neither am I. You've no idea how long I've wanted to do this. Even when I thought you were a man, when I didn't know what you looked like. You were my exception to the Girls Only club."

Well that was really arousing. Spitfire brushed a damp curl away from Vixen's forehead. "How can I reconcile what I want with who I am?"

Vixen leaned against her, nuzzling her neck and touching her, touching her all over, back and arms and shoulders and neck. "One step at a time."

One step at a time. One kiss at a time. One painfully earnest sigh at a time. Spitfire's body trembled all over, from arousal and unspent adrenaline and fear and the awful, stinging slap of rejection from her comrades. She would live in this moment, and not worry about what came later, whether it fit into the plan, or fit into her world. This was right. It felt almost inevitable, like she and Vixen had been circling each other for years, not recognizing the tight, witty banter and constrained violence for what it was: super powered flirting.

Fuck it. She picked Vixen up—who yelped—and plopped her in the command chair. Vixen smiled against her mouth, until she slid down to her knees, hands wandering south. The tactical shirt had a convenient zipper down the front, and Vixen slid it open with excruciating slowness. Spitfire whimpered, nipping her clavicle, leaving little love-bites on her neck and shoulder. Then Vixen was bare-chested before her, and she bent to take one dusky nipple in her mouth.

That was when she found out that Vixen was very vocal. She told Spitfire exactly what she wanted her to do, which was very helpful, and Spitfire wished everyone was so forthcoming. Harder, not that hard, now switch sides, suck, lick, and all the time with Vixen's fingers in her hair, scraping her scalp.

"Hope I'm not being too pushy for you," Vixen breathed.

"Are you kidding?" Spitfire said between licks. "This is great, I don't have to think at all."

Vixen got a handful of her hair and pulled, so she had to look up at her. "Spitfire," she purred, "do you have a bit of a submissive streak in you?"

Spitfire shrugged noncommittally. "I haven't really had a chance to explore that kind of thing."

Vixen bit her plump lower lip and stroked her thumb over Spitfire's cheek. "Ohhh sweetie. Tell me I can teach you about it."

"Maybe? Like you said. One step at a time. One kink at a time."

"I'm so good with that."

Spitfire couldn't look her in the eye for this request and cast her gaze downward. "Can I go down on you?"

"Can you? Is it my birthday or something? Of course, baby!" She wriggled out of the tight-fitting pants, slid forward in the seat, and hooked her knees over Spitfire's shoulders.

Spitfire loved doing this. She loved finding the spots that drove a lover wild. Vixen did more than respond, she showed her exactly what to do. God, that made things so much easier. Vixen took her hand and guided Spitfire's fingers into her and held her by the hair to grind against her mouth. She couldn't remember doing something so amazingly hot with such a rapid escalation. It was such a thrill, knowing that she was the one making Vixen cry out and shake, Vixen wanted to be with her, just her in that moment. She felt it when Vixen came, her whole body shuddering her release.

Spitfire wiped her mouth on her sleeve and grinned up at her. "Alright?"

Vixen was still gasping and trembling. "Holy shit." She opened her eyes, looked past Spitfire at the command console, and went rigid, eyes widening. "Aw, holy shit!"

An alarm sounded from the sensors, and they left off the sexually charged existential crisis. The sensors were hardly necessary; they could see the starships descending through the clouds. The ships had arrived.

* * *

When Spitfire woke up, she wasn't sure where she was or why she was there. The narrative thread of her life had an unexpected gap in it. She was in her armor. The area was unfamiliar—just grass and trees and gray smoke in the sky. Some kind of ships up there, black and spindly like bugs. She tried to sit up, and a wave of nausea came over her. She flopped back on the ground, then struggled for a minute to get her helmet off. The catch released with a soft hiss; she took a big breath of smoke-flavored air and almost gagged on it. Minutes passed, just breathing, staring ahead, watching the sky with all its ships. Why were there so many ships? She suspected they were related to why she was on the ground with the worst headache of her life.

"Spitfire!"

It was a woman's voice. She thought she recognized it, but her brain wouldn't pull up the information for her. She managed to put a hand in the air and wave before dropping her too-heavy arm back onto the ground. Her head hurt. Her shoulder hurt. Her side hurt. Maybe she had fallen? If so, the pain was giving her a pretty good map of how she'd landed.

"Spitfire! Oh my gods, can you sit up?" The voice was right behind her now.

"I don't think I ought to."

"Shit. Ok." She came around to lean down into Spitfire's view. Huh. Why was Vixen here? Why was Vixen checking up on her, instead of cackling madly that she had won? Because she had clearly won whatever fight they'd had. Something went whistling overhead, and Vixen looked up sharply. Something exploded. Pieces of ships were falling from the sky, like monstrous shrapnel.

"Alright, Spit, we're getting out of here whether you can walk or not."

Vixen picked her up, which was impressive because Spitfire was a lot bigger than Vixen was, especially with the armor. The world spun, and the nausea returned. She was not going to throw up on Vixen's hair. She was not. She was not.

"Drop me."

"What? No! Oh, I see."

Spitfire wrenched away from Vixen as she threw up in the grass. Vixen waited until she'd emptied her stomach, then hauled her back up and kept them moving.

Right. Vixen was… a kind of ally right now. She couldn't remember why. She reassured herself she'd remember later, when her head stopped pounding, and the world stopped spinning sideways out from under her, and the sky stopped exploding above them.

They didn't get *too* many strange looks on the subway. Apparently, a woman in armor and a woman in tactical gear didn't really rank for "weird" on the city subways. Spitfire wouldn't know; she always flew. Or drove her Prius, if she wanted to be subtle.

She managed to not throw up again, anyway. Small victories. Vixen half-dragged her out at the last stop, got her up the stairs, through the front doors of a little hotel, parked her on a couch in the lobby, and returned a little while later with a med kit, bottled water, and a key card.

"Come on, Lancelot, let's get you patched up."

"Lancelot was a tool. I'd rather be Gawain."

"Whatever." Vixen helped her up and half-carried her to the elevator, then to a hotel room down the hall. Once there, Spitfire collapsed in a heap on one of the beds. With some coaxing, she got out of her armor. That alone was worlds better. Vixen checked her over and categorized her injuries—all bruising, no bleeding, not on the outside anyway. She got some water and painkillers in her and sat tensely on the opposite bed.

"Well, I think it's just a concussion. And frankly, if all you got was a concussion and some epic bruises after being knocked out of the sky like that, you're doing pretty good."

"I'm starting to remember what happened. When I first woke up, I was super confused to see you there."

"All coming back to you now?" She brushed Spitfire's hair out of her eyes, and it felt good, just to have someone touch her with kindness, gentleness. Had it been that long since she'd been touched like that?

"Yeah." Yeah, she was remembering now.

"Don't fall asleep."

"No." She pushed herself slowly up into a half-sitting position. "Tell me what happened from your perspective."

Vixen folded her legs up. Her long, powerfully

muscled legs. In combat boots. Spitfire loved small
women in combat boots. She refocused on what Vixen
was saying. "…when the alien ships came down. You
took off out of the portal and tried to draw their fire
while I hailed them. Which you ended up doing very
successfully." She gestured to Spitfire's current
condition. "I might not think much of Kettler, but
damn, that armor's something else."

"It's made of unobtainium." She wheezed
laughter at her own joke while Vixen rolled her eyes.

"You're hilarious. Anyway, I saw which way
things were going. When my ship started taking heavy
damage, I took the escape shuttle away."

"Ooh, you have an escape shuttle?"

"Good thing, otherwise, I'd be toast. I don't know
what the aliens are doing now. They won this round.
Never mind they could have just, you know,
communicated and taken the damn thing."

"Do you speak alien?"

"I have a universal translator."

"A what?"

"A magic gizmo." She frowned. "Had a magic
gizmo. It blew up with the ship."

Spitfire wondered what had become of her life
that she accepted this as a plausible explanation. "Did
the Squadron show?"

Vixen's lips drew into a thin line. "Let's check the
news and see what's going on." She switched on the
television and, with some wrestling with the controls,
found a station with live coverage of the event. Spitfire
could make out two figures whirring around that were
probably Squadron fliers. The rest would have a pretty
hard time participating from the ground.

"Hey." Spitfire pointed at the screen, tracking the ships. "There are two different kinds of ships. Like, vastly different."

"Yeah…" Vixen got up to get a better look. "And they're firing at each other."

"Maybe that's your explanation for why they just attacked you. Maybe they thought you were an enemy ship."

Vixen straightened up, and Spitfire could read the exhaustion in the lines of her body. "Or maybe all that group wanted was the destruction of the damned thing."

"What's it do, anyway?"

"Hell if I know!" Her bag was slung on a chair, and she took the Spaceball out of it to look at it. She came over to Spitfire and put it between them on the bed. The surface was etched with strange shapes and textures, which only showed when you moved it a certain way. The interior glowed like a small sun, yellow at the center and fading to red.

A small sun. The thought caught in her head and wouldn't let go.

"Hey. Could this be a generator of some kind?"

"What makes you say that?"

Spitfire hesitated. She didn't want to look like an idiot in front of Vixen. She had a concussion. She probably wasn't thinking straight. This was the kind of thing that might have gotten her laughed at in the Squadron. Not only then, but for years afterward, brought up over and over at her expense. But Vixen waited, not looking the least bit like she wanted to laugh.

"Ok. So, the sun works on nuclear fusion, which produces a tremendous amount of energy. This looks like a tiny sun, and a lot of people are really invested in controlling it, so it must have value to them. Could this thing have a tiny nuclear fusion reaction going on inside it?"

She waited. Vixen didn't laugh. She picked the Spaceball up and turned it over in her hands. "I don't know enough about nuclear physics to say. I mean, on the one hand, I thought it needed a lot of matter to do something like that, which is why, say, the sun has nuclear fusion and even big planets like Jupiter don't." She met Spitfire's eyes over the top of the ball. "But these aliens are also traveling faster than light, and I thought that was impossible too."

"What's the saying? Sufficiently advanced science is indistinguishable from magic?"

"Something like that. Well, it's a good theory anyway, best one I've heard." She got up and put the ball back in her bag and snapped the flap over it. "I don't know why I feel better having it in the bag. It's not like a layer of canvas really helps."

"I don't know either, but I can't argue."

Vixen came back to where Spitfire slouched, and gingerly touched her forehead. "You're going to have a nice bruise there tomorrow. A real war wound to show off."

"I'm going to have nice bruises in lots of places."

"How are you feeling?"

"A lot better than I did a few hours ago. Thanks for patching me up. I love modern medicine, especially painkillers."

Vixen sat down, close to her. "Hey, Spit, it really scared me today, when you got shot down out of the sky. I thought for a few minutes there was no way you'd survived."

Spitfire chuckled. "Afraid to lose your nemesis?"

Vixen didn't chuckle. Didn't even smile. She cupped Spitfire's cheek and brushed her thumb across her lips. "Afraid to lose my new friend."

Spitfire didn't know what to say. She was tempted to be snarky. How could Vixen bear such scalding sincerity? Did she dare meet her on her own terms, with her own sincerity? That seemed incredibly dangerous.

But then, since when had she been afraid of danger?

"I am glad I didn't die and miss out on whatever happens next."

Vixen smiled. "I'll make it worth your while to stick around." She kissed her. Spitfire put her arms around her and drew her close, until Vixen was practically in her lap. They stayed there a long time, kissing each others' mouths and necks and ears and shoulders, while the alien ships fought on the other side of the city.

When the sun went down, they got under the covers together. They deemed clothes unnecessary and discarded them. She tried to dismiss her concerns about her body. After all, Vixen was here with her, had chosen her, that should be enough. Shouldn't it?

Then Vixen started talking. She already knew Vixen was vocal during sex, but this was something else. "Spit, you're so gorgeous," she said, her voice honeyed and soft. "I love your muscles. Fuck, you're ripped. Your breasts are absolutely perfect, God you're so much bigger than I am. I love it! I bet you could hold me up against the wall. Not right now though." She slid down Spitfire's body. "Right now, I have a score to settle."

166

Spitfire clapped a hand over her own mouth to keep from screaming, it felt so good, it had been so long, way too long since anyone had touched her like this, had wanted to make her feel good. Had asked her what she liked, what she wanted.

"You," Spitfire managed to say. "I just want you."

Vixen knew what she was doing. She was talented with her quick, eager tongue, and brought Spitfire to climax easily, then straddled her and rubbed against her until they were both utterly wrung out. Who needed penetration? Not when they were learning each others' bodies so openly. Not when just friction between them felt so good, made time stretch out and lose all meaning. She was left boneless and sleepy and wanted to climb inside Vixen's skin and live there forever. What a strange impulse, she thought, but she was too tired to examine it.

"Thank you," she just said instead. "I … I need this. I needed you. I didn't know."

"Someone's been unkind to you," Vixen said. Spitfire stroked her new lover's face, admiring how the soft yellow light of the lamps outside played on her dark skin. She was just so damn pretty.

"Yeah, I guess so. A lot of someones, really." She didn't want to talk about it. Humiliation and dismissal and underestimation had been all too common a theme in her life. "You're not unkind to me."

"I think maybe suffering has made you into a kinder person." Vixen pressed their foreheads together. "But if it had been up to me, I would have spared you from it."

"Suffering tends to make people go one of two ways, in my experience. You either want to spare others from it, or you want to make everyone feel it." It

167

occurred to her she knew very little of Vixen's past. "I'm guessing you've done your share of suffering as well."

Vixen smiled, but it was a look full of sorrow and grief. "You could say that."

Spitfire leaned in to kiss her. "Well. Here's to not suffering for a little while."

* * *

Spitfire woke up in the morning to an empty bed, and for just a moment, had the gut-wrenching thought that maybe it had all been a ruse, and Vixen was gone. But then she heard Vixen in the shower, singing "Roxanne" so off key she might have been harmonizing. She shook her head and turned on the television to check the news. It felt so old-timey to do that; she was a little lost without her phone to connect her to the outside world. More about the aliens, some collateral damage, a statement by the president, by some military guy, a representative of NASA...

Spitfire lunged out of bed, and almost face-planted on the floor. She recovered her balance and blundered into the bathroom.

"Hey!" she barked, louder than she intended.

Vixen shrieked, and there was some thumping that was probably dropping stuff, and possibly almost falling. Vixen yanked the shower curtain back and gave her a vicious death glare. *"What the fuck, Spit!"* she barked back.

"You have a NASA contact!"

"Yes?"

"Vixen, call him and tell him we have the Spaceball!

"The what..."

168

"Sure, you can't communicate with the aliens anymore, because the whatsit magical thingy in your ship…"

"Universal translator."

"Right, it's toast, but I bet NASA can figure out how to talk to them!"

Vixen pondered this. "Huh. It's a better plan that anything else I've come up with. Yeah. Yeah, let's do that!" She returned to the glare. "After I finish my shower."

* * *

The actual handing over of the Spaceball was somewhat anticlimactic. Communication and analysis revealed there were two factions of aliens after it–one that wanted to destroy it and one that wanted to obtain it. The entire world of Earth, when faced with the bristling firepower of two alien fleets, agreed in the shortest negotiations ever that they did not have a dog in this fight, and would turn the cube over to a neutral ambassador ship that promised to negotiate between the two factions. Spitfire approached the landed ship in her (very dinged up) armor. An alien emerged and she extended the Spaceball to it on her upraised palm (because these aliens were apparently very tall) and the alien snatched it out of her hand with what she suspected was a dirty look.

"Like turning it over hadn't been what we were trying to do from the beginning," Spitfire muttered as she buckled up in her Prius. She found it dispro-portionately comforting to be back in the familiarity of her car, with its air conditioner that only kind of worked, its window that would fall into the door if you tried to roll it down, the well-worn gear shift, the tear in the driver's seat. Yes, this was good.

"Maybe they weren't giving you the stink-eye. Maybe that was the alien equivalent of 'Good job, human superhero, may you live long and prosper.'"

"I'm going to choose to believe it, anyway." She watched Vixen buckle in, smiling.

Vixen fixed her with a careful look of analysis. "And the Squadron?"

The smile died. Spitfire stared out the front windshield, hands clutched on the steering wheel. "They have apologized. Sort of. It was a shitty sort of apology. It was the 'sorry you feel like we did something wrong. We will grudgingly forgive you' kind of apology."

Vixen took her hand. "And what did you say?"

Spitfire shrugged. "What do you think I said? I told them to stuff their apology up their collective asses, and I wouldn't be communicating with any of them." She had wanted to say so much more. She wanted to threaten them, to detail explicitly the damage they'd done to her. So much left unsaid. And probably for the best that way.

"How many times have they tried to contact you since?"

Spitfire unclenched her hand from the steering wheel and looked at her new phone. "Up to 27 now." She dropped it into her bag and started the car. "Where to?"

"You wanna go visit the museum?"

Spitfire laughed out loud. "Oh my God! No! Anywhere else! I'm not helping you scope out new targets."

Vixen grinned, fox-sharp. "Do you know how I pick targets, Spit?"

She quieted her laughter, thinking. "No, I guess I don't. I mean there are patterns…"

"I'm a government operative."

Holy shit. Her brain turned in circles, trying to process and failing. "You're gonna need to explain that more."

"Well. There are a lot of countries that can't straight up buy back their sacred artifacts and cultural history because the museums in Europe and the Americas aren't selling. There is a group of nations that contact me when they think there's a good opportunity to steal something back and return it to the people to whom it really means something. They fund me, protect me, negotiate under the table for my release when I get caught. Which, frankly, hasn't been very often."

Spitfire stared, wide-eyed, as her whole world did a slight shift sideways. "I'm going to need to hear a little more about this," she said slowly. "This casts our entire history in a different light. You're… kind of a superhero."

"Yeah, I know. But what could I say? 'Hey, Spit, I'm on the side of the underdog here, championing the right of poor and war-ravaged cultures to own their history, and you're on the side of colonizers?'"

"Actually yes, you could have said that." Spit dropped her head on the steering wheel. "This is all way more complicated than I knew."

"Frankly you're a lot less surprised than I expected."

"I've been reading. It… fits."

"See? I knew you were too smart not to spot some of the bullshit in our world."

171

Spitfire leaned over the console to pull Vixen into a kiss. This one, she thought. I want this one. And she wants me. Thinks highly of me. She could be… home. Spitfire straightened and nuzzled her, little kisses on her cheeks and forehead and nose. "Stay with me."

"Stay with you where?"

"Anywhere we are."

Vixen grinned so bright and so hard that Spitfire's heart felt like it might burst out of her chest. "You do know that it's a cliché for lesbians to want to move in together immediately, right?"

"Can't help it. I live in a world of tropes. So? What do you say?"

"Yes."

The Little Push

By Christopher Peruzzi

Red fire-lightning sizzled through the air and missed Captain Photon's battle helmet by a hair. The two demon spawn were working to outflank him on his left as their leader did nothing but practice his own unique brand of hellfire target practice on Brightstar City's shining champion.

"You cannot hide forever, Captain!" Baron Beelzebub shrieked madly. "My fire minions are closing in on you!"

Damn! I did not sign up for this, thought Captain Photon, extraterrestrial champion of the Andromeda galaxy, thought. *Where is Doctor Mystic when you need him? Knowing him, he's probably making a house call.*

The bank's structural integrity was already beginning to crumble. Powering his extradimensional cosmic wristbands, the Captain fired a ray blast at the lead demon spawn's head. It hit like a cannonball, and the thing exploded in a white-hot ball of flame. The sudden concussive force blew his netherworld companion back 10 feet.

More dust and debris rained down within the

173

lobby. Baron Beelzebub, flying on the back of his personal demon bat, darted back and forth like a mad hornet in a syrup factory, leaving a fire trail in his wake. Three of his hulking hench-monsters trudged out from the bank vault—each was burdened with heavy sacks of cash in reinforced bags.

"Load the truck, idiots!" the Baron ordered. "We're on the clock!"

"That's a lot of money to take to the shadow realm," Captain Photon yelled. "What are you going to do with it?"

"That's none of your business, Captain Clueless!" The Baron darted to where he thought he'd heard that voice. "It's all part of my master plan to destroy this fragile reality! Besides, do you know how much it costs to run a barony?"

The demon master of malevolence flew his bat around the granite pillar and found nothing.

"Where are you hiding, coward?!" he screamed.

A tremor rocked the building. There was a desperate *tik-tik-tik* sound coming from the ceiling of the old bank building. This building was not made to survive a melee between meta-human versus demonic elementals. Captain Photon knew it wasn't zoned for explosive fire-lightning. Whatever was going to happen between him and the forces of evil had to happen in the next 60 seconds or he and his cosmic armor would be another metal wrapped piece of meat in the rubble.

He was running out of time.

Captain Photon bolted to another large pillar. He closed his eyes and focused on his cosmic con-sciousness powers. In all the years he'd been using this amazing ability, there was never any time when he wasn't astonished by it. Within an instant, he became aware of everything around him on a near molecular level. He knew the exact composition of the concrete rebar rock beside him as well as every other object within the bank and where they were relative to him. It was a feeling that required no thought at all on his part. It was like having a universal cheat code. It revealed every hidden and non-hidden item in the room as well as giving him a one up on the "Heisenberg Uncertainty Principle".

The power had the added benefit of instant wisdom. He found he knew what to do and when to do it. He called it his "intellectus."

With a diving roll to the center of the lobby, the Captain landed precisely where he intended. He swung both his arms independently in what appeared to be a random pattern. His mind unleashed a complex series of subconsciously calculated infinity force blasts. Each blast from his hands found and decimated the demons and hench-monsters within the building—including the three hiding behind the tellers' stand.

The Captain took a second to smile up at Baron Beelzebub, raise his finger to his lips, and blew imaginary smoke from the tip of it.

"You were saying something about 'closing in on me'?" Secretly, he was relieved. The cosmic consciousness confirmed all the innocent bystanders got out of the bank. If things went sideways, he and the Baron would be the only casualties.

"AAAARRGGH!" the baron howled. "You have more lives than a cat! You're harder to kill than a radioactive cockroach on steroids."

In a fit of rage, the Baron flew his demon-bat

directly at the Captain. This was the Captain Photon's favorite part of any battle. If you got your enemy to lose his shit in front, it was almost a certainty he'd do something spectacularly stupid. He braced himself. Again, he used his cosmic consciousness to calculate the exact moment his fist could connect with the demon-bat's head. He'd allow himself a bit of pleasure from this.

After all, Baron Beelzebub was an asshole.

Like a major league baseball player at bat, Captain Photon felt that perfect moment of anticipation where his senses focused in on an oncoming object. He gathered his strength for the ball or in this case the sweet spot of the demon-bat's head.

It never came.

Like a concrete missile, a chunk of detritus connected with the villain's torso and knocked him off his ride, hurling him backwards headlong to the bank vault where he made a Baron Beelzebub-sized dent in the vault wall.

"I thought you could use a hand," a feminine voice said from outside the bank. Despite the fact that it was saturated with bravado, self-importance, and more than a hint of arrogance, it was one he could recognize immediately.

"I was doing fine on my own, Marvella," he said, trying not to let anger creep into his voice.

"Of course, you were," said Mistress Marvella, mystic warrior princess from the magical eighth dimension of Lemuria as she approached him. "But why should you have all the fun?"

A horrible noise of wrenching steel groaned through the bank. The *tik-tik-tik* from the roof sped up to be the building's death rattle.

"Stay back!" he shouted as he flew toward Marvella, propelling them away from the site. Like a gigantic house of cards, the three-story structure folded onto itself and crashed to the ground, leaving nothing but a haze of floating dust and twisted debris.

"What do you think you're..." the heroine started.

"Quiet!" Captain Photon barked. He held her down, pinning her with his hand to her chest. He turned his attention to the site and focused his cosmic consciousness on it.

Nothing.

Well, almost nothing. He sensed that Baron Beelzebub was safe and alive inside the reinforced vault. His space-born senses focused on the pile and found no immediate concerns that couldn't be resolved by shutting down the power and gas lines to the site. That had to be addressed immediately.

Looking down, he glared at Marvella and sighed. He felt a headache coming on.

"What were you thinking?" he said in hushed tone. "You could have been killed." He got to his feet and shook his head. He extended his hand to Marvella. She slapped it away.

"Keep your hands to yourself, space-boy," she said with more than a little irritation. She got up slowly. The Captain stood back and watched her rise. He secretly believed she was made of nothing but concentrated ego and the DNA of marble. To look at her though, she was perfection. From her deep auburn hair, to her flawlessly carved face and her hard steel spun muscles. And then there were her perfect breasts and legs that never seemed to end. She was a heavenly construct of the gods.

It was also a bit unsettling to watch her stand. She didn't stop rising. Her eyes passed his, and kept going until they were a few inches above his head. She stared down at him, getting ready to explode. However, before she could speak, the Captain quickly held up his hand.

"I need to talk to the fire chief before something blows up." He turned from her and headed to the largest SUV marked FIRE.

* * *

Deep inside the sublevel basement of the Citadel of Fortitude, Marvella was working through her anger issues in the gym. Three heavy bags were decimated with fist-sized holes. The semi-curl barbells now had her handprints permanently molded into the iron grips.

Some men brought out the worst in her.

It wasn't that she hated men–far from it. Throughout her crime-fighting career, she'd gone through legions of super-men of all shapes and sizes. Heroes, anti-heroes, and on again/off again villains provided a hand-picked buffet for her personal sexual appetites. Each was an entertaining distraction to what could be a lifetime of angst and soul crushing loneliness. She had fun with some of the more colorful characters. The Elastic Crusader stood out most in her mind with his talent to get into "just the right places."

It was men like Captain Photon who got under her skin.

There was a time, before she had learned to control her impulses, when she'd make a man like that a red smear on a wall. Who did he think he was? It's not like he wrote the book on crime fighting. Given her age and experience, she just as easily could have written a volume on the subject. But, oh no, Mister high and mighty had to show her up in public.

She was running her 17th mile on the reinforced treadmill specifically made for speedsters like The Blue Streak and Captain Mercury when Captain Photon entered.

Marvella pushed harder against the treadmill. The anger had to burn out of her like the last bit of alcohol from a Bunsen burner. Meta-humans did not exercise like normal people; they pushed to the extremes. Marvella's feet fell with the staccato of a machine gun when she worked out. Sweat beaded against her forehead as her speed hit 90 mph.

Photon had removed his blue armor plating and silver chainmail tunic and wore normal workout clothes. The only parts of his uniform that remained were his cobalt-blue cosmic wristbands that stayed with him regardless of what he wore. The bands were spotless and when the light glinted off of them, they glowed with ethereal power. She knew they were a part of who he was now and, like it or not, they'd be with him until he died.

It was clear the Captain kept himself at the peak level of fighting form, conditioned to work at optimum efficiency. Muscles bulged and pulsed at his slightest movement. Even his workout shorts, which would have looked drab on any other man, hugged his ass and thighs like a woman seeing her husband off to a war.

Marvella wished she didn't notice the Captain's strong features and prominent jawline which were window dressing to his piercing ice-blue eyes. He kept his ginger hair short and close cropped. Any advertising firm would kill to make him their spokes model—especially if the campaign required a body to make women melt and face that had "that natural look."

Marvella wanted to put her fist right through it. She focused on her breathing as she passed mile 75 on the machine. Her arms were two blurs, and her legs pumped like pistons in a muscle car engine.

"Hey Marvella," the Captain said, throwing his towel onto a bench.

She bristled at the sound of his voice. He was the last person she wanted to share this workout with. This interruption threw her out of her zone. She grabbed the arm rails on either side of her, hoisted her legs to the footrests, and switched the machine to the cool down mode.

"Space boy," she said in mock acknowledgement. She slowed her run to a slow trot. When it rolled to a stop, Marvella grabbed her towel and dabbed the sweat off of her face and chest.

She watched as Photon prepared for his meta-human resistance training. The Captain was strong, his strength range 40 times that of a normal human meaning he could lift 8,000 pounds during a workout. He pushed his first rep and pumped with the discipline she'd seem him practice throughout his career.

Marvella stood and watched him. While the weight he was pushing was small in comparison to what she'd do in a normal regimen, watching him make the effort stirred something inside of her. His sweat and muscles hit a primal part of her that she did her best to suppress. After all, mindless lust was not her way.

Not *mindless* lust, anyway.

The Captain went down for his second set of reps. This time, it was a bit more difficult. Meta-human or not, he was using his muscles to push. Muscles would exhaust. When they did, it wouldn't matter how much he'd want them to work again. Muscle failure was muscle failure.

"That looks hard," Marvella said.

"So is fighting crime," he said as he grabbed his towel and wiped his face. "Did you want to use this machine?"

Was that a dig? No, he couldn't be that stupid. This is what makes him so insufferable. He could never stop being such a strait-laced jerkwad.

"No, I'm good," she said. "Did you want a spot?"

"I'm a big boy. I can do this."

"Suit yourself." Fuck, he was annoying.

* * *

Photon began his last set. He took a few breaths in and out. He was getting spent too quickly today, but that's why even superheroes had to exercise. If you didn't, entropy would sneak up on you, and kick your ass later.

The first rep pushed down harder than he imagined. He gasped and sucked in a huge gulp of air. He stopped the onslaught of weight an inch before it hit his chest. He pushed against it, and got the weight up again blowing out the air. He held the weight up and then eased the bar down again. Every rep was harder. He strained against the bar for the seventh rep and gave the weight an extra hard push and got it up. He took a deep breath and let the weight down.

I should have had a spotter. This weight could literally cut me in half if I let go.

He had three more reps to go before the machine would turn off automatically. If he couldn't do this, he'd either have to yell for help or get the bar to the holder. He grunted and pushed the seventh rep up. Sweat was beading on his forehead, and his face was going from pink to red.

I can do this.

The bar rose slowly, and his arms were vibrating. He kept pushing. The bar continued to rise and then stood still. He grunted again. He focused and pushed again. This time the weight made it all the way to the top.

There was a part of him that recognized his own stupidity. The part of him that knew he should stop now. He could just rest the bar on the mount. Instead, he lowered it back down to his chest.

That was the part that he knew that Marvella was watching.

He was committed now. He had to get this up. He sipped in three quick breaths and gritted his teeth. The bar rose again. His arms were vibrating excessively. He could summon all of the willpower he had, but it wouldn't help. His muscles were failing. He had to keep the weight off his chest.

Just a little push.

A large hand grabbed the bar and jerked it up to the safety mount. The machine's engine and gravity multipliers ran down and gradually went off.

"I asked you if you needed a spotter," Marvella said furiously. "You could have been hurt."

He closed his eyes, and let his arms go limp to the floor. This was a bitter pill to take.

"I know," he said. His voice was barely above a whisper. "I know."

"Get your ass to the showers," she ordered. "Maybe, if you scrub hard enough, you can wash some of the stupid off of you."

Photon gave her a black look and turned away. *Stupidity is a disease that happens to everyone. Why should I be any different?* He considered this and headed to the showers.

He stopped at the door and turned back to her.

"I'm sorry," he said, shaking his head. "You're absolutely right. It was quite stupid."

* * *

Mistress Marvella's powers were magical and as anyone who had contact with magic knew, magic came with a price. The price she had to pay were semi-regular visits to Delphi the Oracle. As part and parcel to keeping her powers, she was required to pay her respects to the psychic priestess. At first, she thought the meetings were a royal pain in the ass. For years, Delphi, in her role as priestess, had worn the trappings of ritual and formality including acting as though she had a three-foot rod up her ass.

Over the decades, however, the pomp and circumstance had gradually worn away. Delphi had softened. Instead of dreading their meetings Marvella came to know her as an old friend and counsel. Sure, she had to show a healthy amount of respect to her priestess through cordiality and position, but those two things had evolved to common courtesy.

Delphi was her closest friend.

Marvella drew her sword and traced a door in the air. A portal opened to the eighth dimensional realm of Delphi's temple, and she walked through it.

The temple was a magical construct which had changed over the years. When Marvella began her rituals, the temple consisted of a lot of white marble, green ivy, and casually placed water fountains that would make a Greenwich Village decorator faint from aesthetic overload. As Delphi's attitude to the meetings became more intimate, both Marvella and the oracle met in a location which looked more like an old woman's kitchen.

"Blessings and salutations to the holiest of oracles," Marvella said as part of the ritual. "I am your servant."

"Greetings Daughter of the Mystic Flame," the old woman replied. She greeted Marvella with a kiss on the cheek. "I was expecting you."

While Delphi looked like an old woman, in reality, she was not. The beings of the eighth dimension were sentient constructs of energy. Form was an inconsequential concern to Delphi. She could appear to be fat, thin, young or old. With Marvella, Delphi took the appearance of a strong, matronly, older woman. She found this form was both comfortable and comforting.

"Of course, you were." Marvella said smiling. "I think that comes with being an oracle."

The oracle laughed and poured them both some tea. "How are things?" Delphi asked raising her voice at the end of the sentence. Delphi was getting better at this. Marvella was almost convinced Delphi didn't already know the answer.

"Okay, I guess," said Marvella. She knew she wasn't being totally honest, which was stupid because

Delphi could smell bullshit no matter how much Marvella tried to hide it.

"I know that face," said the old woman. "What's wrong?"

"Nothing," she said. "Really."

"Are we really going to play this game?" Delphi sighed. "You know what I am. Spit it out."

"It's this man. He's making me crazy."

"Crazy? How?"

"I don't know," Marvella said. "Half the time, I want to jump his bones. And the other half, I want to beat the living shit out of him."

Delphi smiled, and the face she wore wrinkled. "Remember, that's not your purpose. When the elder gods of the eighth dimension granted you these powers, it was not for wanton destruction."

Marvella was getting nostalgic for the days when Delphi had the three-foot rod up her ass. This kind of talk made her feel like a child—which at her age was embarrassing. "Yes, I know... Peace, Justice, Liberty, Equality and Accountability." She almost added "brave, clean and reverent".

"Don't ever forget that."

"It's only that he gets me so mad."

"Hmmm," the old woman said. "It sounds like a match made here."

"That's ridiculous," Marvella scoffed.

"Is it?" the oracle said. "Let's do a reading. I think we can clear this up."

There was a time when Delphi would speak in riddles and make a huge production of her psychic messages, or spend her energy being mysterious and ominous. Marvella was glad they were beyond that.

"Let's have some fun," she said with some mischief in her voice. Delphi waved her hand and materialized a deck of common Rider-Waite tarot cards. "Ever since you told me about these, I've been dying to try them."

"But they aren't…"

"They are when I use them," Delphi raised her eyebrows and smiled. "While a poor carpenter blames his tools, a good carpenter can use any tool."

Delphi shuffled the deck and then drew three cards. She laid them out face down. Like a magician performing a trick, she presented the cards with a flourish.

"Here they are—past, present and future," she said. "Let's see your recent past."

She turned over the first card. It was a picture of a man holding three swords. Two were in one hand and one was in the other. Two men were walking away from the man in defeat and two swords lay on the ground.

"Humiliation and a pyric victory," she said. "You're holding a lot of anger, and it's doing you no good."

"And?" Marvella said. "I know that. The bastard showed me up in public."

"Did he indeed?" The old woman cocked an eyebrow which said volumes to her companion. "Anger is a funny emotion. If you can't control it, it will consume you. There is a time and a place for it. This is not it. No good will come from focusing on this."

Delphi turned over the second card. On the bottom, it simply said The Lovers. A naked woman

186

was on the left, a naked man on the right, with an angel under the sun between them.

"Regardless of what you think, he is your partner," Delphi said matter-of-factly. "If your anger is blinding you to this, you need to let it go."

"He's a dick," Marvella folded her arms across her large chest.

"I'm not getting that from the cards."

"He's a jerk," she fired back at the old woman.

"Grow up," Delphi scolded. "You may be older than you look, but you have a lot to learn."

Marvella pouted. She was secretly hoping that Delphi would be an ally with this. She should have known better. Whatever Delphi was, she wasn't going to give or take shit. She was going to get the truth, like it or not.

"Flip the third card," said Marvella. She was sick of hearing that Captain Photon was anything other than a self-righteous ass.

Delphi turned over the last card. It was a young man giving a child a cup of flowers.

"Remember the past," said Delphi. "Understand that people have their own pain."

"Pain? Really?"

Delphi looked at her flatly. "I am an oracle," she said. "Have I ever lied to you?"

"No, not really."

"No, not ever," Delphi said. "It is not my fault that you misinterpret what I tell you or have different expectations. This is what it is. It is meant to give you understanding for when the moment comes. No more. No less."

Marvella finished her tea and bowed to Delphi.

"Farewell, Holy Oracle." Mistress Marvella said bowing.

"Farewell, Daughter of the Mystic Flame," said Delphi. "Use this knowledge wisely."

* * *

Chemistra, the caustic countess chemical warfare, melted a hole through the testing laboratory of ApexChem, Brightstar City's pharmaceutical processing plant. On her way there, she blew up a hospital, an orphanage and a convent.

By the time Photon arrived on the scene, Blue Streak had engaged their newest villain. Photon could see he'd been hard at work trying to contain the large yellow clouds of organic airborne compounds which rose from the testing lab, but Chemistra had managed to throw off the speedster who now lay in a heap on the ground below. Photon didn't plan to fall into one of her traps.

"Hold it right there, Chemistra," he said hovering behind her inches off the ground with his arms crossed, "Put your hands up where I can see them."

Moments later, Mistress Marvella arrived. She looked over to the Captain and said, "Space boy," with a sly smile on her lips. "I'm here for the party."

"What is it with you people?" said Chemistra. "You come here like it's a game or something. Shouldn't you be mourning your teammate, the Blue Streak?"

Photon settled down onto the ground, and once there, focused his cosmic consciousness on the laboratory area. The Blue Streak was alive and would be well… eventually. His senses also made him aware of the exact location of Compound #9, an experimental pheromone treatment. He knew that's what she was after as well as the potential threat it posed.

He whispered softly to Marvella, "We have to get to the back vault before she does. If she gets that formula, we'll be helpless against her."

Marvella nodded. Petty rivalries would wait. Business was business. If Chemistra could take down a speedster like the Blue Streak, they would have to up their game to the next level to be successful.

"I'd love to stay and slay you two," Chemistra taunted as she grabbed her rebreather and dropped a gas grenade at her feet. "But I have a world to conquer."

The gas grenade exploded and filled the laboratory with thick white smoke. Marvella knew, even with his great cosmic consciousness, Captain Photon would be helpless against any projectile Chemistra used under that cover. She needed to get to the vault. Whatever Chemistra planned to steal, the villain wasn't going to leave without it.

Marvella closed her eyes and focused everything into her other senses to get her to the formula before Chemistra. Marvella reasoned that if she couldn't see Chemistra, Chemistra couldn't see her either. The worst thing that could happen would be getting hit by a wild shot. She moved straight ahead, knowing she'd eventually hit the rear wall where the vault was. Her meta-human hearing focused on that goal as she listened to anything that might be a threat. She heard foot falls and waited.

They stopped.

Photon followed Marvella and moved toward the smoke. He touched his feet to the ground where his cosmic consciousness identified the residual chemicals of the smoke were non-toxic. His senses also revealed the vault was 20 feet north-northeast from where he stood. Fortunately, he knew exactly where his opponent was in this insanity.

He closed his eyes and let his senses target Chemistra with his infinity force, then hit her on the side of the head with the precise force to knock her out. While he couldn't see her fall to the ground, his intellectus confirmed it.

He flew to the vault.

Photon knew the moment Mistress Marvella heard him land in front of the Compound #9 vacuum chamber. Unfortunately, she mistakenly took him for Chemistra and swung her fist. She landed a solid punch to his jaw. He reeled backward, shattered the container, and splattered the formula on both himself and Marvella.

* * *

When Captain Photon awoke in a strange bed, he was more surprised than anything else. While he'd never spent any time in this particular bedroom, he recognized it as one of the ones within the Citadel of Fortitude. The super-team spared no expense when it came to the welfare and comfort of its members. This bed was king-sized. His, at home, was a twin. And, with the exception of his extradimensional wristbands, he was naked.

Mistress Marvella stood at the other side of room, staring at him intently.

"I'm sorry," she said. "I swung blindly. Luckily, I hit you and not a civilian. That kind of punch would have killed anyone else."

He moaned and rubbed his eyes. His head hurt like someone had stuffed 40 pounds of cotton wadding through his nostrils. There was also a smell that he couldn't quite identify. It was part floral and part biological.

"How do you feel," she said.

"I feel like a man who wished you wore boxing gloves."

Marvella laughed and sat down on the bed. She put her hand on his chest and a sudden electro-chemical charge buzzed through him. It was as if a small man in his brain found the libido switch, turned it on, and asked, "What does this do?"

Why did she have to be so damned beautiful? Sitting up he felt himself stiffening and not as a result of her punch.

"I was worried about you," she said softly. Mixed with the genuine concern, he sensed a warmth that radiated from her lips, and suggested possibilities that would make a monk give up his vow of chastity and dedicate the rest of his days to writing love sonnets, and to studying the Kama Sutra.

He looked deeply into her dark Mediterranean eyes. The deeper he peered into them, the more he felt like a dinosaur falling into the La Brea Tar Pits. He could struggle all he wanted, but there was no escaping.

He reached for her hand and caressed it. Another charge ran through his body, this time stronger. The little man in his brain not only found his libido switch,

191

but the passion dial next to it and was turning it slowly upward.

"You going to be okay, Space Boy?" Marvella stared into Photon's blue eyes. No, not just blue. They were the sky of a spring day after a terrible storm. Or maybe sparkled like an arctic glacier. Beneath those eyes, there was the deep understanding, regardless of whatever was happening, that everything would be all right. A man in despair could look into those eyes and follow the Captain into the deepest pit of Hell.

A woman would look into those crisp blue eyes and fall in love.

"You can call me Rusty" said Captain Photon hesitantly. "That's what my friends call me."

She watched as his eyes widened and she wondered if his powers could sense what she wanted. To her, it was if her body was sending out a blinking neon sign screaming, "NOW!"

Marvella drew him close and kissed him letting the full heat of her desire unleash. She may have been a warrior, but what she really wanted right now was a good fuck. Her heart pumped every gland and pheromone it could get its hooks into, doubling whatever Compound #9 was already pushing from her. She'd wanted him before the chemical addition. The chemical was simply heightening what was already there.

"I... ," Rusty said.

"Shhhh," she whispered bringing her finger to her lips. She threw the bed covers off him taking in his sexy, naked body. With a quick practiced motion, she removed her top letting firm breasts stand out. After shedding the rest of her costume, she stood to her full height of six and a half feet. Facing the Captain—

Rusty—Marvella planted a knee on the bed. She trailed her long finger all the way down his six-pack washboard abs to his full erection. "I want this."

She took it, and Rusty had no reason to stop her. Her tongue started at the bottom of his shaft and with the weight of a feather teased up to the head. Her tongue lightly danced and played at the tip where she used quick darting licks around the top two inches and then back. She repeated the cycle.

Rusty's body went wild. He pulled Marvella's head up when he sensed he might release too soon. Instead, he reversed the biological onslaught and kissed her full on the mouth, while cradling her ample breast in his hand.

He used his cosmic consciousness power to tune into her rhythm.

No, not yet. He knew her body wasn't where it needed to be. The consciousness zeroed in on her right nipple. He gave it a squeeze.

Marvella took a fast sip of air as the rush of endorphins seized her. *Gotcha!* He gave her breast another squeeze, timing it to her biological needs. Being able to know what she wanted was a heady use of his abilities.

With the increased pressure, Marvella panted, and her breath came with a slow building moan. Her leg dropped to the floor with such a concussive force, the floor shook. She grabbed Rusty and hoisted him up from the bed. With one arm, she pulled him to her and used the other to guide him in.

She was hot and welcoming. He was engulfed in waves of pleasure as Marvella took him and used her arms to pump him toward her, while he used his own bit of flexing to push into her to places she'd never felt. Just a little push. The first inkling of what would be a series of multiple orgasms hit her like a jackhammer.

"Ohhh... Yes... OHHH!!" She squealed wildly as they began their unending barrage. Losing control, she threw herself back onto the bed with such force the supporting legs broke. Rusty continued to thrust until he was again building to his own climax. He moved to get their need synchronized and accelerated to bring Marvella to a new level of ecstasy. He brought her up, up, up and up again. Then, when they both arrived at that stratospheric edge, he screamed and exploded into her with an incredible blast of a release.

He withdrew and fell next to her, panting. Not since the Koraxian Armada invasion three years ago had Rusty felt so exhausted. He lay with Marvella as she purred and nuzzled against him. He snaked his arm underneath her and held her, enjoying their warm afterglow.

"I think you're feeling better, Rusty," Marvella said. She kissed him softly on the lips. Each kiss was light and brushed both his lips and his neck.

"That was incredible," he sighed.

"You were incredible," she said with a smile. "I knew you were a strong man, but when it comes to orgasms, you're a real hero."

"I will never forget this moment," he said to her and meant it. She was so beautiful and passionate, he knew there would always be a part of his heart with her name indelibly carved into it. Regardless of where he was or what guise he wore, he'd never stop thinking of her.

Marvella kissed him once again and caressed the outside of his face. Staring into his eyes she looked at him as if to say, "everything will be all right." She laid her head against his chest and closed her eyes.

Rusty lay there next to her and waited for his pulse to slow. When it finally did, he enjoyed the comfort and connecting as they drifted off to sleep in each other's arms.

* * *

Returning to her civilian life was never a pleasure for Marvella. But just as it was necessary to visit Delphi, it was equally necessary for her to return to her fragile mortal self. She'd been doing this for decades. Fight crime, save lives, be strong. She had to remember humility was a virtue, too. *This is part of who I am*, she thought.

Rusty was out of the hospital. No new villains had surfaced, so it was time to go through the process of turning. Starting with the north, she gave thanks to the Earth. Then, she turned to the west, she gave thanks to water. She turned again to the south and thanked fire. Finally, she turned to the east and thanked air.

Her mind adjusted itself to her new and much smaller stature. She picked up her cane and made her way back to her modest apartment. Today, the cook was going to make her favorite pasta dish.

She walked away from the alley and ambled the rest of the way to the nursing home. The smell of flowers was still in the spring air and the weather was getting warmer. There was a hint of rain in the air. When it rained, her arthritis acted up. The city would smell like roasted coffee from the local plant afterward.

As she walked, she noticed a new pain in her ankle. It felt like another bone spur. That was part of this life. She thought of it as just another surprise she'd have to deal with. It wouldn't matter much. She only had to cross the street from here.

"Can I give you a hand?" a rough voice said behind her.

Mistress Marvella, now Agnes White, a retired florist, turned to the older man, "I beg your pardon, sir?"

At first glance, she took the older man for a transient, but that was wrong. He looked to be about 70, wearing an olive drab fatigue jacket complete with sewn on patches and two captain's bars on his collar. His face was weather-beaten with the satin smooth skin patch of a burn scar down his neck. His arms looked strong, and told a story of a life where most every day he had done some form of manual labor.

"Can I help you get across the street, ma'am?" he said. His voice was weary, yet there was an undercurrent of strength and discipline only found in those who had served their country. "A woman with your dignity and grace should have an escort."

Agnes was tired and her foot hurt. It was a good time to accept a little kindness. "Why, thank you, sir," she said. She took his arm and her hand slowly, but not intentionally, trailed to his wrist where it bumped on something. A medical bracelet she assumed.

"You can call me, Rusty," the old man said. "That's what my friends call me."

She looked at the soldier again, this time more closely, and saw a few strands of ginger left in a sea of white.

Agnes smiled. You'd never see the wristband

under his jacket. Those bands, the ones that would glint blue with an extraterrestrial glow when the light hit them just right. She looked at his hand, covered in burn scars that went up under the bands.

This is my Captain. The man just can't help himself from doing good.

"Are you a veteran, Rusty?"

"I am, from a war forgotten except by those of us who are still around to remember it." They got to the other side of the crosswalk. Rusty patted her hand gently before letting it go.

Remember the past. Understand that people have their own pain. Delphi's words rang in her head.

"Would you join me for tea, Rusty?" asked Agnes. "I'd love to have some company."

"Thank you, ma'am. I'd like that."

She kissed him lightly on his scarred cheek, "For my strong man. You're a real hero."

He paused and she watched as he wondered. Would he see beneath the years? Behind the frail façade? And then, he smiled.

"You're incredible," he said.

She looked into his eyes again and returned the smile. As Delphi predicted, everything was going to be all right.

Foolproof
By Louisa Bacio

Chapter One

CRUNCH.

A flash of red and the side of her foot slammed into Lackey One's stomach. With an oomph, he hit the alley's brick wall.

Lackey Two attacked from the side, and that wondrous woman didn't even flinch. Without looking, she extended her arm, chopping him in the Adam's apple with the side of her hand. *Whoosh*! And he went down.

From the other side of the alley, Lackey Three blocked the entrance. Beyond, life in Downtown Long Beach continued on as if an epic battle of good vs. evil wasn't taking place. A light above his head flickered on, and at that moment, he made eye contact with me, and shook his head.

In the fastest I'd ever seen him move in our short acquaintance, he ran. That's what I get for hiring henchmen off the dark web's equivalent of classifieds.

Loser.

She faced me. How she knew I was there in the dark depths, I had no idea. At least she shouldn't be able to fully see me, only my silhouette. From my vantage point, every feature was accented—the signature red patch over her heaving chest, those long, long legs that just kicked some bad-guy ass, her high cheekbones, flushed from the physical activity, and those ultra-pouty lips that she now parted.

"It's safe to come out now. They're gone," she called out.

Wait. Did she think I was a victim, and she'd saved me or some type of shit like that? Maybe I'd be able to use it to my advantage.

"Uh, thanks." As quick as possible, I opened a door on my right and slipped into the restaurant's backroom. Adrenaline churned through my body, although I wasn't sure if it was because of the fast escape or raging attraction to Robyn Redbreast.

Dishes clinked as the wait staff cleared for the night and prepared for tomorrow's service. Someone laughed. I slipped off the black trenchcoat, and hung it on the hook behind my office door, replacing it with a crisp white chef's jacket, and flipping the dark purple felt fedora onto the top of the locked filing cabinet that housed employee files and financial records.

My head sank into my hands on the desk as I sank into the chair. L'amore Italiano was in the red. We paid out more than we brought in, and we couldn't stay afloat for much longer. The choices were getting to the point of letting it burn and collecting on the insurance or robbing a bank.

"Goodnight, boss," called out Marco.

"Have a good one."

The back door clicked shut. It wasn't just about me. People depended upon me to survive.

I hated her—that masked crusader who thwarted my every evil deed. She'd out-maneuvered and out-smarted me every time over the last few years. But I couldn't let Papa's dream of this restaurant fail. This time, I'd devise a plan that promised to be foolproof.

She made me think good was bad, and bad was good. But if she thought she knew me, I knew her better. All she made me want was to see her fail, and maybe be a better villain.

Challenge accepted.

* * *

I stood outside the L'amore Italiano, gathering my emotions and catching my breath. I'd stashed my getup in the car. Just my luck, right before a first date, I'd have to battle some hooligans along the way. One last time, I checked my watch: only a few minutes late. Hopefully, the lady-in-waiting would be understanding.

We'd known each other in high school, but didn't hang with the same crowds. Her group got into way more trouble than mine. Not that I looked down upon her, but you know. Rumor had it, she lived in a group home in an area of Long Beach my mom didn't appreciate me frequenting, especially after dark.

We'd both taken AP English though, and she stood out, smarter than she let others see. She played it cool, like the grades didn't matter to her or she didn't care what others thought. I only wish I would've tried to get to know her back then. So much time wasted.

At the time, I didn't know I preferred women, and maybe she didn't either. Only recently when mutual friends got together at Cherise's restaurant, we hit it off. The moment I saw her—snap. It felt like sliding home. I got her number, we texted a few times, and now here we were here.

I was supposed to have been there before the placed closed. The front door was locked, so I knocked. Hopefully, she hadn't already left. After a few minutes, I raised my hand to try once again, and from the other side I heard the bolt sliding open. Cherise blocked the entranceway, one hand on her hip.

Despite the attitude, or maybe because of it, she looked hot in tight black jeans, a form-fitting black tank, topped off by an ultra-cute white jacket—usually seen on those hellish kitchen shows. Her curves spilled over her top just enough for me to want to cup them and sink my face there. Something about her shape made me think of the figure I'd seen while kicking ass on those three dudes out back.

"Decided to show up, did ya?" She snapped her gum, bringing me back to the present.

"Listen, I'm sorry. I…"

"Oh, I'm sure you have a good excuse, err reason. But I learned long ago if someone doesn't care enough to show up on time, well, then they don't care enough."

She moved to shut the door, and I slid my foot in. Stalker-much? "Really, I didn't want to be late. It's rude, and I don't blame you if you don't forgive me, but I hope you'll give me another chance."

At that moment, my stomach rumbled. I'd skipped dinner to eat with her and, especially after physical activity, my body needs extra calories to process. One could say I had a fast metabolism, and that was an understatement.

She dropped her eyes to my offending body part. "Oh, for Christ's sake. As if my Papa would let me allow someone to go hungry." She moved aside, making an opening for me. "Come on in."

Before she locked the door, she stuck her head out and looked up and down the street, as if expecting someone else. It was late, past 11:00 and no one else was out on the street.

A warm glow emanated from candles on one corner booth. The table was set for two. She indicated the direction with a nod of her head. "Grab a seat and I'll be back with some pasta."

Heat radiated from a basket. I pulled back one side of the red and white-checkered napkin: bread. Ravenous, I tore a piece, dipped it in olive oil and spices, and *hmmmed* as the taste spread through my mouth.

"You sound like a woman who likes to eat."

When I opened my eyes, Cherise stood before me with two plates. I hadn't even heard her approach, which was odd since my senses normally keyed into my surroundings. I must have been more depleted than I thought.

"It's good. The perfect amount of crunch on the outside with the soft inside." I was rambling. Being around her put me on edge, made me feel nervous, when usually I was the one in control.

"Thanks. I baked it fresh for you. You're lucky it's still hot." She slid the plate in front of me. "We're going simple tonight. It's one of my favorites, pasta bianca with broccolini and turkey meatballs. Wine?"

"Yes, please."

After pouring two glasses, she scooted around the

bench seat next to me. Not close enough to touch, but close enough for me to feel the heat coming off her thigh.

"Salute," I raised my glass toward her. "Old friendships and new beginnings."

She slightly cocked one eyebrow and considered me. "I'll drink to that."

All of this—the posh eats, the normalcy—was so in opposition to what I knew about Cherise.

"How come if your family owns a restaurant like this, you ended up in foster care?" Yeah, I wasn't known for my diplomacy, and tended to be blunt. If it bopped around my head, I tended to say it, or ask it, and didn't think of the repercussions.

"Never told anyone. It's a sad, short story," she paused, and I leaned in so she knew I was listening. "Mum was a user. Dad wasn't much better, and he died in a drive-by shooting when I was young, without knowing about me. After I graduated high school, and emancipated from the system, I tracked everyone down, and met my paternal grandfather," she held her hands out, gesturing toward the dining room. "When he died a few years later, he left it all to me."

Her hand rested on the table, and I placed mine on top, and gave a gentle squeeze. "I'm sorry."

She turned her hand upward, grasping mine. "Not your fault."

"Still… I'm glad you found your grandfather." The words resounded, hanging unseen in the air between us. I wanted to take away some of her hurt no matter how impossible it seemed.

Whether she moved or I moved, I'm not sure. But her thigh was flush against mine, and our gazes met. It was enough to propel us forward. Our lips met and that sense of homecoming struck. Our pasts didn't matter, what did was the here and now. And maybe a future?

Soft, delicious with the slightest hint of the meal we'd shared. The details made it all that much more real. I leaned into her, slipping my hand around her back. She possessed all the charms I lacked, soft and caring, despite the hardships of her life. I may have grown up privileged, but I was all edges. I hadn't developed a deep empathy for those who committed crimes for an alternative reason.

Our kiss deepened, and everything I'd been missing in a connection with someone else hit me, hard. She was everything I needed. "You. Are. So. Delicious."

Her breasts pushed against me, and I admit, I copped a feel, cupping the side curve, and breaking contact to nuzzle the generous offering. "Oh, Cherise."

"Cece," she corrected, breathing heavy.

"What?" Momentarily, I stopped, what did she say?

"Cece. Only people who don't really know me call me by my full name. I'm Cece."

Clearly, I hadn't known her—until now. "Cece. Would it be too forward to tell you, you have gorgeous tits?"

"Oh, what a sweet talker you are." She pressed her hand to the back of my head, and basically offered up those luscious breasts.

There was no asking twice. Greedily, I slipped down the neckline of her shirt and briefly appreciated her lace-edge bra. Maybe it would be something I'd enjoy later. Right now, I needed more. With my thumb, I brushed down the material, exposing her already hard nipple. That's what I wanted.

One stroke of my tongue and she moaned, pressing tighter against me. She didn't need to encourage; I was ready for this very girl dessert. Almost on instinct, I fit my other hand between her legs, seeking the warmth I most wanted. The moment my hand hit home, she thrust her hips forward.

"Robyn!"

Nothing else. Her body language told me she was more than willing to continue our date. It may have been the first one, but we'd known each other for years. With one final swirl of my tongue, I pulled back, and brought her shirt closed. "Willing to blow this joint, and come home with me?"

"Took you long enough."

Chapter Two

Never in a million years, did I imagine myself here. In Robyn-the-perfect's home. Yeah, I admit, I crushed on her in high school. But even back then, she seemed so good, and I came from bad blood. She was clearly better than me. My family life was fucked, and she always had it altogether.

Yes, I'd pushed to improve myself over the years. I graduated from the JC with my degree in hospitality and did all the extra culinary coursework to be certified with the state. She probably went straight to a four-year genuine university.

Her hand holding mine, Robyn opened the condo's front door. She lived in a complex above the Pike in Downtown Long Beach, the ones built to "gentrify" the neighborhood. Within a few steps of popular restaurants and major brand-name stores. I bet if we looked out the window at the right angle, we might glimpse the Aquarium and maybe the Pacific Ocean beyond.

"Wait. I mean, what are you doing these days? Look at this place. It's fucking amazing. Do you rob banks or something?" The words spilled from my mouth. It's not like I suspected her of doing anything untoward or subversive, like me, but really. If she was legit, I wanted in on the secret.

"Private security."

The explanation wasn't much, honestly, but in the moment, who was I to ask more questions? I'd waited too long for this moment, and I had no idea if I'd ever get a second chance with her. I'd leaving the drilling for later. No, wait. I lived by the motto it was now or never. If I didn't make it happen, it never would.

"You might have started things back at the restaurant, but now you're all mine."

As if by instinct, I sought her bedroom. For someone so in control, she let me lead so easily. Her bed was perfectly made, and with a simple voice command, she turned on the side-table light. Ah, techno-savvy, too.

Every inch of her body featured carved muscle. I ran my hands over biceps, enjoying the tone. While I couldn't remember the last time I'd stepped in a gym, she either lived in one or was graced with better genetics than I imagined.

"While I very much enjoyed how you dressed for me, I'm ready to see you out of all… this."

Piece by piece, I stripped off her clothes. Good Lord, she was even more beautiful below. In the light, I just about glowed white. She embraced her darker skin tone and didn't sport one tan line. I took a minute to admire the entire package of her beauty, from her shapely long legs, all the way up to her tough-looking, short scarlet-hued cut.

"When did you shave all your hair? I mean, I love the faux hawk, but wow, it's like red."

She laughed. Being so close to her, the action reverberated through my body.

"Low maintenance. I appreciate your long locks. It gives me something to hold onto."

And that she did. We tumbled onto the bed, all hands, pulling at each other's clothes, and found ourselves naked on the smooth sheets.

"Beautiful." She stroked a hand along my side sending shivers.

In the low light, I caught a glimmer in her eye, almost wistful, as if she sought something more from me. The thought struck with a pang. I didn't know if I had more to give except tonight. Tomorrow, I had to get back to my real life. Right now, she was my fantasy come to life.

"You know, just because we're chicks, doesn't mean you have to be all touchy-feely. I'm totally good with feely."

I topped her, sliding down her body, and bracing my hands on her inner thighs. Fuck-me, she was clean shaven, not an inch of hair on her pussy. With my fingers, I spread her swollen lips and pressed the hood of her clit. It popped, ready to be worshipped.

"You don't have to." She flexed her muscles, trying to close her legs.

"Oh yes, I do."

And then I feasted, losing myself in the sensation of every sigh, and simper. For such a strong woman, she fell apart under my touch. How I wanted to possess her. I craved the desire to take her. I pushed three fingers into her, slicking my tongue over her clit, back and forth, over and over, until her entire body tensed, and she clawed at my shoulders.

"Cherise! That's it. Right there."

As Robyn convulsed, I vowed to make her learn my preferred name, either by punishment or pleasure.

* * *

The woman had more skills than I imagined. Maybe I always fantasized about her dark side. Truth, I'd stereotyped her, but who knew she'd be so good, in bed?

Despite the aftershocks coursing through my body, I wanted to return the orgasmic favor and take a delightful excursion of her body. "Mmmm, thank you." I guided her upward, tasting myself on her lips. "You deserve a treat for that."

While we kissed, I explored her body. Propped on one elbow, I used the other hand to draw her closer, categorizing every nuance. Her breasts were at least twice the size of mine, and the more turned on she became, the tighter they seemed. I sucked on the side of her neck, not caring if I left a mark that anyone might see, before moving down to her collarbone, and luscious nipples.

Cece arched into my touch, quiet, accepting my direction, taking in every slight pressure to turn this way and that. I worked my way down her body, worshipping every swell. Her slight belly told me a story of hours behind the stovetop, feeding others. Right when I reached that apex between her thighs, I moved my hand to her hip.

"Turn over."

She hesitated. I felt it through her skin. She'd probably counted on me immediately giving head, returning the favor. Even for a superhero, I didn't always play by the rules. Not that she knew that.

What I wanted was that ass. She teased me in those tight jeans, bringing plates to the table. How often did she grace others with even more—leaning over to get something out of the oven. I'm sure the people in the back of the house, in the kitchen, ate it up as quickly as I devoured her food.

"What are you doing?" she raised into my touch, even involuntarily, she must have sensed my desires.

"These curves," I shifted, settling one hand under her pelvis, my fingers seeking her heat and angling her up. "They need to be worshipped."

From behind and below I ate her out, thrusting my tongue into her, and alternating between running it along the perineum, that sensitive strip between her snatch and her asshole.

"God, so dirty. You're so..." she shuddered, not continuing whatever she was going to say.

She wanted dirty. I'd give her dirty and more. Keeping one hand on her clit, I angled my thumb and index finger on my other hand to push her ass checks apart. For someone with fair skin, her rosebud was such a pretty contrasting pale pink... *rosé, like a fine wine*.

Time to finish this challenge. I tongue-fucked her, pushing the tip of my tongue past that firm outer rim, while flicking my fingers against her sensitive sex. The first few moments, she stiffened, maybe unsure of my ministrations, but then she became pliant and compliant.

With each thrust, she rocked back, taking me a little further into her. She deserved all the attention, all the riches.

Her moans filled my ears, making me want more from life, making me want her. Maybe I could have it all—the secret superhero side, and the love of my life.

Maybe I didn't have to worry about keeping to myself. If I could protect the city against all the bad guys, like the ones I'd battled earlier, maybe I'd be able to protect her.

"Robyn! You're filthy. I've never. Don't stop."

I didn't plan on it. I planned on taking her now and all night long, and not giving her up anytime soon. "That's it."

Her orgasm hit, and extra wetness drenched my fingers. I slowed the pace, yet keeping the pressure, trying to eke out every ounce of pleasure from her body.

"Enough! Aunt."

"What?" I laughed. "Aunt?"

"Yeah. Why should men always be given the power?"

I shook my head. "You know you're something, right? I'll be right back." Before cuddling, I took a quick trip to the bathroom and brushed my teeth. Then, settled next to her, holding her close.

"Never imagined you had the bad girl inside you," Cece said.

People see me one way, and usually I don't let anyone into the other side. "Maybe you brought it out in me."

"Don't blame any of that on me. It was all you. Filthy. But let me warn you, when I come at you, you'll remember it forever."

Despite coming, my sex pulsed at the implied promise, and in the back of my head lurked the thought, if I was extra good, maybe she'd decide to stay.

Chapter Three

A flash of shining red hanging out of the closet caught my eye. I looked back toward the bed where she lay sleeping. I didn't regularly dig through my bedmate's things, but she'd been a bit edgy about what she'd been doing since high school, and I wanted to know more about her.

The door was a mirrored roller, and I pushed on it as gently as possible. It squeaked and stopped, like something was on the floor blocking the path.

Robyn murmured and flipped over, twisting the sheets with her. Any minute now, she might wake.

On tiptoes, I grabbed the hanger and pulled out the garment. The material fell in a cascade... a cape? One that looked familiar. My mind flashed to images of the masked Robyn Redbreast, kicking ass in the dark alley the night before—right before I was supposed to meet her at the restaurant, and she was "running late."

What the fuck? Yes, the name was the same, but I didn't peg her as the type. I knew those delicious curves and that shock of short flame-red hair. Where was the rest of the suit?

"Mmmm. Where did you go?" The woman in question sat up, sheets clutched to her chest.

"Look what I found?" I held up the cape, tempted to put it on and spin. Did it give superpowers like Spiderman's or Batman's costumes, or was it all her natural ability?

Her eyeliner had smudged during our love-making, giving her an even sexier, smoky look. How was that fair, when I looked like a raccoon in the morning?

"Halloween costume from last year," she shrugged, maybe a bit to nonchalantly. "What else do you want me to say?"

"The truth."

She got out of bed, all business now, walked by me naked, pulled out a robe and shut the closet door. "It's not nice to snoop."

"Are you going to deny it?"

"What?" she fake-snorted. "You think I'm a superhero or something?"

I threw my hands up. "I was there. In the alley. I saw you."

She froze. "The woman in the shadows, that was you?"

"What of it?" Reflexively, I crossed my arms over my chest. "What if I told you that I was the person who'd hired those guys that almost kicked your ass."

"There's no way!" She pointed her index finger at me, then seemed to think better of it. "Why?"

"I had a job and needed a few dispensable men." She'd foiled me and shined a light on the differences between us. The pain of the truth laced through my heart. I failed at everything. Every damn thing. "You're a superhero. I'll never be a super villain."

She pulled me close, embracing me. The warmth from her body bled into mine. If only her goodness blanketed the evil deeds I'd done, that I wanted to do. Or at least attempted to do. She'd, in fact, stopped me from completing many of them.

What did I offer her? I'd only eventually pull her down into the murky pit of despair I lived in.

Over dramatic much? Hell yes.

"That's all right. You can always be my sidekick."

"What the fuck?" This time, I said it aloud. I pushed against her, breaking the connection. "So what am I, some pretty arm piece? I come in second? Don't rate as high as you?"

"Come on, baby. I didn't mean it. It's as an endearment."

"Endearment." My focus on her narrowed. If I was throwing out clichés, I'd say I was seeing red.

"I'm sorry. I made you mad. Please don't be mad at me. Be happy we're able to have this talk."

"Happy? Are you really telling me how to validate my feelings? Next, you'll be telling me I have nothing to be upset about."

"There's gotta be something I can say to make this up. Something I can do?"

Gotcha! I totally had many things I wanted to do with her... naked. It started with stripping her, tying her to my bed and making her scream with pleasure.

But first before we get to the sweet treat at the end of the sex dessert menu—it's totally a thing I didn't get to just make up—first, she's going to do something for me. This time, I'm going to win. I'm going to rob the orphanage, and she's going to help me. And she's going to like doing it.

* * *

215

"There's no way. I'm not going to do it." I'd be willing to do just about anything for Cherise, except for what she was asking. In my world, there was a firm line between good and bad, and I never crossed it. Not even for love. Or really good sex.

"What if I told you the owners were bad," the temptress ran her finger down the V of my neckline, hard enough to leave a trail. "They don't treat the kids well. I know… They need to be protected."

My hands balled into fists. She knew how to entice me, in more than one way. Although, we'd only been together for one night, it's like she'd been studying me for years. And I her. She knew exactly what made me tick.

"The owners collect money from the state for each kid," she rubs her fingers together in the universal sign for dough. "Yet, I have to drop food off for them because they go hungry, otherwise. They keep it for themselves. Just the other day, one teen boy was sent to the hospital for a broken arm."

"There's a process for all that. Report it. Let the officials handle it." My heart hurt hearing stories, but I couldn't let her goad me.

"Sure. You're right. As if the system never fails. As if kids don't fall through the cracks." She picked up her clothes, piece by piece, and I watched her the entire way. "If you're not going to help me, then I guess I'm going to have to do it myself."

At that, she glanced toward me, and damn it, I was lost.

We agreed to meet in two days in the alley near her restaurant and then head over to the group home. After she left, I did some research. Long Beach didn't

216

have any "orphanages" anymore. We didn't live in an "Annie" alternate universe. What the city did have was group homes that housed mostly older kids who didn't fit in elsewhere, that were more organized, and not exactly family settings. The one Cherise had talked about had a few reports filed over the years, and one missing killed that was written off as a runaway.

I arrived before her, ready to talk her out of going and handling the job myself. She didn't have the best track record, and I was used to working alone. It was better that way, and safer.

"So we meet again." The woman who'd haunted my fantasies stepped out of the shadows where I now knew she enjoyed lurking. She wore a tight lavender bodysuit with a flared deep purple skirt. Gorgeous. Her dual light/dark side echoed through all her choices. Would it even be possible to tempt her toward good?

"Long time no see." On the surface, the chitchat was idle, but a deeper connection flowed between us. If I pulled the right strings, she may see things the right way, my way.

The sound of a revving car's engine screeched down the tight alley, and lights flooded my vision. I threw my arm up to block the light. Doors opened and a few men poured out. I stood between them and Cece.

Here we were again, indeed. Had she called them? Was this a trap?

"Watch out!" Cherise screamed.

Reflexively, I turned toward her. Someone sucker-punched the side of my head, and I staggered. It was the break they needed. Hits came from all sides, and instinct took over. I twisted, kicking, blocking, making connections with soft flesh.

217

Ooomph! Pow! Boff!

A blur in purple fought on the opposite side of the pack. I couldn't let anything happen to her. The bad guys outnumbered us, but I'd easily taken this many before.

They shifted as a group, and we got a moment's reprieve. I learned over, catching my breath and gathering energy. "Hell!"

As fast as they'd attacked, they retreated. The two of us combined were probably too much for them to handle.

"Gah!" I wanted to chase, but I also wanted to make sure Cherise was all right.

"Are you all right? Don't be so hard on yourself," she reached out to me. "There were a lot of them. The odds were against us."

I wasn't used to losing. I'd let them go, just like that. "Against us? If I didn't have to worry about you, I could have taken care of them all."

"Me? Are we back to that? A liability? A hindrance? Someone you have to worry about."

The hurt on her face should have stopped me. Some warning sounds that I was about to fuck up something good should have rang, but I was past that point. "When have you ever won? You said it yourself! You always lose, and now look at me…"

"Serious? You're blaming being a loser on me? Oh, no." She mmm-hmmm and muttered a few other things under her breath, before wagging her finger in my direction. "I don't need this, and I don't need you."

With that final say-so, she turned like a runway model on her black knee-high boots, with a flash of that damn skirt, and headed to her restaurant. When she reached the door, she glanced at me. "And don't think you're going to take any sort of shortcut through here either. You can walk all the way around."

Tears of fury blurred my vision. The woman pissed me off like no one else. Maybe it was better if we weren't together. My heart fought with my head. There wasn't room in my life to be the superhero and her lover. The two roles were at odds with her refusal to change. That nagging feeling hit again. What if she was right? Did she need to change?

Right and wrong. Good and bad. It had always been so simple, until she crushed the boundaries. Cherise wasn't a one-dimensional villain in a comic book. She didn't conform to any boxes. She didn't think outside the box. After living the life she had, there was no box big enough or strong enough to hold her.

By the time I'd reached the street, my anger had cooled. To the right lay her restaurant with its red awning. Maybe I should head that way and check in with her, see if anything was worth solving, before heading home? She was angry though. I'd said some horrible things. It might be better to give her the night to shake it off.

A sharp pain hit my thigh, and I flicked at it. A dart? A car pulled to the curb on my left, and the whoosies hit. The figures of men coming toward me blurred, and they dragged me into the backseat.

* * *

By the time I'd gotten inside the restaurant, guilt struck. Robyn had been trying to make me happy, do my bidding, and ultimately protect me, and all I brought was danger. Maybe I really was bad for her.

219

And maybe I could catch her before she left. I picked up my pace and headed toward the front door, pushing it open. I got to the street in time to see some dude shove Robyn into the back of a car. The door slammed shut, its taillights flashed, and the car flipped a U-Turn and took off in the opposite direction. I ran. Right before it turned, I saw her hand slam against the back window, palm against the glass.

They'd taken my woman, and I had to get her back. Quickly, I memorized the license plate before the car got too far away. If I called in a favor or two, I might be able to get a friend in the department to run the address. It meant relying on someone else. But right now, I didn't have many choices. In order to get her back, I'd have to open up.

Chapter Four

Drowning. I swam toward consciousness, but everything echoed, and a fuzzy haze filled my mind. It was like when the tide sucked me under when I was twelve, and I fought to get to the surface.

In a burst of light, I came awake, gasping, and took stock of my surroundings.

"Look who finally decided to join us," a guy on my far left said.

Someone had bound my wrists behind the chair but left my legs free. If one of them were dumb enough to get close enough, I might still be able to kick, trip or grip them.

"Don't engage the prisoner," another guy interrupted. "We don't want her to know too much."

If it was the same group I'd fought earlier, it meant there were at least three of them.

"You know kidnapping me was incredibly stupid, right?" If I kept them talking, then they wouldn't have time to kill me. The main problem was it was almost impossible to plan an escape and keep three thugs occupied at the same time. "She's not going to stop until she finds me and takes you all out."

"Can't you shut her up?" The thug I liked to call Georgie said. Yes, I'd already named them. "I'm tired of her smack already."

"I got something I could stuff in her mouth," Pudgie, who fit his nickname for all the wrong reasons, offered. "She might even like it after being with that Cherise broad."

"Don't touch her," Georgie said. "She's right. If we hurt her, the other chick will never stop looking for us."

Hurt me? Were they that much of idiots? I'd be able to identify all of them. If they were going to get away with it, they'd have to kill me. Fortunately, between the three of them, they didn't seem that smart. Sooner rather than later, one of them was going to figure that out.

Back and forth, I worked my ring over the rope they'd used to bind my wrists. Over the last 20 minutes, I'd loosened the knot, and felt the ties fray. None of them had been Boy Scouts or had taken sailing lessons.

The problem was, I didn't recognize any of these guys, and had no idea why I was on their hit list. They weren't any of the henchmen I'd fought the other night. I'd recognize them. Not even runners-up. I hadn't put any of them away before. I didn't know of any secret plot to do away with me. Nothing. So if I didn't know the reason why I was being held, it was going to be even harder to figure out how to get them to release me.

"Hey, Jones, how long before you think she finds us?" Georgie addressed the third guy, who sat with his legs slung over a chair, facing the backrest. Of the three of them, he scared me the most. He wore a white mask over his face, and from what I'd seen, he was the only one carrying a gun.

"Not long now. She probably already ran the plates and is heading here now."

So they knew she'd be coming, and actually

wanted Cherise to find them. "Damn, you don't want me. You want her!"

"You're smarter than you look," Jones said. "Maybe too smart for your own good. I've never liked intelligent dames."

The three desperadoes gathered in a huddle and argued in heated whispers about their plan for when she arrived. I continued to work at the bindings. My watch buzzed with a notification. They must have forgotten to have taken it.

From the corner of my eye, I checked out their location and faked a stretch to check out the message. It was from Cherise: *Incoming. Hold your breath.*

What the?

A window broke open with a crash and a smoking can hit the cement. A cloud of gray spiraled toward the men, and they began to cough-curse. Pudgie hit the ground first.

"Grab her," the masked Jones sputtered.

By "her," he meant me, and I was ready. Georgie approached me. His eyes bulging and one arm covering his mouth. Just a little closer...

Wham! I hooked my ankle around his leg, knocking him off balance, and whapped my head against his. The extra movement snapped the final threads holding me, and I was free. My lungs ached from the exertion, and I took a few precious seconds to rub feeling into my wrists.

The side door burst open, and I caught a flash of lavender. My heart lifted. Jones struck at her. I opened my mouth to shout a warning and inhaled the toxic concoction.

Cherise pulled something from her waistband,

and a bright spark struck Jones, his body vibrating. Yes! She'd brought toys!

"Don't worry. I got you." Cherise wrapped her arms around me, gently putting a mask over my mouth. "That's it. Slow."

She helped support me outside. Look at me, the damsel in distress, and her the rescuer. "Don't let them get away."

"It's all right. They're not going anywhere, and I called the police."

Realization hit hard. "You saved me."

She brushed a tear away from the corner of my eye. "I could say the same thing."

* * *

Almost losing Robyn scared me the hell out of me. She'd only been captured by those guys because of her acquaintance with me. I'd staked out the group home and intervened too many times. They'd come looking for me and grabbed her instead. I'd flirted with the darkness for so long I'd forgotten the feel—and importance—of someone's love.

We left the scene before the cops showed up. I'd told my friend at the station the situation and knew we'd eventually have to give statements. First, I brought Robyn back to her place, and explained the whys, especially why we shouldn't be together.

"Ridiculous," she replied. "And you know, I won't let anything happen to those kids, right? We'll take care of the situation, even if it means getting licensed as foster parents."

We sat on a balcony off her room and the light breeze flicked her red hair. When she brought her wine glass up for a drink, the red marks on her wrists from the rope glared.

A lump grew in the back of my throat, threating to choke me. I fought the urge to run. Better to stay and face this situation. It had been brewing like a pot of foaming pasta water, fast and furious and threatening to bubble over.

"Why can't I keep you out?"

"Me? Because you know I belong in your heart and in your life. We're meant to be together."

"Easy to say, but my brain…"

Robyn reached, curling her hands around mine and bringing them forward. That magical connection that we shared, that never happened with anyone else, flowed between us. How could something so right, down to the deep of my soul, possibly be bad?

"Sometimes you need to trust what your heart says and not try to overthink it," she said.

Humph. "Easy for you to say. You're… good."

That sassy brat quirked an eyebrow and stole a half-smile from me. I felt it, that tug up on one side of my lips. I wanted to be mad at her. I didn't want to want her. Not loving her made all this easier. But that was a losing battle.

"Am I? Because I'm fighting on the opposite side as you? Are we really 'enemies,' or are we simply both trying to do the best that we can with the, ah, skills we have? Are we both trying to survive?"

"Listen to you, making an argument."

I stole. Hired henchmen. Fenced. Damn: Organized crime. For what though? To keep orphaned children safe and fed? To pay employees at my restaurant? My mind listed all the good deeds she did. The conflict tore me apart. There had to be another way.

What did people do when faced with the direst situations? What would I do to survive and to protect those I loved? All those "villains" she'd fought, attacked, to protect others, were they all bad or were they like me?

She'd infused herself into my heart, and now she was getting into my head.

A lock of the long hair on top of her head had straightened over the day's exertions, and it tangled with her long lashes. Those already full lips puckered and she attempted to "puff" it out of the way. Adorable. I had better ideas for that hair. I broke free one hand and didn't tuck it behind her ear, but tugged, gently, bring her face close to mine. Her eyes widened, crinkles forming at the corners.

Why question what we had?

She brought my hand over her heart, which beat at a superhero's pace—"faster than a speeding bullet, more powerful than a locomotive." I knew all the mythology and had no rulebook when it came to her.

Her sweet breath brushed against my lips. "Do it. You know you want to kiss me. I dare you."

I crushed my mouth against hers, taking away all the frustrations. She tasted like freedom. How? So non-specific, but it's what came to mind... like the crisp air on a winter's morn after a huge storm chases away the layer of gunk that clogs the sky.

I stood, bringing one of her wrists to my mouth. "Do they hurt?"

She shrugged. "Not really, but I'm sure you could make them feel better."

"Mmmm." I licked the red lines, wishing to erase them and the fear of the night.

"I heal fast. You don't have to be too gentle."

Heat flared, and I propelled her arm behind her back, holding her to me. She'd pushed me so far, and I'd fallen over the edge. The line between villains and superheroes may be black and white, but we were diving into uncharted gray territory here. I wanted to do things to her, with her, that no decent crime stopper should be thinking about.

Robyn purred low and rubbed her body against mine. She'd known what she'd been doing and probably was playing me on purpose.

Ask me if I cared.

She nipped at my bottom lip and broke the connection between us. "Ouch." I licked the sore spot, and tasted copper. "You bit me!"

"I thought someone liked playing rough."

Her chest heaved, tempting rounded globes threatened to escape from a black stretchy tank. How did she ever manage to fight anything in that outfit! I'd seen her in action. And the henchmen? Did any of them attempt to grab a feel? Goddamn it. I pushed the thought out of my mind. She was safe, with me.

"I'm not messing around."

She flicked those long lashes at me and held her ground. "I thought that's exactly what we were doing." She slid her free hand over my hip. "Come on, Cece. Don't you want to play?"

That's exactly what I wanted, and what I wanted to hear—my chosen name on her lips.

"Even the good guys get to have a little fun every now and then, don't they? You deserve a night off."

No, I deserved a night to get off. With her. I stepped closer, making direct eye contact, until she took a step backward, and another, until her ass hit the wall behind her. I placed my hands on either side of her. Sooner or later, she might get tired of me. But right now, we were more than equals.

My index finger slid under the strap on her shoulder easily, and I brought it down to her mid-arm. "You're not wearing a bra?"

"Restricting." She smiled, and the curve of her lips sent shivers of pleasure straight to my pussy. Was she completely nude under that tight-ass super suit?

Moving faster, I brought the other strap down, essentially trapping her arms to her side. The material of the neck pushed up her breasts like a gorgeous offering to the goddesses. In this case—me.

It would be impolite to ignore such a pretty feast. Her nipples were a few hues darker than her skin. They pearled into hard nubs under each stroke of my tongue. A gust of wind caught her cape, sending the scarlet material billowing around us like a red shield of invisibility.

"That feels so fuckin' good, like I could come with just your mouth sucking my tits," she said, all hushed.

Such a delicate flower, this one. But I liked her crass tone. She wasn't afraid of me. She didn't bow to me. She didn't expect perfection from me, which all made her even more perfect and so very wrong for me.

"Let's take this inside."

She made me want to be a better woman. The plan had been foolproof, but instead I was the fool.

I loved her—that masked crusader—and fortunately, she loved me, too.

Just Be Yourself
By Rachel Kenley

Maya's head hurt. No, her whole body hurt. And the smells and sounds around her were unfamiliar, wrong. She didn't open her eyes. Her training told her she needed to figure out where she was and what had happened first. If someone saw she was awake it could draw attention, and without knowing her situation that could be dangerous. Worse than not knowing where she was, was not knowing *who* she was. This was one of the problems with being a Metamorph, especially one employed by the Extreme Excel Administration, an unofficial, but well-funded, government agency.

There were an increasing number of Excels in the world, people with gifts which made them more powerful than average humans. The comics and movies got that right. Those with strength, or flight, or telekinetic abilities operated in full view and were called superheroes. Their agency was highly publicized. However, for more insidious gifts—phasing through solid matter, fire throwing, mind reading—it was better to keep them hidden and find a way to use it secretly.

Maya discovered her ability in her teens when, after being bullied, she left the girls' room looking like the most popular girl in the school. It wasn't until she was getting kissed by the other girl's boyfriend that she knew what happened. It took months to be able to learn and control her ability. She tried to keep a low profile, but during her senior year of college the Administration visited her and offered her the opportunity to train and work with them. The work sounded exciting and the pay was substantial.

In the last 15 years, she'd infiltrated drug cartels, sleeper cells, political lobbies. She'd stolen evidence, seduced warlords and silently assassinated dictators. She'd worked as a female and a male, whatever the assignment entailed. She and her team had been responsible for a great deal of peace and the end of unsolvable problems. It was their specialty. When regular tactics didn't work, the EEA stepped in and did what was needed. It was exciting and dangerous work, with some murky moral issues. Maya couldn't say whether she actually liked it. After so many years, it was all she knew.

At the moment, however, she didn't know anything so until she could figure out what happened, she wouldn't let anyone know she was awake. With her eyes still closed, she took in the information her other senses told her. There was steady beeping from a machine. Muffled talking, as if on the other side of a door. She couldn't tell if anyone was in the room with her, but for some reason she was fairly certain she was alone. She tried to get a sense of her own body aside from the pain. She was lying on her back in an uncomfortable bed. Not a good sign. She naturally slept on her side. She lifted her arm a fraction and felt a pull. There was something attached to her.

She was in a hospital.

Her heart rate increased, and the sounds of beeping increased in tandem. A monitor. Using years of training, she brought her breathing under control, concentrating on the beep until the sound was slow and regular again. She waited to see if anyone noticed the change and came to check on her, but she remained alone.

Why was she here? What was the last thing she remembered?

She'd been dressed in a gown of gold, her hair and makeup done in a glamorous style. She looked in the mirror as she put on a pair of oversized gold earrings and saw a dark-skinned woman with almond shaped eyes, desirable by any standard of beauty but especially appropriate for this part of the world. A man came up behind her, put a heavy jeweled necklace around her neck, then kissed her there. An extravagant gift proving she'd done her job well. All he saw was the arm candy other men would envy. She shivered and smiled as he expected. He took her hand and put his on the small of her back as he guided her to a waiting car. She didn't make eye contact with the driver, but she knew him well. They'd worked together on other missions.

It was a short drive to their destination. A party where her time and effort would pay off, and she'd meet the other people in power. Well, meeting was an overstatement. She wouldn't be introduced. She'd be seated with them, but expected to be beautiful and silent. Sometimes her ability to blend in and be invisible was her greatest asset. And as she sat there being the ideal accessory, the cameras hidden in her earrings would take pictures of everyone and send the information back to those who needed to know.

231

Everything was in place. After nearly a year of getting close to the key players of a dangerous regime, she and her team were ready to finish the job. Tonight, she'd slip her escort the poison she'd brought, get out of the compound by looking like one of the servants, then escape to the air pad and return home.

It had gone wrong at the field where the plane was waiting. Gunfire. Explosions. She saw one of her team members go down, bloody and likely dead. A bullet had gone through her arm and she'd fallen, hit her head. She tried to get up, to get to the plane but another explosion had blown her off her feet. That was the last thing she remembered.

Knowing she was in a hospital only gave her part of an answer. Whose hospital was it? Enemy or ally?

Who was it safe for her to be?

Maya thought about her appearance in the mirror on that last day. Was that who she looked like or had she reverted to someone else? She hadn't looked like herself in years, didn't even know what that might be. Not knowing her current form, she decided she'd shift only a part of her appearance so as not to cause alarm. Her eye color. That wouldn't attract attention since they were closed. She thought about what she wanted and made the shift.

Then screamed as pain radiated through her body.

* * *

Eric was running down the hall before the sound ended. He knew who it was. When they first brought Maya Schell to his hospital, the Metamorph was slipping in and out of consciousness, shifting from person to person, and screaming in pain. They'd had to sedate her to do an examination. Scans showed severe head trauma which was likely what was causing her ability to malfunction. As soon as the medication wore off the cycle of shifting and pain started again. There was no way for her to heal while awake, so they'd kept her in a medically induced coma for over a week. In the last days, they'd started the process of bringing her around. He'd hoped she'd wake safely and pain free, but from the cries coming from her room, that wasn't the case.

He arrived in her room before the nurses. She was sitting up in bed, her head in her hands. Her form was steady which was an improvement, but the tears streaming down her face told him as much as the scream did.

The heart rate monitor sounded as though it might explode. She looked up and met his eyes. Her pupils were huge, her skin pale. "Help me," she cried.

A nurse came in with a hypodermic of sedative and went to the IV to add it. "Let me," he said, taking the drug and turning to his patient. "Maya, I'm Dr. Eric Larson. You're in a hospital and you're safe. I'm going to administer something to help with the pain. We've kept you unconscious for several days to allow you to heal. I'd like to give you as little medication as possible and see how you do. Can you count to 10 with me?"

She did, her voice breaking with almost every number but the time they finished, she was calmer, the monitor showing a more normal rate. He adjusted the bed to raise the head. She closed her eyes, leaned back against the pillow and asked, "Where am I? What happened?"

He pulled a chair next to her and sat down. "You're at the EEA medical facility in Switzerland. I

233

don't know the details of what happened other than you were ambushed when trying to leave the Middle East. Apparently, there was a second Excel team from a hostile country who'd been shadowing you. They attacked as you were leaving."

She didn't say anything for a while, and he thought she might have fallen asleep. Finally, she said, "My team?"

"I don't know if any of them survived. You are the only one they brought here."

"What's wrong with me? I know I'm sore and bruised, I can feel that everywhere, but when I tried to shift it felt as though my head exploded."

"We are still trying to find out what's going on with your ability and your health. You had a severe concussion when you arrived. You couldn't maintain a form for more than a few seconds when you were awake, and you were in constant pain. An MRI on your first day showed swelling in your brain which is improving. You're currently holding your form, but something is still off."

"How long have I been here?"

"Over a week," he said.

"How many people have been in to ask you about me?"

He smiled. She understood the Administration. Metamorphs were valuable to the EEA and, although he hadn't been told the details of her last mission, he knew the types of assignments they were given. He'd patched up a few after missions went wrong, although nothing like what was happening to Maya. "I had one visitor the day after you arrived, and they've been calling to check up several times since then."

"And how are things in—?" She named a country that was a key participant in the ongoing Middle East power struggle.

"I hear there was a death of someone in a position of power and repercussions are likely to be serious. They're not saying how he died."

"I'll bet they aren't." She looked at him and he found himself captivated by her eyes. He was mesmerized not so much by their color, which was a beautiful golden brown, but that they held a lifetime of knowledge and sadness. For reasons he didn't understand he wanted to ease that sadness, give her a genuine reason to smile. "How long before I can leave?"

"At this point there's no way of knowing. What happened before the pain started?"

"I tried to shift my form."

Form, not body. Interesting. "All of it?"

She paused and what little color she had drained from her face. "No, just my eyes. I didn't know where I was. I wasn't sure what was safe to do."

"If a shift that small caused that much pain then it's clear you have quite a bit more healing to do."

"How much time did they give you?"

Yes, she knew them well. "The Administration is hoping you'll be ready to fly home in a few days, a week at the most."

"Your tone suggests you don't think that's likely."

"As I said, you've improved, but given what happened with the smallest shift, I'm reluctant to let you leave or give them a timeline."

She nodded and lay back again. "What now?"

He said nothing and something in her expression made him think she didn't expect him to answer.

235

* * *

Over the next week Maya was in agony almost constantly, and it wasn't limited to physical pain. Either she was trying to shift and feeling as though someone was trying to rip her head off her shoulders, or she was talking with psychiatrists and doctors who were trying test after test to learn—without success— what was wrong. The swelling in her brain was gone, and her physical body was healing normally. The rest of her, not so much.

In addition to not being able to change her appearance, she'd been having nightmares. In some, she was back at the airstrip when the attack on her team happened. In others, she was in empty rooms, locked away from everyone and everything and, no matter what she did or who she became, she couldn't get out. Those were the worst.

And on top of everything else, Dr. Eric Larson was driving her crazy.

Not because of anything he did or said, but because his kindness and interest in her was the most unnerving thing she'd experienced since her early Metamorph episodes. It wasn't like when she was 15 and she'd suddenly and unintentionally shifted into her sister during dinner—her sister had screamed, her mother fainted. This was worse.

Ever since joining the EEA her life was about training, using her skills, and completing missions. When she finished one, there'd be a short break and before she knew it, she was being briefed and readied for the next. Year after year. Person after person. until she almost dreaded the down time between assignments since she didn't know what to do when she wasn't being someone else. She lived in an apartment the EEA provided which had only a few more homey touches than the hospital room. She'd barely seen her family since her college graduation and that was fine with her. This was her life. She was a quick learner, a talented shifter and a focused operative. It made her an excellent agent.

And a lousy patient.

Day after day she did nothing but sit around waiting for the next test, hoping this one would help lessen the constant pain or give them a diagnosis so she could leave and get on with her life.

The only thing she looked forward to was her visits from Dr. Larson, and she didn't like that she looked forward to those. Every morning he'd bring her coffee along with his. He'd sit by her bed or he'd join her on the couch by the window and ask about how she slept, how she was feeling. If he wasn't too busy, he'd tell her what he could about the other patients he was seeing or the research he was doing. He'd come back at the end of the evening to review how her day was, let her know if they had any new results for her.

Generally, she liked talking to him and he was, she admitted, nice to look at. She guessed his height to be around six feet. He had warm brown eyes and hair which was always tussled because he had a habit of running his hands through it when he was frustrated. And those hands—strong and capable. More than once she'd thought about what they might feel like on her skin.

As the days dragged on, he asked personal questions in addition to medical ones. What did she like to read? To watch on television? What movies did she enjoy and what was her favorite wine? When she didn't have an answer, and she often didn't, he looked at her with something she thought was sadness and that pissed her off. He brought her books, fiction and nonfiction, which helped fill the time between his visits. And they laughed together, especially at his atrocious imitation of the head nurse, which was surprising and lovely. Last night, after a particularly rough day that included a full body MRI and other testing, he brought *Some Like It Hot* for them to watch on his laptop. Now she had a favorite movie. She wondered what he might do next.

In the morning, when he made his usual visit, he said, "I want to try something."

"You sound serious."

"I am. Nothing seems to be making any significant improvement to your condition. We need to find a way to get you well and I have an idea."

"Great, because I'm dying to try something new."

"Sarcasm is a good sign. Means you're feeling closer to normal."

"Don't bet on it," she said. Besides, she didn't know what normal was anyway. A setting on the dryer, she'd once heard. That was about right.

"That's part of my idea. I want to get you to a baseline that works for you. You said the pain has lessened but isn't gone." It was true. When she tried to shift it was nearly unbearable without medication, but it didn't go away at other times. It was always there. "What if this is because you're shifting right now?"

"What do you mean?"

"Is this what you really look like?"

She was confused. "Is 'what' what I really look like?"

"Is what I'm seeing the real you?"

At first Maya had no idea what he was asking. And when she understood the question, she didn't know the answer. The realization was a shock. She'd chosen to stop looking like herself a few months after she learned of her ability. She returned for her junior year of high school as a prettier version of the person she was when she left. It wasn't a drastic enough difference for not be recognized, but it was dramatic enough to get her some positive attention from the in crowd. A few alterations as necessary, and by senior year she was part of the homecoming court. She'd never gone back. "I doubt it."

"That's what I thought. Do you know what you look like right now?"

"I think so, but I could be wrong. After all those shifts you said I went through and given the fact that I was on assignment when this all started, I could look like anyone."

He handed her a large mirror. She almost didn't take it from him. Suddenly she was afraid she might not like what she saw. But she needed to know. She took the mirror and looked at her reflection. She saw what she thought of as her Neutral. Her hair was light brown, straight to her shoulders. Everything about her said "average." It was a look she'd perfected in her first year at the Administration. Not unattractive, but not so pretty as to warrant a second look. It allowed her to blend and not draw attention both of which had their advantages.

"Is this what you thought?" he asked.

She started to say yes—then noticed something was wrong—her eyes. The first thing she'd tried to actively change once regaining consciousness a week ago. In her Neutral they were a simple brown. Now they were blue and bigger than she was used to seeing. "My eyes are different than what they usually are when I look like this."

"Wrong color? Wrong shape?"

"Both, but not wrong. This is my original color, but I haven't worn it in years."

"Interesting. And the rest?" She explained about the Neutral, how she developed it over her first year at the EEA. "So, this is not how you should look without any shift?"

"I suppose not, but it's all I really know at this point."

"I found something I think could help. When I had this idea, I reached out to the Administration and asked them to send me all the photos of you they had on file, specifically any pictures they had before you came to work there."

"Did they have any?"

He nodded. "You changed in high school, didn't you?"

"How did you know?"

"The pictures from your freshman and sophomore year show a different bone structure from the later ones."

"That's when I got my abilities and started to alter my regular appearance. I improved it a little every few months so no one would notice. Or at least that's what I thought, but the Administration found me anyway. Once they did, it was easier to join them and not have to worry about my abilities being discovered."

"Don't be too hard on yourself. They have ways of finding Excels. Anyway, I took the picture from your sophomore year and scanned it into the computer." He turned his laptop around to face her. "Recognized her?"

The face that stared back at her was familiar. Like someone she vaguely remembered but hadn't seen in a long time. "Somewhat," she said, and he took the computer back.

"I put the scan through the software police use to age kidnap victims to create what you'd look like now. Want to see?"

No, she thought. "Okay," she said.

He turned the screen around again and she was faced with... herself. Only not. She could see where the Neutral came from, how she'd taken her own features and either made them a little smaller, like her eyes, or smoothed them out, like her sharp cheekbones and slightly pointed chin. She didn't know why the girl she'd been hadn't liked how she looked because the person she was today thought the woman in the picture was quite lovely.

"Amazing," he said softly.

"What is?"

"How do you feel? How's your pain."

She hadn't noticed but now that he asked, she did. She couldn't stop the smile. "Well thank whatever deity you believe in. It's gone."

"That's not the only thing that's gone." He handed her the mirror again and this time she saw the woman from the laptop image, only a little older. "You shifted as you were looking, and if what you say is true, then the pain is gone because you are finally in your natural state. Welcome back, Maya."

241

She couldn't remember the last time she'd honestly cried. During her training with the EEA she learned to cry on cue because there were times when it helped the role she needed to play, but tears that were truly hers? When Eric said welcome back, she couldn't stop them. Her eyes welled, her throat closed and when he moved to the bed and his arms came around her, the tears became wracking sobs.

She cried for everything she'd held back in the last few weeks—her fears over her health, the pain she'd endured, the loss of her team members, all but one of whom had been confirmed dead. And she cried for the 14-year-old girl in the picture who'd thought so little of herself she'd made herself disappear.

"I'm sorry. This is a little beyond the scope of your duties," she said when she was finally able to calm down and pull back. His hands stayed on her waist and she welcomed his strength and warmth.

"Not at all. I'll assume it falls in the 'other duties as assigned' category."

She managed a smile. Looking at him as he returned the smile, she wanted to kiss him. Just a quick kiss on the lips she'd been staring at for days. It might turn into something more. Then he'd pull her into his arms and maybe they'd… *No, wrong, Maya. Back off.* She was a patient. He was her doctor. She'd eventually have to leave. She couldn't let her thoughts go this way.

"Doing better," he asked.

In what sense, she thought. "Yes, thank you. How did this 'treatment' occur to you?"

"There was an increase in pain every time you shifted, but there was pain even when you weren't.

While I was thinking of you last night it occurred to me maybe you were still shifting all the time or at least staying in a form that wasn't your own."

"You were thinking of me last night?"

"I was. I mean, it was thinking about your case."

He was cute to begin with, but stuttering—and was that a touch of a blush—made him cuter. Not that she wanted to notice. But it did feel wonderful when he held her and maybe his attention wasn't as annoying as she thought. "Well, whatever you were thinking—thank you."

"You're welcome."

* * *

Eric wanted more than her thanks, and he shouldn't. When she cried in his arms, he breathed in the scent of her and, even though she'd been using whatever the hospital provided for showering, there was something distinctly *her* that came through. Something he knew would linger in his memory long after she was gone.

Which was not something he wanted to think about. The EEA had been calling several times a week since her arrival wanting to know when she'd be ready to be discharged. He assumed that meant they'd bring her back to America and send her on another assignment, but the truth was he wasn't certain she would ever be capable of that again. He'd never thought about it before, but he didn't think the EEA had job reassignment plans for Excels who couldn't perform their previously needed duties. There were no "desk jobs."

He was pleased with the breakthrough she'd made this morning, but it wasn't enough. They had a way to stop the pain but not a way to prevent it. Nothing on her most recent MRI showed a physical reason for her continued issue, but he'd had other patients whose ability malfunctioned permanently after an injury. Just as they couldn't predict or create Excels—and the EEA had been trying for decades— they couldn't always figure out what to do when something went wrong with an enhancement. Sometimes it was beyond his ability to diagnose and cure.

But what did that mean for Maya?

Were there shorter, simpler assignments she could be given? Could he find a blocker that would allow her to shift for longer periods with manageable pain? Maybe he could create an implant of some kind that put out a consistent dosage of medication without dulling her abilities or her other skills, because she couldn't be seen taking drugs on assignment, couldn't risk being caught or having them taken away. He was worried, though, that she was beyond this sort of treatment.

He needed to push her and himself. He needed answers and so did she, because if his theory was true, Maya had some difficult decisions to make, and so did he.

* * *

Where the fuck was he?

He hadn't come to see her in over day. The nurses kept telling her he was busy and sending a different doctor who did a cursory check on her in the mornings. And then the food stopped. They brought her nothing but clear soups and beverages. When he finally came to check on her in the middle of the third day, she threw a cup of water at him.

"Guess I don't need to ask how you are," he said with that maddeningly cute smile. She wanted to wipe it off his face. Only a few days ago she wanted to kiss him. Now she wanted to smack him.

"I'm starving, damn you. No one will give me anything to eat."

"Didn't they ask you what you wanted?"

"Of course."

"And what did you say?"

"I said anything was fine."

"And then?"

"Then they asked me to be specific, and when I wasn't, they left and brought nothing but broth. Am I on a liquid diet because of a new test or something?"

"No."

"Then what?"

"They're waiting for you tell us what you want."

"Food," she said.

"I'm sure you do, but could you narrow that down a little bit?"

"I don't care. Anything as long as it's palpable, and even that isn't a priority at this point."

"I want you to be a little more specific."

"What do you mean?" Was he deliberately being cruel? What was he getting at?

"I want to know what you want to eat. Do you want eggs, a sandwich, a T-bone steak, raw oysters? What do you want?"

She was starting to understand what he was getting at and it made her uncomfortable. "It doesn't matter. Anything is fine."

"Actually, it matters a great deal, Maya, and no, not anything is fine. You've been telling me about your life, and it's clear that who you are and what you want hasn't been a priority in a long time. I understand why that is, but I think for you to improve, you are going to need to get through some of the other non-medical issues that are blocking you."

"You're a shrink now?"

"Not by training, but by experience. I've seen all sorts of Excels, usually at their medical worst and the healing almost always goes beyond the body. Given the fact that your problems are clearly related to your inability to hold your true form, I think it's important that you know what you want and ask for it."

Part of her training had been years of learning how to use whatever was available to help her mission. She looked around the room to see what she could fashion into a weapon. She was ready to kill him. She'd already tossed the water. The book she was reading would have as much of an effect. "Have them send me a peanut butter and jelly sandwich. I don't care." Her words lacked any authority, unfortunately, because as she said them, she sensed her body shifting into another form and with the shift came pain. She winced.

"I could gloat," he said, "but given how uncomfortable you look, let's try this again. This medical facility is large and well equipped. We can make anything you want." He pulled a chair next to her and looked into her eyes. Every time he did that she relaxed and was drawn into the warmth of his gaze. Today, she didn't want to be drawn in. She was mad at him. She wanted to get better and get out of here.

Didn't she?

"Think about a meal you enjoyed. Something that tasted so good you were sad when it was gone and couldn't wait to have again."

She knew what he was asking, but she didn't have an answer. She combed through her memory, but most of what came to mind were meals eaten on missions. Foods she often didn't recognized and occasionally didn't like, although no one could ever tell. Was there something she once liked? Something someone made her. Something... "Pasticcio," she said without thinking.

"What's that?"

"A Greek dish my mother used to make. It's ground beef or lamb and pasta and béchamel sauce. It takes forever to make because there are so many steps, so she only made it on special occasions, like my birthday. I tried to make it once. It was an utter disaster." She laughed at the memory. "But, oh, it was so good."

"Well I'm guessing you've hit on the truth because you've returned to your true self. I have no idea if the kitchen has ever made it, but I'll tell them, and we'll see what they come up with. In the meantime, I'll have them bring you a grilled cheese sandwich and soup for lunch, so you don't starve before then."

"And cheesecake," she said as he started to leave. "For dessert."

"Any kind in particular?"

"Chocolate."

He nodded. "Sounds good."

"One more thing."

"What's that?"

"Will you join me for dinner."

He smiled and this time she was happy to see it. "Absolutely."

* * *

It was silly, but she was looking forward to dinner, both the food and the man. She'd asked the nurses if it was possible to have real clothes to wear, and they'd found her some underwear, leggings and a big sweater. It was the most normal she'd looked and felt in weeks.

When he wheeled in dinner her mouth watered the moment she smelled the food. He uncovered the dishes with the largest portions of Pasticcio she'd ever seen. And there was a whole cheesecake, not just slices, for dessert with a bowl of strawberries on the side. She almost clapped with glee when it was laid out.

A table and chairs had been set up earlier and they immediately sat down to eat.

"You mmm'd," he said.

She opened eyes she didn't realized she closed. "I did what?"

"Made a happy sound when you tasted the food."

"I did not." He raised an eyebrow. "I might have. This is really good."

"As good as mom used to make?"

She blinked as unexpected tears threatened to fill her eyes. "I think so. I don't really remember. It's been so long."

"Then we'll enjoy now and not worry about that."

She nodded in agreement.

They talked about everything and nothing over the course of the meal—his research, the book she'd started reading, movies she remembered and ones he wanted to share with her. It was all so normal, and she enjoyed every minute.

"I need to stretch out," she said after they were done. "I can't remember the last time I ate that much, but I couldn't stop."

"I agree. I need to make more special requests from the kitchen. That was terrific."

They moved the couch and after he sat, Maya leaned against him. He put his arm around her and that, too, felt normal. She let the warmth of his body comfort her. As he rubbed her arm with his hand, she turned to look into the eyes that had come to mean so much to her. They sat there looking at each other, a thousand words unsaid, then he pulled her close and kissed her.

Maya allowed herself to fall into the kiss, tasting the chocolate and strawberries from their dessert and something uniquely him. Her body hummed and tightened with an ache she hadn't experienced since her first serious college boyfriend. Other than the occasional one-night stand with other Excels, most of her sexual experiences had been on assignment. She'd been trained how to please a man and had good results, but this was different.

Very different.

Her hands shook as she wondered what to do.

Eric must have noticed because he asked her his favorite question, "What do you want?"

"This is like the food thing, isn't it?"

"Absolutely. I want to know what you want, but more than that, I want *you* to know what you want."

She never imagined being asked something like this could be sexy, exciting, but it was. All Eric wanted was to know what was true for her, and she wanted to give him that.

"Undress me," she said. "I want to be naked with you."

He reached for the hem of her sweater and pulled it over her head. She had a moment to wish her underwear was sexier, then decided it didn't matter because she wouldn't be wearing it much longer. She unbuttoned his shirt and in moments it was on the floor with her sweater. He leaned forward and kissed her neck as he reached behind her to undo her bra.

When he brought his mouth to hers in a heated kiss, she ran her hands down the back of his neck and across his shoulders. She loved having him so close, the feel of his chest hair against her skin. Too soon he moved away but continued kissing her as he moved down her body. He kissed between her breasts then sucked her nipples to hard, sensitive peaks.

"Do you like this?"

"Yes," she said.

"Harder, softer?"

"Yes, both. More." She felt his laughter against her skin, and he returned to sucking one nipple while teasing the other. He made circles with his tongue then moved to lick beneath her breasts, which was a new sensation she'd have to remember to tell him she liked.

When he kissed his way lower, her body tensed in anticipation and need. He stopped at the material of her panties and nipped at her skin. She moaned softly as her body trembled. Liquid heat rushed between her legs. He continued to tease her, running his fingers along the edge of the fabric covering her pussy, never touching there. Her legs opened wider to show him what she wanted, but he continued to torment her.

"Please," she finally whispered.

"Please what?"

"Touch me." She was surprised at the demand in her voice.

"Like this?" He placed a hand on her stomach.

"Not exactly."

"How about that," he said moving his hand to her knee.

"No, damn it. I need to feel you stroking my pussy."

"I love it when you're more specific." He slipped a finger under the thin fabric and into her wetness.

"God, yes," she called out as she melted over him.

"You are so sensitive, so wonderfully wet" he said, his breath whispering over her skin.

"You do that to me," she said honestly. She couldn't remember responding to any other man the way she did to him. Not even before the Administration.

"Take off your underwear, Maya," he said. "I want to see that you want this as much as I do."

Without thinking, she reached for her panties, lifted her hips, and slid them down her legs. It was exciting seeing him watch her strip away this last piece of covering. Being naked in front of him made her feel

251

more exposed, more vulnerable, as well as strong and desirable.

"You are so beautiful," he said, and there was something special about those words because he was saying them to *her*. He was seeing her. No act, no switch, no role. It meant everything. She wanted to tell him but before she could say anything, his mouth covered her pussy and his tongue teased her clit in the barest hint of a touch. Her body responded completely, and she cried out with the pleasure.

And he didn't stop. So many of her sexual experiences were men getting her ready enough and then stopping to take what they wanted, but not Eric. His mouth and his fingers continued to taste and touch and torment in the most wonderful ways.

"I'm... I'm going to..."

Instead of saying anything, he slid a finger inside of her, then a second. Stretching her, taking and touching.

There was no stopping her orgasm. It raced through her like an electrical current and lit every part of her. She put her forearm over her mouth so her screams wouldn't bring any medical personnel running, then surrendered to the pleasure he brought her. Her back arched, her toes stretched out. Every part of her was alive.

As she came down from her climax, he gentled his touch, giving her more shivers. He kissed his way up her body finally ending on top of her, kissing her lips. She tasted herself on him and found it exciting.

"You stopped asking what I wanted."

"You made it very clear anyway."

"I suppose I did. Now I want more."

"You're sexy when you're greedy."

"Take off your clothes," she said.

"Greedy and demanding. I like it."

It took only seconds before he was as naked as she. He stopped to take a condom from his wallet and sheath himself. She opened her legs wider. He grabbed her hips and with one forward movement he filled her.

His cock felt so right, their connection so intense. As they found a rhythm, one of his hands left her hip and moved to her clit. When he touched her again, she let out a small cry of "Oh God, yes." She was still so sensitive, so swollen.

She looked into his eyes and saw mirrored there all the passion and need she was feeling. His ache was hers. Her desire was his. It was everything she'd ever wanted—and so much more.

"Tell me," he growled as her breathing sped up.

"I'm on the edge, Eric. I'm going to come again." It was as though she'd never come down the first time.

"Then don't hold back," he said. He moved his finger faster on her clit and his cock deeper into her pussy.

"Yes, yes, that's it," she said. And then it was there, surrounding her. Her nails dug into his back and her hips came up, taking him more fully.

"My turn," he whispered, and he drove himself into her. She met his thrusts, aching to give him the pleasure he had given her. His hands gripped waist as he moaned, "Oh, yes. Maya, yes."

She tightened the walls of her pussy and was rewarded with his gasp. She wrapped her legs around him and pulled him closer. His orgasm crashed through him and as he came she could see he wanted to call out as she did.

There wasn't much room on the couch for them to hold each other, but they made do. She'd never been happier. If only there was a way to stay with him. But she knew the truth of her situation and knowing it, she decided to enjoy every moment she could with him for as long as she could. It would have to be enough.

* * *

Eric needed a plan to keep Maya with him. In the days after they'd first slept together, he found ways to spend more time with her. He had her moved from the hospital room to one of the private suites which were given to longer-term patients. It was more comfortable and helped in the healing process. In this case, it gave them more privacy—and a bigger bed. She was able to wear regular clothes and he particularly enjoyed seeing her in skirts. She had great legs. He liked them best when they were naked and wrapped around him.

Last night, he'd broken all protocol and brought her to his apartment which was in the residence area of the medical campus. She'd shifted to look like one of the nurses when they left the building so no one would think anything of seeing the two of them together, but once they were alone, she became herself. It had been another perfect night. He went through the motions of work, research and seeing other patients, but he was often distracted with thoughts of Maya. Which was probably why he didn't notice the imposing man in uniform in his office until he rose from the chair where he was sitting and waiting.

His receptionist left the week before to get married and move to Germany. He needed to fill the job to avoid surprises like this, but it hadn't been a priority. He made a mental note to call human resources.

"Dr. Larson?"

"Yes?"

"I need to talk to you about Maya Schell."

"And you are?"

"General William Cabot."

Eric thought about asking for credentials but given the medals on the man's uniform and the fact that he made it through security to get to Eric's office in the first place, he decided to keep quiet. He sat behind his desk, knowing he was using it as a shield—knowing it was useless for whatever was coming—and asked, "What can I do for you?"

"When will the Metamorph asset be ready to return to the States? We have several assignments in the works, and she's needed in the field." This wasn't the first time Eric had been asked a question about a patient and had them referred to as an object. It never sat well with him. Excels weren't product. Today it bothered him more than usual.

Especially because he was part of the problem, part of the system that fixed them and put them back in harm's way, like a field doctor on the front lines of a battlefield. He supposed there was little difference especially since the person he was speaking to was all-military. But now that he loved her, he didn't like the thought of putting her back in harm's way.

Yes, he loved her. He'd admitted it to himself recently and was aching to tell her, but not until he knew how to keep her with him.

"Dr. Larson?"

"Yes, sorry. When will she be better? I don't know. Her head injury appears to be healing, but there is pain when she shifts, and her ability to hold a form is still impaired. At this point, I can't say with any certainly how long before she can return to work or if she will ever be able to do so at the level she did in the past."

"If you can't fix her, I need to know as soon as possible. She'll need to be retired."

This was the first time he'd heard the expression. "Retired?"

"Doc, that asset knows more about our country's stealth operations than I do. Hell, she's been doing this longer than I have. She knows enough to hurt a lot of people. When the asset is no longer viable, we have methods of erasing and replacing their memories, then giving them new lives. Sort of like witness protection except the person being protected is our national security."

Her memory gone, her identity wiped. Maya gone. He couldn't stand the thought. If she improved, she'd be taken back by the agency. If she didn't, she'd be taken another way. Unacceptable. He couldn't lose her. He wouldn't.

* * *

"You have to let me help you," he said the next night when they were in bed together.

"How?" Eric had told her earlier in the evening about his meeting with the general, but she'd been more interested in touching him, kissing him, feeling him inside her again. He'd tried to insist, but by the time she unbuckled his pants, he was willing to put off the conversation. The last week had been the happiest of her life, and she didn't want to think about what might happen next. Her ability still wasn't working without pain, and she'd accepted that this might be a permanent condition. Unfortunately, if she couldn't go back to the EEA, then what came next was a change she couldn't bear to think about.

"General Cabot came to visit me today."

She knew the name. "He wants me to go back."

"Of course he does, but you can't shift for long periods and you can't go on these assignments heavily medicated."

It wasn't a surprise that they were still calling for her, but she hoped for a little more time with this wonderful man. "I have to go. This is all I am."

"No, Maya, no. This is all you've *known*. There's a difference."

He was right, but she didn't know what, if anything, could be done about it. "I understand, but it's not that simple. There are protocols to follow when Excels with my ability and experience are pulled from the field." When he didn't answer she turned on the bedside lamp to look at him. Seeing his expression, she said. "So, you've been told."

"Yes, the General was 'kind' enough to explain it to me. I never knew this what happened to operatives I couldn't help. I'm so sorry."

"It's not your fault. Every job has a downside. Some are a little more dramatic than others. Truthfully, this wasn't something I ever worried about. I don't keep in touch with my mother or sister. I think they were relieved when I left. My ability made them very uncomfortable. Before now there was no one I would miss or who would miss me." Her eyes filled with unexpected tears, and he pulled her close and kissed her. His warmth and strength were the most wonderful thing she'd ever known. If she couldn't stay with him, it would be better, she thought, not to remember him at all.

When she curled up against his chest, he asked, "Do you want to stay?"

"I do. And more than that, I want to stay the real me."

"Then we need a plan."

A week later the new receptionist escorted the general into Dr. Larson's office, offered them coffee or tea, then went back to her desk. The general didn't know the doctor had an open phone line that allowed his receptionist to hear what was going on.

"Has she been found, Doctor?"

"No, General Cabot. We've had security out looking since we discovered she was gone yesterday morning. They've added dogs to the search, but there's no trace of her."

"How could this happen?"

"She'd been moved to a private room over a week ago, minimal security. We thought making her more comfortable might speed the healing process."

"She wasn't given a Nulling Band?" Nulling Bands removed an Excel's power rendering them normal. "Isn't that standard procedure?"

"As far as we knew she couldn't use her ability for any length of time and when she did, she was usually in terrible pain. Since that's what we were trying to fix, a Nulling Band seemed counterproductive."

"Apparently she had you all fooled."

"Yes, sir. I'm very sorry."

The general gave a sharp nod. "We'll continue the search. Who knows how far she's gotten by now, but if her ability isn't working properly, we'll find her. We need to go over your security here for the future."

"I understand. I wish there had been more I could have done for her."

"Yes, well, it's out of your hands now."

The general left without any additional pleasantries and when the door to the outer office closed, the receptionist waited a few more minutes then went into to talk to the doctor. Once there she put her arms around him and shifted. "What do you think?"

"I think you'll need to continue working as my receptionist for a while, and I don't know if you'll ever be able to be yourself in front of people here, but I do think you'll be safe from the EEA."

"I'll manage. Fortunately, I don't need to hold the adjusted visual for very long."

"Fortunately, I needed a new receptionist."

"That too," Maya said. "You know, as the years go on, I can look like anyone you want. I can change to fit your desire. Some men would find that a wonderful quality in a wife."

"I don't want you to look like anyone other than yourself," Eric said. "I love you."

"I love you, too."

"The real you, inside and out."

"That's one of the things I love the most," she said and kissed him to show him how true it was.

259

Law, Love, and the Whippoorwill

By Austin Worley

Madison Harper trudged into the darkened kitchen and poured herself another cup of day-old coffee. Its musty stench churned her stomach, but she guzzled the rancid brew anyway. Only a quick jolt of caffeine would ward off exhaustion long enough to wrap up all this pretrial paperwork from the Bricktown Boys case. Then she could curl up in bed. Alone. Again.

If only we'd managed to work things out...

Soft footsteps crept across travertine tiles, and Madi frowned. *Who in the... is that Topsannah?* She scoffed at her own question. Of course it was Topsannah. It had to be! Nobody else ever dropped by, unannounced, in the middle of the night. *Then again, didn't I change the locks after we broke up?* Three more footsteps and a low whisper derailed her train of thought.

"Hello, Madame District Attorney."

Her heart skipped a beat. Before everything fell apart, Topsannah always opened their midnight trysts with that familiar greeting. But this time... it sounded all wrong. Flat instead of singsong. Muffled instead of distorted. Callous instead of sultry. A chill swept down her spine.

261

This was *not* Topsannah.

Madi whirled around to find a mountain of a man silhouetted against the patio door. Darkness concealed most of the intruder's features, but it couldn't hide his gait. Fluid. Measured. Like a panther stalking its prey. Moonlight spilled across him as he drew closer, revealing blue jeans, a biker jacket... and an elegant helm. Translucent stars and stripes covered its faceplate. Only one man wore such iconic headgear: Ironsides.

Shit!

Unlike most of the costumed criminals who plagued Oklahoma, Ironsides had built a name for himself well before the Crash of 2026. Other hitmen balked at contracts on public officials—such high-profile murders attracted too much attention—but he *exclusively* targeted them. One Senator, the Director of the CIA, six FBI agents and a US Attorney topped a list of 84 public servants, all slain by his hand. *And I'll be the 85th.*

The mug slipped from her shaky grasp. Porcelain shattered. Cold coffee splattered everywhere, but Madi didn't even flinch. She *couldn't*. Terror locked up every muscle in her body.

"Ah, that doe-in-the-headlights look on your face... it's even sweeter than the payment for this contract." Porcelain shards crunched beneath the assassin's combat boots. In the blink of an eye, Ironsides slipped a big revolver out of his jacket and shoved it into her face. "Always fun to ice another prosecutor."

Madi gulped. "Why?"

"Isn't it obvious? Pigs like you decide the fates of others every damn day. No fuss. No fanfare. But when the tables turn and your fate rests in my hands, you lot turn into sniveling cowards." He thumbed the hammer back to full cock. "Are you cut from the same cloth, little piggy? Or will you die with your dignity intact?"

Before she could reply, something zipped past her and Ironsides. *Is that a… cockroach?* No. Round, black, marble-sized, it curved toward the patio door before rolling into a grout line. Moments later, a whippoorwill's forlorn cry filled the kitchen.

Ironsides spun to face it. "What in—"

KA-THOOM!

Everything flared white. Her eyes burned from the sheer brilliance. For a second, silence reigned. Then, incessant ringing filled her ears. A shockwave thrummed through flesh. Acrid smoke seared her lungs. Every instinct screamed. *Now's your chance! Run!* Blind, deaf, Madi stumbled out of the kitchen. Tile heaved underfoot. *God, can tonight get any worse?*

Strong arms swept Madi off her feet and swung her around. Familiar arms. The kind she used to fall asleep in every night. They shoved her against the wall. Something hard and heavy pressed against her chest. *Body armor?* Perfume drowned out the smoke now. Lilac and a hint of hyacinth.

Bursts of color still obscured most of her vision, but they couldn't hide the glowing eyes an inch from her face. No, glowing *lenses*. In a cowl. Mottled gray and brown blanketed it, a full-body set of ballistic plates, and the newcomer's knee-length cape. *The Whippoorwill!* Oklahoma City's most fearsome vigilante. And Madi's ex-girlfriend, Topsannah Price.

Gauntleted fingers gripped her by the shoulders, dark lips mouthed words, but Madi didn't understand.

This damned ringing… she couldn't think through it. A few seconds passed before it finally began to fade.

"Madi?!" Panic dripped from her name. "Madi, can you hear me? We don't have much longer!"

"What the *fuck* is going on?!"

"No time to explain." The Whippoorwill rolled off her and drew two escrima sticks from an elastic band around her thigh. "There's a blue Mustang parked along your front curb. Climb in back. I'll be right behind you."

"But—"

"Run for it on my mark," she whispered, gesturing toward the front door. It hung wide open on the opposite side of the foyer, just 15 feet away. *But what if Ironsides shrugged off that stun grenade?* The door lined up perfectly with an arch leading into the kitchen. The same arch she'd blindly stumbled through. The same arch Madi and Topsannah flanked right now. Fleeing out the front door meant Ironsides would have a clear shot at her back.

Before she could point out this problem, a silhouette lumbered through the archway. Whippoorwill drove both sticks into its throat. Hard. Gasping, wheezing, Ironsides stumbled back into the kitchen.

"Now!"

Madi bolted.

BANG!

Lead whizzed past like an angry hornet. Her hip clipped an accent table. White, hot pain shot up and down her side. Madi stumbled, then lurched outside. Sure enough, a blue 2025 Ford Mustang sat parked next to her mailbox.

Keep moving!

Brushing auburn curls out of her face, she limped

through the yard. Damp, dead grass tickled her bare feet. *Just a few more steps...* Four yards separated Madi from the Mustang now. Three. Two. One. She wrenched the rear door open and dove inside. Premium leather seats cushioned her landing.

"Eh, you made it! Long time no see, huh?"

A young woman sat in the driver's seat, tucking a coal-black strand of hair behind her copper-toned ear. The lenses of her domino mask cast a blue glow across the dashboard. Mottled blue and orange patterns decorated ballistic plates worn over a black nanoweave bodysuit. *The Kingfisher.*

"Didn't you retire, Rosa? Head off to study veterinary medicine at Oklahoma State?"

"Bah, that's just a... hiatus." Rosa Coronil—the street kid Topsannah adopted as her own—grinned. "Nobody ever really retires from the cape and cowl life."

"Does that mean you know why an ex-CIA operative just tried to murder me in my kitchen?"

"Do frogs grow hair?" She shook her head and sighed. "I'm just home for Thanksgiving. *La vieja* didn't bother briefing me on the case. Never does, these days."

Hearing Topsannah described as 'the old lady' brought a smile to Madi's face for the first time all night. *God, I remember when I thought 36 was old...* She glanced toward home, and that smile vanished. Her front door still hung open, framing a pit as dark as any black hole. *You said you'd be right behind me, blossom. So, where the hell are you?*

The universe answered her question a second later. Whippoorwill sprinted across the lawn, drew a neon pepperball gun from her utility belt, and fired back into the shadows. Breathless, she yanked open the passenger door and shot three more pepperballs before ducking into the Mustang. "Go, go, go!"

Tires squealed as the V8 engine roared to life. Movement flickered off to the right, and Madi turned in time to see Ironsides stagger onto the front porch. Doubled over, coughing, revolver raised. Bullets peppered their tailgate as they flew down the suburban street. "Really?!" Rosa growled. "I *just* buffed out the dents from last time!"

In a flash, they were out onto May Avenue. Whippoorwill holstered her pepperball pistol. "Kingfisher, activate Chameleon Protocol."

"Aye, aye, *vieja*." Rosa tapped a button on the steering wheel, and an electrical hum coursed through the Mustang's body. When the hum faded, its paint scheme had morphed from bright blue to a forest green.

"Thanks, baby bird."

Rosa cringed.

"What? You have your terms of endearment. I have mine." Groaning, Topsannah pried off the cowl. Black hair shorn into a messy, utilitarian bob fell to her sharp jawline. Beads of sweat blazed trails across dusty russet cheeks. "Take us back to the Nest."

"The Nest?!" Rosa blanched. "Lawton's almost an hour and a half away. We're five minutes out from Perch 13!"

"And risk Ironsides compromising one of our safehouses? Unacceptable." Warmth crept into Topsannah's voice as she glanced into the backseat. The frosty vigilante gave way to a gracious rancher. "Besides, I'm sure our guest would prefer a hot meal and a real bed."

266

God, she's just as gorgeous as the day we met. Not worth the trouble, but gorgeous nonetheless. Setting aside some unworthy thoughts, Madi leaned forward. "Hey, can somebody *please* explain what the fuck is happening?"

A sheepish grin flickered across her face. "Right. I'm sorry we left you in the dark so long. Remember when Ironsides assassinated Mayor Cargill a couple years back?"

"Yecch!" Visions of blood, brains, and bone played behind Madi's eyes. "I tried to forget it."

Topsannah offered her a sympathetic nod. "The client for that job hired him on a darknet known as 'Hashashin.' After Ironsides slipped through our fingers, I infiltrated it and created a system to monitor for any contracts in Oklahoma. It pinged me Monday morning. An anonymous user offered $5,000,000 for your head."

Madi sagged against the back of her seat. *Five million dollars? To kill me?* This... it sounded like a bad joke. Or a nightmare. Maybe both.

"Do you have anywhere to lie low?"

"Wouldn't protective custody be safer?" Her brow furrowed. "Even Ironsides can't carve through an entire metropolitan police department."

"The OCPD are compromised."

"What?!"

"The. Police. Are. Compromised."

"No, I understood you the first time. *How?*"

Topsannah grimaced. "I traced that anonymous user to a contraband smartphone in the possession of Oklahoma County Inmate #210553720: Jude Ellis."

Just the name left Madi fuming. During his tenure

as commander of the Oklahoma City Police Department's Bricktown Sub-division, Major Jude Ellis built a culture of corruption in the once thriving entertainment district. Shakedowns. Frame-ups. Embezzlement. Perjury. Even murder. Only a concerted effort by Internal Affairs investigators, her office and the Whippoorwill had managed to root out his so-called 'Bricktown Boys'. *But what if we missed a few weeds?*

Cradling herself, Madi sighed. *Topsannah's right. I can't rely on the police. Especially if Ellis still has friends on the force.* Only one alternative came to mind. "Daddy owns a cabin down by Lake Texoma. Way out in the sticks. This time of year, I doubt anybody would notice if I holed up there for a while."

Rosa shook her head. "Too obv—"

"It's perfect," Topsannah cut in. "In the morning, we'll head straight for Texoma." Lightly gripping Madi's knee, she leaned into the backseat. "By the Great Spirit, I swear I'll protect you. With my life, if need be."

A sly grin crept onto Rosa's lips. "Do I smell the makings of a rekindled romance?"

"No!" They answered in unison.

Topsannah glanced at the cowl in her lap. "Finding time for the two of us was always a challenge. Much as I love Madi... as much as I pray she loves me... some things will always be more important than my love life. And ignoring them would be *unforgivably* selfish."

"That's not the only reason we didn't work, and you know it!" Nostrils flaring, Madi jabbed a finger at the back of Topsannah's seat. Fresh agony throbbed through her hip, but she ignored it. "Yeah, all those

268

cancelled dates and ruined holidays and lonely nights annoyed the hell out of me, but I could tolerate them. Barely.

"What I *couldn't* tolerate was the secrecy. Did you make it home in one piece? Are you off on some undercover mission? When should I expect to see you again?" She snorted. "Hell if I ever knew! You never texted. Never called. Dropped in and out unexpectedly. My job is hard enough without lying awake every night wondering whether my little prairie blossom is dying in a dumpster somewhere."

But you still wonder, a little voice in her head whispered. *Don't you, Madi?*

Meanwhile, Topsannah winced and twisted around. Her jaw dropped. Mahogany eyes widened. "Madi... you're bleeding."

The world wobbled, then clouded. Pain pulsed through her hip again. Madi pressed a hand against it. Warm stickiness soaked her nightgown. *What if the accent table wasn't what clipped me?* Hesitantly, she raised her hand to eye level. Blotches of crimson glazed pale flesh. "Uh oh."

She fainted.

* * *

Every time a whimper rose from the infirmary, Topsannah almost puked. *This is all my fault.* Steel plates clanged underfoot as she paced across the bunker. *Shoulda acted sooner. Shoulda hit harder. Shoulda taken the bullet myself.* Wasn't that why she'd become the Whippoorwill in the first place? To take bullets so nobody else had to.

269

Focus, Price. Guilt wouldn't protect Madi from this assassin; that required a well-designed stratagem. Pacing toward the supercomputer at the Nest's heart, she cleared her throat. "Flycatcher, pull up everything we have on Ironsides."

After the past few days, the basics were already burned into her brain. Real name: Sam Nichols. Sixty-three years old. Seventy-nine inches tall. Two hundred and forty-three pounds. Enhanced strength, sharpened reflexes, and bulletproof skin thanks to CIA experiments designed to create the perfect wetwork operative. Burned after a botched mission in 2022, spawning an intense hatred for government officials. Performed dozens of contract killings over the next 19 years, never failing to find his mark. Pathologically afraid of capture. A real piece of work.

While the computer collected more detailed information, Topsannah glanced at the pile of Whippoorwill armor she'd stripped off earlier. Part of her hated it. Hated how the identity's demands destroyed her relationships one by one. Craig. Madi. Even Rosa grew more distant. *And yet the Whippoorwill is the only reason I still have a chance to patch things up with Madi.* The Great Spirit sure loved irony.

Her gaze drifted toward the far end of the Nest, where row after row of display cases stood. Each of them held a reminder of the evils she'd faced. A diamond drill bit wrenched from the Golden Driller's prosthetic arm. Colt Peacemakers and Winchester Model 1873s seized from the Wild Bunch. A bloody Leveler manifesto. Beyond them stood a 20 x 30 foot bulletin board—as tall and wide as the Nest itself— covered in letters and thank you notes.

So many plots foiled. So many lives saved. So many monsters brought to justice. Remembering them all should've drowned her in joy, but it didn't. Not the way nights with Madi had. *Ugh, what a mess I've made.*

Automatic doors whooshed, and Rosa wandered out of the infirmary. Splotches of blood stained her scrubs. "Good news, the wound wasn't even half as bad as it looked. Some soft tissue damage where the bullet grazed her, but nothing a few stitches couldn't handle."

"So Madi should be fine?"

"Probably." She shrugged. "I'm a prodigy, not a prophet. Unforeseen complications are always a risk. Monitoring her recovery myself would be ideal, but I can't afford to miss practice this week. Bedlam, you know? Just keep an eye out for signs of infection, limit her physical activity, and everything should be fine."

"Thank you, Rosa." Topsannah held up trembling hands. "I never could've sewn those stitches myself."

Slender fingers wrapped around her wrists. "Remember how we used to fight the post-mission jitters?"

"Rosa, not right—"

Too late! Lean muscles honed by years of martial arts and football had already hauled her out of the command center. *Spirits, when did my baby bird get so strong?* When she'd first found Rosa, the poor girl was little more than skin and bones. Now, the young woman she proudly called her daughter could compete with professional athletes. *Kids… they grow up too fast.*

Giggling, Rosa towed her past the arsenal's titanium doors. "C'mon, pet the horsies with me!"

271

Topsannah half chuckled, half groaned. "You're *such* a child."

"And proud of it!" She quickly tapped an access code into a keypad on the wall, then practically hauled her up the staircase leading out of the Nest. "Where would I be without childish enthusiasm? Brooding in the dark like you? Yuck! We're humans, *vieja*, not nightjars. Sometimes, we gotta step into the light."

While sneakers and cowboy boots clanged up the stairs, gears whirred, and a steel hatch rolled away. The pungent mix of fresh straw, horse sweat and manure washed over them as they emerged into an empty barn stall. Rosa unlatched the gate, then rushed over to a stall holding a mare and her colt. "Is Caspar still a cutie pie?"

Topsannah grunted. "He's becoming quite the biter."

Leaving Rosa to coo over the mouthy colt, she strolled over to the barn doors and surveyed her domain. Cattle grazed along a low ridge to the east, as they had since her great-great-great-grandfather was allotted 160 acres of Comanche tribal land by the Dawes Act.

If only the rest of my people fared so well.

Her gaze drifted toward the horizon, where a small wind farm stood silhouetted against the rising sun. Two dozen turbines in all, each built using her patented design. A design which had given birth to Price Renewables and the immense fortune behind her private war on crime and corruption in Oklahoma.

Clean energy helping clean up our streets. She smiled. Even if vigilantism couldn't return Oklahoma to its pre-Crash glory days, knowing the company she'd created had made the world a cleaner place helped her sleep at night.

"Ow!"

Topsannah glanced over her shoulder to find her baby bird cradling a nipped finger. "Not half as cute now, is he?"

"Not even a quarter!" Grumbling, Rosa stomped over and hugged her. "Just another sign I oughta head back to Stillwater. After last night, I need a good day's rest before the coaches run me ragged."

"I'll be rooting for you next Saturday… even if you do look *hideous* in those Halloween-colored uniforms."

"At least my alma mater won't be named after a bunch of cheaters." Breaking from the embrace, Rosa sobered. "Hey, a word of advice—loop Madi into whatever it is you're planning down at Lake Texoma."

Topsannah crossed her arms. "I know what I'm doing."

"Oh? Is that why Madi left you?"

"Don't go there, Rosa!" Nostrils flaring, she stormed back toward the Nest. A red haze descended over the world, and warmth flooded her face. *Didn't I raise her better than to… to butt into other people's business?!* Topsannah spat at a bale of straw.

Footsteps quickened behind her. "Stop shutting out everyone who cares about you. Breaking up with Craig to 'protect' him, keeping secrets from Madi, refusing to even consider my advice. At this rate your life will end up cold and empty. You deserve better than that, Mom!"

Mom. Such a strange word to hear out of Rosa's mouth. Even after the adoption, the girl opted for the playful *'vieja'* or a curt 'Topsannah'. Never a plain old 'Mom.' And certainly not one so... desperate. It cleared away the haze, cooled her cheeks, and stopped Topsannah in her tracks.

"Look, I know how hard it is for you to fully, completely open yourself up to someone else. Even me. But if you want Madi back—and I *know* you do—there's no other option. So just try, okay?"

She's right.

Still, parts of her refused to admit it. There *had* to be other options. Alternatives she hadn't considered. Anything to avoid exposing Madi to all the danger and darkness which came with being the Whippoorwill. But right now, nothing came to mind.

Dammit, why is Rosa always right?

"Okay," she muttered. "I'll try."

* * *

Sunset painted Lake Texoma a medley of sparkling colors. Gold, orange, red, all fading to pink and purple. Crisp autumn air needled Madi's lungs as she paced across the deck for a better view.

"You shouldn't stand out here."

Phone in one hand and a bottle of Pepsi in the other, Topsannah leaned against the cabin's sliding glass door. Her carbon nanoweave bodysuit glistened, highlighting the contours of every tensed muscle beneath.

As if the sunset wasn't beautiful enough.

Setting aside some unworthy thoughts, Madi chuckled. "C'mon, blossom. It's been a week. He's probably off in search of easier prey by now. Besides, doesn't Ironsides only kill up close and personal?"

"He *prefers* to." Wary eyes scanned the forested shoreline like a hawk hunting mice. "Up close, far away, it doesn't matter. You're still a sitting duck. For all I know, Ironsides could be snorkeling across the lake right now!"

Madi shot a sideways look at Lake Texoma. Suddenly, watching the sunset didn't seem like such a good idea. "I guess you're right." Her gaze drifted toward Topsannah's phone. "You gonna call Rosa?"

"No." Her lips twitched. "I'll explain later."

They headed back inside and upstairs to the guest bedroom. Football blared on the TV. "What was that supposed to be?" Topsannah growled as she took a seat on the bed. "You can't blitz a quarterback like Simpson!"

Shaking her head, Madi traipsed over to the closet and unzipped her half-empty suitcase. Whippoorwill gear lay in a heap beside it. "The cabin has two more bedrooms. I still don't see why we need to share this one."

"All of them are at least three seconds away." She sipped Pepsi. "Those seconds could mean the difference between life and death. Especially when a professional killer is involved." Her voice trembled, then cracked. "I can't stomach the thought of you dying because I was too far away to help. But if it makes you more comfortable, I can always sleep on the—"

"No, you're fine."

Fishing a tablet out of her suitcase, Madi frowned. *Why does she still care so much?* The question nagged at her as she flopped down beside Topsannah and began sifting through a mountain of unread emails. *Does she wish things had turned out differently, too?* Curiosity and hope fluttered in her stomach, but she quashed them. Reopening old wounds wouldn't accomplish anything.

Hours passed while Topsannah quaffed Pepsi and watched the game, and Madi examined new case files and pondered appropriate charges. *This is… actually kinda nice.* Sitting so close to the most feared woman in Oklahoma brought a familiar sense of security. A sense she'd missed the past few months.

"You know," Topsannah said, tossing her empty bottle into the trashcan, "I never thanked you."

"For what?"

"Being the best damn district attorney I've ever known." Sighing, she stared at the TV. "Every blow the Whippoorwill strikes… sure, it helps protect the public. Temporarily. The injuries I inflict can keep a criminal off the streets for days, weeks, maybe even months. But you—the convictions you secure can put them behind bars for life. I can't fight crime and corruption without you."

Madi blushed. "It goes both ways, blossom. When I took office, my law enforcement partners were some of the biggest crooks in the county." A bashful smile tugged at her lips. "Then I found you. A vigilante. A hero. The kind of woman I could always rely on."

Blinking back tears, Topsannah hung her head. "But you couldn't rely on me in the end, could you? I shut you out. Figured, 'If Madi doesn't know I'm in danger, she won't worry about me.' Ugh, I was so *stupid*!"

"Shhh, there was plenty of stupidity to go around."

Topsannah rolled her eyes. "Says the summa cum laude graduate of Harvard Law."

"Honest!" Madi leaned in close. Close enough to

smell the sweetness on her breath. "All those times I complained about how you ran off to be the Whippoorwill instead of spending time with me… *that* was stupid. And selfish. Like you said, some things are more important than our love life."

Sniffling, she wiped away tears. "I'm sorry, Madi. For being so stupid."

"Me too."

All the tension between them faded, and Madi became acutely aware of everything. A spark in the air. Cotton sheets beneath her. The scent of lilac and sugar. Rhythmic breaths washing over her face. Their lips just inches apart.

Not worth the trouble, remember?

Quashing the thought, she took her prairie blossom by the hand. Fingertips brushed familiar calluses and scars.

Topsannah shivered. "There's something I need to—"

"Kiss me!"

"But… we… you said—"

"Damn what I said," Madi whispered. Then she pounced, knocking Topsannah back against the pillows as their lips locked. Her tongue still tasted like Pepsi. Madi groaned into the kiss, then groaned again when corded arms gripped her in a vise. They tumbled over. Strands of black hair tickled Madi's nose. Icy fingers traced the contours of her body. One brushed the gunshot wound. She winced.

"Sorry!" Topsannah's lips twisted into a sly grin. "Let me make it up to you…"

Calloused hands crept beneath Madi's T-shirt, carefully avoiding her stitches, and slipped it off. In a flash, her bra clasps came undone. Tender kisses blazed a trail onto her chest, then lower still. One of them engulfed a hardened nipple and sucked until Madi cried out in pain and pleasure.

God, I missed this. How long had it been since they'd fucked? Seven, maybe eight months? *Might as well be an eternity.*

A swift tug yanked her panties and pajama bottoms off as more kisses trailed across the softness of her belly, through tufts of damp red hair, and onto her folds. Slick warmth trawled between them. Slowly. Teasingly. Then Topsannah found her clit.

In an instant, the tempo shifted. Long, sensual licks gave way to quick, fluttery ones which kindled a tickle in her depths even though nothing had delved into her pussy. Fear, agony, stress… Topsannah's tongue drove away a week's worth of trouble.

Dark lips joined in, sucking at her swollen clit. Low moans of satisfaction vibrated against it and thrummed through Madi. Warmth built in her belly alongside the tickle from earlier. She flopped back against the pillows, shuddering.

"Don't stop," Madi whimpered. "Blossom, don't stop!"

An icy finger tentatively circled her pussy before sliding inside. Then another. And another. Soon they glided in and out, stroking a bundle of nerves Madi had almost forgotten about. The tense, ticklish heat between her legs coiled tighter and tighter, like the spring in a wind-up toy. Tight enough she almost burst.

Then Topsannah pulled away, licking her fingers clean. "Beg me. Beg me for release like you begged me to kiss you."

278

"Please, blossom," Madi whined as the last echoes of her touch faded. "*Please* let me finish."

Topsannah struck her most sensitive points with surgical precision. Almost as if she was just some supervillain to be defeated. Such a naughty notion led Madi right back to the edge. Those soft lips sucking her folds, that exquisite tongue lashing her clit, those nimble fingers plunging into her pussy... they shoved her over.

Waves of delight pulsed through Madi from head to toe and back again. Trembling, she wrapped both legs around Topsannah and ground against her face. Rings of muscle clutched at the three fingers stuffing her pussy until an ecstatic wail erupted from somewhere deep, deep inside. Somewhere primal. For a moment, the whole world went blank.

When she finally floated down from her dreamy high, Madi found Topsannah lying beside her. Dark lips glistened with beads of nectar, but her nanoweave bodysuit remained zipped up all the way to the collar. Madi frowned. "Aren't you gonna... ?" Hazy pleasure still muddled her thoughts, and the words slipped away. "I can... don't you want me to...?"

Topsannah shook her head. "Pleasuring you is good enough. Besides, I need to—"

"Oh, hush!" Madi followed up the command with a fierce kiss. Quick swirling motions licked the sweetness from her lover's lips, and she savored the taste of herself. Light. Sweet. Almost syrupy. Reluctantly, she pulled back just a hairsbreadth. "Forget about what you *need*. Just for tonight. What do you *want*?"

Shivers and a sharp breath answered her question. "I want *you*. Your touch. Your tongue inside me."

Giggling, Madi reached for the bodysuit's zipper. "That can be arranged."

Zipper teeth rasped against the metallic slider, and Madi's heart almost hammered out of her chest as she peeled back the fabric to reveal sweat-slicked muscles. Only black boy shorts and a sports bra concealed Topsannah's nakedness now. *Practical as ever.* One fluid motion rolled the bra up and off.

Dark nipples swelled as Madi cupped both russet breasts. *So round and soft.* Not at all like the rest of her body's hardness and sharp angles. She kneaded them for a moment, then ran her fingers lower to trace Topsannah's litany of scars. *Ironsides is a damn fool.* If none of these wounds could stop Topsannah, what chance did he have?

Her thumbs slipped into the damp boy shorts and eased them off to expose Topsannah's hairless pussy. Sopping folds glistened in the dim light. *God, I've never seen her so wet.* Madi brushed a finger over them, then raised it to her lips. Metallic. Tangy. Familiar. Slurping up the juices, she gazed hungrily at Topsannah. "Queen me."

Next thing she knew, Topsannah straddled her face. Lilac perfume mingled with the sweet scent of arousal. "Remember our old safety signal?"

Distracted by the warmth and wetness so tantalizingly close, Madi drew a blank. "Um… shove my thumb up your ass?"

Topsannah chuckled. "No, but that's good enough for now. Ready?"

"Ready!" Madi tunneled her tongue between dewy folds and up into Topsannah. Slowly at first, then faster and faster. Her lover's taste drowned out every other taste in the world. Corded thighs clamped over her ears and tugged at auburn curls, but the pain didn't matter. Only fucking Topsannah mattered.

"*Ohhh,* Madi…!"

Hearing her name moaned like that spurred Madi onward. She reached around and squeezed toned asscheeks, using them to pull herself closer. Close enough that breathing at all meant breathing in her little prairie blossom's nectar.

"Madi, I'm gonna—"

Topsannah bucked like a bronco before she could finish. Holding her down, Madi switched to lapping at her clit. A wordless squeal leapt from her lips, and she shuddered once, twice, three times before drenching Madi with warm sweetness. Utterly spent, she slumped off to the side.

Madi lay motionless for a moment, basking in the afterglow. Then she remembered why they'd come here in the first place. Visions of Ironsides and his expressionless faceplate loomed before her mind's eye. She tried to forget, to stamp them out, to think of something else—anything else—but nothing seemed to work. *Well, almost nothing.* Rolling onto her side, Madi reached out. "Can we go again? Please?"

"Not… I gotta… just give me a few minutes." Panting, Topsannah took her hand and scooted a little closer. "Fistfights, car chases, deathtraps… nothing ever takes my breath away quite like you."

Madi grinned. *This is how life ought to be.*

Whether a minute, an hour, or an eternity passed before they fell apart again, Madi couldn't say. Bedlam still blared in the background.

"That defensive stand makes it Fourth and Goal

from the one-yard line," an announcer said. "Looks like the Cowboys are bringing out their kicking team to tie this thing up and send it to triple overtime."

Topsannah nuzzled her cheek.

"Rosa Coronil nailed a field goal from 53 yards out earlier tonight, so this shouldn't present much of a problem."

An icy finger began tracing circles around her belly button.

"The kick is—no, it's a fake! Coronil steps back to pass, dodges a tackler, gets hit as she throws. Garber dives for it… touchdown! And with that, the Oklahoma State Cowboys win Bedlam for the first time in—"

Madi sat up to find the TV muted. Returning the remote to its place on the nightstand, Topsannah met her gaze. "There's something you need to know. Something I tried to tell you before we… got distracted."

Well, that's ominous. Nevertheless, she nodded. "Okay. I'm listening."

"We didn't come here to hide. Rosa was right—this cabin's connections to your family make it an obvious bolt hole." Pausing, Topsannah snatched her clothes up off the floor. "Besides, hiding from Ironsides is an exercise in futility. He'll simply lie low, allow you to believe the coast is clear, then strike at a time and place of his choosing."

Flushed, sputtering, Madi struggled to find words. "But… how… you… why *are* we here?"

"To lure him into striking at a time and place of *my* choosing." Carbon nanoweave slipped over glistening muscles, and a zipper purred. "Think about it. Ironsides almost killed you once already. He 'fended off' the Whippoorwill. He knows I'd never approve such an obvious hideout, so he'll figure you're alone. Possibly injured. Isolated. Defenseless. Easy prey. Eager to claim the price on your head, he'll forgo extensive surveillance and charge onto a battlefield *I* control."

Not an awful plan. Still, her face and ears burned white hot. "You didn't think to tell me I was *bait*?"

"Not until today. And that's the worst mistake I've made in a long time." The vigilante's voice crackled as she strapped armor plating over her bodysuit. "For whatever it's worth, I'm sorry."

Madi snarled. "Unbelievable. You say keeping secrets is stupid, then go and do it anyway!"

Wilting, Topsannah donned her cowl. "The plan was already in motion by the time I fully understood how destructive locking my friends and allies out of the loop could be." Electronics distorted her voice now, but they couldn't hide undertones of sorrow. "Like I said, I wanted to explain earlier—before we kissed—but things unfolded so quickly…"

Madi crossed her arms beneath her breasts and glowered.

"Hate me if you like. No doubt I deserve it." The mottled gray-brown cape rustled as Whippoorwill fastened it around her neck. "But… if you can ever find it in your heart to forgive me, I promise you this—no more secrets."

Before she could reply, every light in the cabin flickered. Then they blacked out all at once. *Strange. Didn't Daddy install a backup generator last year?*

"He's here!" Whippoorwill plucked a flashlight

from her utility belt and tossed it to Madi. "Get dressed. Hide. And remember what I told you last time." Soft lips pecked her cheek. "By the Great Spirit, I swear I'll protect you with my life if need be."

* * *

Crouching behind a half-wall between the entryway and kitchen, Topsannah licked her lips. Madi's taste still lingered there. Light. Sweet. A flutter filled her chest and floated higher at the same time her intestines tied themselves into an ever-tightening knot. *What did we just do?* Was tonight the rebirth of their love affair? Or had her reticence torpedoed any hopes of reconciliation?

Footsteps on the porch swept all those questions away. Soft, smooth, they slunk toward the front door. Judging by the shadow he cast through the kitchen window, Ironsides had swapped out his signature helmet for a set of night vision goggles. Another hint he didn't expect much trouble. *Perfect.* Topsannah reached for the pepperball pistol at her hip only to find an empty holster.

Dammit! Must've left it in the guest room with Madi...

Her gaze flicked toward the staircase, but lock picks already rasped at the front deadbolt. An operator like Ironsides would have the door open before she could run upstairs and get back into position. *Time for Plan B.* Gloved fingers slipped a strobe grenade from a capsule on her belt. Tiny prickles covered the marble-sized gadget, allowing it to cling to almost any surface and flash bursts of blinding light in every direction. *You ruined my night, Sam. Let's see if I can ruin yours.*

A draft blew into the cabin, and hinges groaned softly. *He's in!* While cautious footsteps padded across the doormat, she tapped her cowl. Its lenses immediately recalibrated to block out any light at 555 nanometers, the same wavelength her grenade would strobe at. As she hurled it over the half-wall, Topsannah Price faded away. Only the Whippoorwill remained.

A forlorn cry filled the cabin.

"No!" Floorboards creaked as Ironsides spun to face her hiding spot. His pistol thundered. Lead ripped through the half-wall, but she was already in motion. Bits of plaster and sheetrock pattered off the back of her cowl. Whippoorwill lunged around the corner, escrima sticks drawn.

Disarm. An offhand strike crashed across his knuckles. Bones splintered beneath steel. The revolver—a long-barreled .44 Colt Anaconda, by the look of it—clattered to the floor. Howling, Ironsides cradled his ruined gun hand.

Disorient. Before he could recover, a mighty overhand blow smashed his night vision goggles to smithereens. The assassin reeled.

Drop. Ducking a blind punch, Whippoorwill swept both legs out from under him. Air whistled through grit teeth as 243 pounds of hired killer slammed into the doormat.

Debilitate. Triumph swelled in her chest as she leapt, thrust an escrima stick at his vulnerable solar plexus... and watched it sail through empty space. Whippoorwill glanced up in time to see the kick, but too late to avoid it.

Cartilage popped. Blood filled her mouth and

nose. A gasp sucked spittle down her windpipe. Both sticks flew off into the darkness. Then her cowl smacked against the hardwood floor. One lens flickered and died. Half blinded, she lurched upright just as Ironsides scooped up his revolver.

No!

Instincts seized control. Whippoorwill scrambled to her feet and bolted toward the only source of cover—a living room off to the right.

BANG!

Sparks erupted from a wall-mounted TV as she dove over the sofa and crashed through a glass coffee table. Armor plating and nanoweave fiber deflected most of the fragments, but only half her face enjoyed such protection. Jagged shards carved the rest of it into bloody ribbons.

BANG!

Another bullet ripped through the sofa. Stuffing swirled around her like a blizzard. Heavy boots trudged toward the stairs. *Get up!* Whippoorwill pushed herself up onto all fours, but the effort ground splinters of glass against her flesh. Agony blazed in a dozen places. *The pain doesn't matter. You don't matter. Protecting Madi... that's what matters!*

Fresh vigor flooded achy muscles. Hurdling the sofa, she bounded toward the staircase. Ironsides was already halfway up. Just as she reached the bottom step, he twisted around mid-stride. The revolver belched fire and lead again.

Whippoorwill tumbled onto the hardwood, breathless. Speckles of light danced before her eyes. Pain flared again, but not the hot, searing kind from a gunshot wound. Dull. Deep. Throbbing through her

286

bones. Gauntleted fingers found the bullet lodged in her breastplate. *Great Spirit, watch over me a little longer.*

Wheezing, she surged upstairs. Every muscle in her body screamed. Just a few paces ahead, Ironsides stalked toward the guest room. He paused just inside the doorway, squinting into the dark.

Oh, no you don't!

She leapt. Gauntleted fingers grabbed the doorframe as if it were monkey bars and harnessed her momentum to launch herself into a jump kick. Both boots slammed into the small of Ironsides' back and drove him into the floor. Thick muscles heaved underfoot, and she fell on top of him.

In a flash, the assassin shoved her off and scrambled to his feet. Moonlight glinted off the Colt Anaconda as he leveled it at her face. Memories of a twice-sworn vow welled up. *"By the Great Spirit, I swear I'll protect you. With my life, if need be."* Her throat tightened. *Guess it needed to be.* If only she could talk to Madi one last time. To express her love. To apologize again for keeping so many—

Movement flickered off to the right. A woman's silhouette crouched near the bed, something bright yellow clutched in her hands. Was that a pepperball gun?

POP!

POP!

POP!

All three pepperballs hit Ironsides in the chest and burst on impact. Clouds of ghost pepper extract billowed. A soft mist coated her skin. Then the burning began. Even with a cowl, it spread to

Whippoorwill's eyes and fire filled her chest. She tried to cough it out, but that only made things worse. Tears and snot streamed down her face. Meanwhile Ironsides doubled over, wheezing like a heavy smoker.

POP!

POP!

POP!

The clouds of pepper spray thickened, choking the life out of her. Ironsides retreated across the threshold, his bearded face a deep red and his eyes almost swollen shut. "Ah, the little piggy has some fire in her belly after all!"

Chuckling, he swung the Colt toward Madi.

Time slowed to a crawl.

Memories cascaded through her head. Their chance meeting during the Courthouse Crisis. Breaking the Wild Bunch together. Courtship in the shadows. Unmasking herself to Madi. Fierce kisses and long nights tangled in each other's arms.

A new fire filled her chest. One kindled by love, not pepper spray. It flared bright, blotting out every ache and pain. Shattered nose, bruised ribs, half a dozen cuts... they all felt so far away now. Determination welled up as the flames spread. *Madison Harper won't die tonight. Not if I have anything to say about it.*

Roaring at the top of her lungs, she threw herself at Ironsides. A fifth bullet hurtled through the ceiling as they collided with the banister. It held for a moment, then splintered. Both of them tumbled off the second story landing and into the entryway below.

WHAM!

Her whole body went numb on impact then

exploded into crushing pain a moment later. Fresh tears stung lacerated cheeks. She wanted to scream but couldn't find any air. Everything flickered. *Don't black out,* her inner voice whispered. *You've still got a fight to win.* Gasping, wheezing, she tried to push herself up.

Ironsides regained his footing first. Hardwood creaked as he hobbled over and drove his boot into her side. Ribs snapped like dry twigs. At least one bent back against a lung, setting nerves afire with each breath. Everything flickered again. Whippoorwill tried to scramble away, but only made it half a step before slumping against the staircase.

Time for Plan C.

What was Plan C again? Something about a phone call? Law enforcement? Somebody's psych profile? Those bits sounded right, but too much haze filled her head to piece them together properly.

"You fought well, pretty bird. But not well enough." Heavy footsteps lumbered closer, and something pressed against the base of her cowl. "Checkmate."

Helicopter blades whirred overhead. In an instant, the details of Plan C came flooding back.

"You think you're some kind of chess master, Sam?" Even though it hurt, Topsannah chuckled. "You're a novice who only looks one move ahead!"

Sirens wailed in the distance.

Ironsides recoiled. "How did they—"

"An anonymous tip, called in hours ago by yours truly." She grinned, then spat out a glob of blood. "Half the Marshall County Sheriff's Department is coming up the road with the FBI are hot on their heels.

Boats from OHP Troop W are closing in on the lakeside, and one of Troop O's helicopters is circling. Face it, Sam—you're surrounded."

"Don't you remember I'm bulletproof?!" The assassin's voice wavered ever so slightly. "They can't hurt me!"

Is that self-delusion I hear? Topsannah glanced at him over her shoulder. "Oh, they know *all* about your impenetrable skin and your vulnerability to lachrymator agents like tear gas or pepper spray."

Color drained from his wrinkled skin. Chest heaving, Ironsides paced back and forth across the entryway. "Alright. Maybe a bunch of pigs *are* about to cordon off this place. Maybe they can take me down. But they won't get here for a few more minutes. Plenty of time to blow your head off and hunt down the lawyer bitch."

The Colt Anaconda trembled as Ironsides shoved it into her face.

Praying the FBI's behavioral profile on Sam Nichols was correct, Topsannah took a deep breath. "Go ahead, then. Kill me. Scour the cabin for Miss Harper. But just remember—every second you waste on us, those pigs are tightening a noose around your neck. Soon, escape won't be an option. They'll capture you, shackle you, put you on trial in a federal court. Maybe you'll get the needle. Maybe you'll spend the rest of your life in a 7 x 12 cell at ADX Florence. No matter what, you'll never be a free man again." She paused to let the idea sink in. "Is killing us worth your freedom?"

Waving his revolver, Ironsides staggered backwards. "You're trying to get into my head, aren't you!"

"The longer you think about this, the tighter that noose gets."

"Shut up!"

"Tighter."

"No!"

Topsannah slipped into a soft, maternal tone and tipped her head toward the deck. "Run for it while you still can. Show those pigs they can't corner a free man like a rat!"

Hyperventilating, he glanced between her and Lake Texoma's tranquil waters. The Colt Anaconda rose.

BANG!

His sixth and final shot blew a gaping hole in the sliding glass door. Cursing to himself, Ironsides busted through the ruined glass and loped across the deck. With one last frenzied cry, he leapt into Lake Texoma.

I can't believe that worked. Against a man less terrified of capture, it almost certainly wouldn't have. Propping herself up, Topsannah prayed the FBI agent who'd profiled Ironsides would live a long and healthy life.

Bare feet scurried downstairs and into the entryway. Hazel eyes widened as they swept over her. "Blossom, what did he do to you?"

"It's no—AAAAAA!"

"Take it easy." Soft hands cupped Topsannah's bloody face. "Keeping secrets, using me to bait a trap. I ought to be furious right now! But you saved my life. Again. And that's a debt I can never repay."

"Nonsense. If it weren't for your quick thinking upstairs, Ironsides would've blown my brains out." Topsannah smiled weakly, even though it hurt. "Don't you think that means we're even?"

"Only if we forget about every other time you've rescued me." Blushing, Madi wrapped her in a warm embrace. "Whatever the future might hold, whatever we mean to each other, just know I'll always have your back."

Her smile widened. "Likewise."

* * *

As the old gas guzzler's engine died with a rattle, Deputy Patel unbuckled and threw open the driver's side door. Meanwhile, her partner—Corporal Derrick White of the Oklahoma County Sheriff's Department—unwrapped a fresh stick of chewing gum. "Ready, Miss Harper?"

Madi gulped, then leaned over to peer through their unmarked car's heavily tinted windows. The tint blocked so much light she could barely discern the towering, stepped-back outline of the Oklahoma County Courthouse even though it stood fifty feet away.

Hard to believe it'd only been three weeks since she'd last climbed those steps to prosecute a Bricktown Boy. Three weeks full of terror and mayhem. Remembering them left her hands too jittery to unbuckle her seatbelt.

C'mon, pull yourself together! Wasn't this why Major Ellis had hired Ironsides in the first place? To terrorize anyone who wanted to hold the Bricktown Boys accountable? Madi sat up a little straighter. Her jaw stiffened. *Don't let him intimidate you. He doesn't deserve the satisfaction.*

Taking a deep breath, she turned toward Corporal White. "As ready as I'll ever be."

By now, Patel had popped the trunk. She hefted a big black briefcase, circled around to Madi's side of the car, and eased the door open. "What did you stuff into this thing, ma'am? A library?"

"More or less." Flashing a faux smile at the deputy, Madi stepped onto the sidewalk and took the briefcase. In truth, experimental ballistic plates accounted for most of its weight. A gift from Topsannah. Supposedly, even anti-materiel rifles would struggle to punch through it. *Let's not put that to the test.*

Wary eyes surveyed her surroundings. Straight ahead, Assistant District Attorney Palmer trudged up the courthouse steps. His signature red tie flapped in the wind. Off to the right, a clerk fished car keys out of her purse. In the distance, a man wearing an OKC Thunder hoodie jaywalked across Park Avenue. *No signs of trouble.*

Yet.

Taut muscles loosened as White and Patel led her past a row of bollards. Part of Madi wished they were the Whippoorwill and Kingfisher instead. *No way this doughy corporal and his partner can protect me from Ironsides.* Hell, they probably wouldn't even slow him down.

Old anxiety returned with a vengeance. Guts all knotted up, Madi glanced over her shoulder. The clerk rummaged around in the back seat of her car. Meanwhile, the Thunder fan strode down the sidewalk with his head bowed. Such a mundane scene.

What did you expect? After his botched attack on the cabin, everyone from the Rio Grande to the Arkansas River wanted a piece of Ironsides. No way would an operator as smooth as Ironsides risk capture to attack her at a courthouse in broad daylight.

The clerk screamed.

Madi whirled around just in time to see the hooded man raise a big revolver. Morning light glinted off its barrel and the elegant helm obscuring his face. A helm covered in translucent stars and stripes. *Ironsides!* His finger squeezed the silvery trigger.

BANG!

BANG!

Corporal White pitched forward. Then his knee exploded in a shower of blood and bone.

BANG!

BANG!

Too late, Deputy Patel reached for her service pistol. Both shots drilled through her tactical vest before she could clear leather. She spun, tripped, and fell face first into the handrail. Hard.

Heart in her throat, Madi stood alone atop the courthouse steps. *So, this is it. This is how I die.* Then she remembered the briefcase. Instructions from Topsannah looped through her mind. *"Stop. Drop. Cover."* Kneeling now, Madi raised the briefcase to shield her head and neck.

BANG!

The briefcase slammed into her nose. Bursts of color blotted out the real world. Something popped. Warm stickiness dribbled onto her lips.

BANG!

Madi lurched backwards. Agony rippled through her belly. Then the back of her skull smacked into concrete. She dropped the briefcase. Fresh bursts of light flared. Frantic fingers groped for a gunshot wound. They found a hole in her favorite blouse, but not the carbon nanoweave bodysuit underneath. *You're a lifesaver, Topsannah.*

Aching, breathless, she sat up to find Ironsides marching up the courthouse steps like a spring thunderstorm rolling in from the west. Every other step, he loaded another bullet into the big revolver.

She'd only survived this long thanks to Topsannah's tech. Not to mention a little luck. Would it weather six more shots? Doubt churned her stomach. *Where the hell are you, blossom? We planned for this!*

Movement flickered atop the Metropolitan Library. A gray-brown blur dove off its roof. Dark fabric trailed after it, then flared into a facsimile of feathered wings. The figure swooped up, gliding ever closer. Forty feet. Thirty. Twenty. Ten. A flying kick struck right between the assassin's shoulder blades. He slammed face first into concrete.

CRUNCH!

The big revolver flew from his grasp. Cracks spiderwebbed their way across the star-spangled faceplate, but it didn't shatter. Ironsides bellowed. Meanwhile, Whippoorwill harnessed her momentum to tuck into a roll and come up with both escrima sticks drawn.

Madi breathed a sigh of relief. Salvation had come at last!

* * *

Panting, Whippoorwill surveyed the battlefield. Both deputies were already down. One screamed. The other lay motionless on the courthouse steps. Madi sat behind her, propped up on an elbow and gasping for breath. Nose bloody, one stiletto snapped in half, a rip in her pantyhose. No serious injuries, though. *Let's keep it that way.*

Ironsides gripped the handrail and hoisted himself up. Two jagged fractures and countless smaller ones marred his faceplate. Superficial damage, but if one of those cracks reached the seam between ballistic glass and helmet, the whole faceplate would shatter. Then her ace in the hole could put him down. A thousand simulations back at the Nest proved it. *Now to bring those simulations to life...*

The hitman's head snapped to the left. His fully loaded Colt Anaconda rested on a step maybe six feet away. *Oh, no you don't!*

Memories from the past few weeks cascaded through her head. The rescue, this reconciliation with Madi, all the blood and sweat she'd poured into fighting Ironsides It couldn't be for nothing!

Whippoorwill lunged, ramming an escrima stick into his temple. Steel chipped glass. Tiny fissures radiated from the point of impact. *That's for shooting Madi!*

Growling like a rabid dog, Ironsides hurled a wild haymaker at her face. She sidestepped. A backhanded blow from her other stick crashed across his cheek. Cracks inched closer to the seam. *That's for breaking my ribs!*

She'd barely finished the thought when a stiff right hook slammed into those same ribs. Agony lanced down her flank with every breath. An escrima stick clattered off concrete. It took a moment before Whippoorwill realized she'd dropped it. *Should've listened to Rosa. They're not healed yet.* Reeling, she retreated up the courthouse steps.

Ironsides followed, cackling. "Time to clip your wings, pretty bird!"

Can't take another hit like that. Size, strength, speed… he had every advantage. Victory hinged on putting him down before those advantages could be brought to bear. Teeth grit, Whippoorwill tightened her grip on the escrima stick and lunged back into the fray.

A well-aimed thrust caught Ironsides right below the eye. Or, at least, where it ought to be. Chips of glass pattered off her cowl, his head jerked backward, and a shard of the faceplate almost popped loose. *That's for everyone you've murdered!*

Bellowing like a wounded boar, the assassin charged. Thick fingers wrapped around her throat, then choke slammed Whippoorwill into the courthouse. A fleshy thud filled the air. Her other escrima stick slipped from gloved fingers. The world convulsed. Flickered. Dimmed. Pressure crushed her windpipe.

No, this can't be for nothing!

She punched his faceplate. Again. And again. At last, chunks of ballistic glass came loose. A steely blue eye glowered through the gap they left behind.

"All your fury, all your strength, and you barely managed to break some glass?" Ironsides tightened his grip. "Pathetic."

"Remember last time, Sam? The cabin?" Wheezing, Whippoorwill slipped a can of pepper spray from her belt and sprayed it straight into that evil eye. "You're still the novice who only looks one move ahead!"

Howling, Ironsides dropped her and clawed at the remnants of his faceplate. More shards of glass broke off as tears streamed from his eyes. Fingernails gashed wrinkled skin, but that rubbed spray into the fresh wounds. His screams faded into muffled sobs.

"Kingfisher and I concocted this mixture just for

you." She grabbed his flailing limbs and hogtied them with a spool of wire from her belt. "Five percent major capsaicinoids. You'll be lucky to see through that eye again, much less aim with it."

He sobbed louder.

Whippoorwill glanced toward the downed deputies. One was up and moving now, applying a tourniquet to her crippled partner's leg. *He's not gonna make it without help.* Heart skipping, she tapped the side of her cowl. "Kingfisher, I need an ambulance at the courthouse!"

"Already on its way, *vieja*."

Sure enough, sirens echoed through downtown Oklahoma City. Whippoorwill breathed a sigh of relief. "Good work, Kingfisher."

Faux indignation tinged Rosa's voice. "Have I ever given you anything less?"

"Never, baby bird."

Signing off, she rushed over to Madi and helped her up. "Come on, Madame District Attorney. Let's get you someplace safe."

"No way." Madi kicked off her ruined heels, snatched up the armored briefcase, and marched toward the courthouse doors. "I've got a trial to win!"

* * *

"The defense rests, Your Honor."

Judge Taylor nodded, then smacked his lips. "The court will now hear closing arguments." Beady blue eyes drifted toward Madi. "You're up, Miss Harper."

Drawing a deep breath, she stood and smoothed out a wrinkle in her pencil skirt. Months of preparation and a three-day trial all came down to this. *Time to put the last Bricktown Boy behind bars.*

"Ladies and gentlemen of the jury, what we have here is the most *brazen* case of corruption and abuse of power I've witnessed in 11 years as a prosecutor." Madi paused, jabbing a perfectly manicured finger at the defendant. "And this man, Sergeant Alvin McBride of the Oklahoma City Police Department, is responsible."

High heels click-clacked softly as she approached the jury. "You watched *18* separate pieces of security footage from the OCPD's Bricktown Substation. Each of them showed Sergeant McBride stealing firearms from the armory or evidence lockers. Semi-automatic pistols. Pump-action shotguns. Assault rifles. Even a grenade launcher! *All* these weapons ended up on the black market.

"You heard from six eyewitnesses to Sergeant McBride's crimes. Two are co-conspirators within the OCPD. The other four bought his stolen guns at midnight rendezvous in or around Oklahoma City. All of them told you the same story. Alvin McBride sought to profit from his badge by selling stolen weapons to criminals!"

One by one, she made eye contact with each of the jurors. They all leaned forward, brows furrowed. Several nodded slowly. One shot a disgusted look at the defendant. *Good. I've got this jury hooked.* Now to reel them in.

"The defense insists this is all part of an elaborate plot by the Whippoorwill to frame Sergeant McBride for crimes he didn't commit. That she doctored video and coerced witness testimony. Why?" Madi shrugged. "The defense can't tell you. However, *I* can tell you their claims are baseless. A digital forensics expert confirmed the footage is authentic. All six eyewitnesses deny their testimony was coerced. The defense keeps repeating their debunked conspiracy theory for one simple reason—they don't have an actual case."

Sighing, she turned toward the sky-blue state flag beside Judge Taylor. "For the past 15 years, scandal after scandal has rocked our state. Embezzled education funds. Civil asset forfeiture schemes. The Bricktown Boys. This is your opportunity to stand up and say you won't tolerate corruption. To declare 'Enough is enough!' Do what your conscience demands. Do what the law demands. Do what the facts demand. Convict Alvin McBride on all 44 counts of embezzlement and evidence tampering."

Madi paced back to her seat, breathless. *God, I hope they listen.* While McBride's attorney made a hash of his closing argument, she studied the jury's reactions. Half of them glared daggers at the defendant. Juror Eleven curled her lips. When the defense brought up its Whippoorwill conspiracy again, the foreman's eyes almost rolled out of his head. Madi smiled. *This trial is as good as won.*

Soon the bailiff ushered the jury off to deliberate, and Madi glanced at one of her ADAs. "Palmer, I'm gonna go grab another cup of coffee. Text me if anything comes up."

"Will do, ma'am."

Fresh air washed over Madi as she strode out into the hallway. All her worries blew away like dead leaves on an autumn wind. Alvin McBride faced decades behind bars. Some of his fellow Bricktown Boys would die in prison. And best of all, her office was one step closer to stamping out corruption in Oklahoma County. *It's almost storybook.*

"Hello, Madame District Attorney."

Madi froze, overwhelmed by memories of the attack in her darkened kitchen. But this time... this time the voice sounded *right*. Smooth. Singsong. Sultry. Instead of Ironsides, a tall woman clad in cowboy boots, blue jeans, and a rancher jacket lounged on the bench across the hall. An Oklahoma University baseball cap hid most of her face, but that sharp jawline was unmistakable. "Topsannah?"

"The one and only." Her lips twitched. One was swollen and bloody. "Cleaning up that mess down in McAlester took longer than expected. Sorry I missed closing arguments."

"Don't be. You've got better things to do than listen to my dulcet tones." Like foil a mass breakout at the state penitentiary. Thanks to Whippoorwill's intervention, not one convict had escaped. *And she still found time to visit me.* What a woman.

Topsannah rapped her knuckles on the bench. "So, how soon should we expect a verdict?"

"God only knows." She glanced toward the courtroom. "It's a clear-cut case, but they've got almost four dozen charges to deliberate."

"Yeah." Her lips twitched again. "Yeah, you're right."

Scowling, Madi crossed her arms. "Something tells me you didn't come here to watch the McBride trial."

"Am I so easy to read?"

"Sometimes." She took a seat beside Topsannah. "Why did you really drop by, blossom?"

At first, only silence answered the question. Then

301

cowboy boots began to tap out a nervous beat. Deep breaths whistled through a broken nose. When she finally spoke, her typically steady voice trembled. "What happened in the cabin... I can't stop thinking about it. About us."

Memories of that wild night welled up. Calloused hands under her shirt. Kisses across her stomach. Tension melting into bliss. *Just like old times. Better times.* Madi felt a tingle in her loins. *If only she'd shared her plans. If only Ironsides hadn't shown up.* Then everything would've been perfect.

Her dark eyes downcast, Topsannah whispered. "One night of sex. What does it mean, Madi? Nothing? Are we just friends? Exes who found temporary comfort in each other's arms? Or something more? Did we rekindle what we once had? Forge a new bond? I *have* to know for sure."

Madi frowned. "You could've asked anytime in the last eight weeks. Why wait?"

"Because I was afraid." Her voice wavered, then cracked. "Afraid of what your answer might be. But now, uncertainty is worse than any answer."

"Blossom—"

"Please, listen. Just a little longer." Topsannah took her by the hands. "Nine months alone taught me a valuable lesson. Life means so much more when we share it with someone else. Someone who celebrates our triumphs and mourns our tragedies. Someone who holds us together and lifts us up. Someone like you, Madi." Tears spilled down russet cheeks. "In the cabin, before we fought Ironsides, I meant what I said—no more secrets. Complete transparency. I promise. Please... will you take me back?"

The words struck like a string of kisses. Sweet. Tender. Passionate. Part of Madi longed to kiss back. To melt into her prairie blossom's embrace and never let go. But what if they were just empty words?

No. Even an actor would struggle to mimic the raw emotion dripping from Topsannah's voice. Besides, hadn't the Whippoorwill shielded her from Ironsides? She'd fought for Madi, bled for Madi, damn near died for Madi. Only one emotion gave birth to such dedication–love. Unconditional love.

She planted a ferocious kiss on Topsannah's lips. Hints of blood mixed with more bitter notes from caffeine pills and energy shots, but right now that taste was the most wonderful in the world. Corded arms tensed in shock, then pulled her close. For the first time since the cabin, Madi felt safe.

Dimly, she sensed someone else in the hall. *Let them see.* Madi didn't care. Inhibitions, reservations, old quarrels—they all seemed ten million miles away. The scent of the woman she loved became suffocating as Topsannah's jacket—so soft and warm—pressed against her. She ached to draw a fresh breath.

Panting, her lover broke free from the kiss. "So, back together?"

"Back together." Madi grinned. "Let's make it last this time."

Author Bios

Since selling her first short in 2010, **Louisa Bacio** (http://www.louisabacio.com/) has published more than 40 contemporary and paranormal erotic romance stories with 16 publishers. Bacio shares her household with a husband, two teenagers and a multitude pet craziness. She teaches college classes in English, journalism and popular culture.

Julie Behrens is the author of "Chasing Tail" and "Capricious," which won the 2014 Best Bisexual Books Award in Erotica/Romance, as well as a number of short stories in anthologies. Her publishing history can be found at www.juliebehrens.com. She enjoys a wide range of hobbies including knitting, art, gardening, RPGs, and horseback riding. She lives near Dallas, Texas with her children and menagerie of animals.

E.D. Gonzalez is passionate about writing diverse, humorous fiction featuring superheroes, treasure hunters, ghosts, and anyone else with a story to tell. Her short stories have appeared in various literary magazines, including *The Watsonian, Wizards in Space* and *Potomac Review*. She regularly contributes to Book Riot and Foreword Reviews. When not writing, she collects comic books and watches entirely too many cartoons. You can occasionally find her on Twitter @Eileen2theStars.

Naomi Hinchen lives in Cambridge, Massachusetts, where she works as a video game developer. This is her first published story. She also co-writes and stars in the podcast *Crime & Space*.

Stella B James is a Southern girl who appreciates strong coffee and martinis as dry as her sense of humor. When she isn't writing about the complications of life and love, she can be found reading romance novels of any genre, drinking prosecco while watching whatever she has left over on her DVR, or talking herself out of buying yet another black dress. She has published several short stories with various publications and is currently writing her first romance novel. You can find her short stories on her website, www.stellabjames.com. Check out her Instagram @stellabjames, where she shares her writing and inner musings.

Rachel Kenley is the author of seven novels as well as several short stories and novellas. She started reading romances at 14 and credits them with her lifelong fascination with relationships and how they influence our lives. She desperately needs her morning coffee, enjoys shameless flirting and believes in the importance of retail therapy. She can be found online at www.rachelkenley.net.

The world is a dark and scary place for a neurotic like **Christopher Peruzzi**. When he's not writing short horror stories or articles regarding zombie contingency preparedness, he is blogging on Hubpages.com for his

Superhero Academy 101 about all things regarding the Marvel and DC universes. His short stories, *The Undead Rose* (published in the *Once Upon an Apocalypse* anthology) and *When You Wish Upon a Star* (published in *Miskatonic Nightmares*), are best read in a gloomy, dark room with a nightlight. He currently writes for litLAB, a branch of New Brunswick's coLAB Arts, which works hand in hand for social causes. His story *Degrees*, a post-apocalyptic message on ecology will be followed by his piece *Give Me a Beat* on free speech. Chris earns his living as a Senior Technical Writer for a top financial solutions company. He lives in Freehold, NJ, with his wife, Sharon, and menagerie of pets.

Elizabeth Schechter has been called one of the top erotica and alternative sexuality writers in the world. Her writing credits include the award-winning steampunk erotic romance *House of Sable Locks*, the Celtic fantasy *Princes of Air,* and the ongoing *Heir to the Firstborn* serial, her first foray into New Adult fantasy. She was born in New York at some point in the past. She is officially old enough to know better, but refuses to grow up. She lives in Central Florida with her husband and son. Elizabeth can be found online at http://elizabethschechterwrites.com, or on Facebook at https://www.facebook.com/Elizabeth.A.Schechter. You can also find her on Patreon, at https://www.patreon.com/EASchechter.

Kim Strattford lives in Northern Virginia and grew up on romances of all sorts, courtesy of her mother, who let her read them (perhaps a few years before she ought to have). When Kim retired, she turned her eye toward writing her own romances. She is a member of RWA and has stories published in such collections as *Powerless Against You: A Romantic Superhero Anthology, When the Sea Swallows the Sun: A Sweet Romance Anthology, The Robotica* anthology, and *The One Who Got Away* anthology. When she's not writing, she likes sipping good whiskey, collecting Zoya nail polishes, and reading (of course!). See more at www.kimstrattford.com.

David T. Valentin is an aspiring short story writer and novelist based in New York City. He's currently working on a nonfiction book, *The Binge Watcher's Guide to Avatar the Last Airbender*, one of the latest books in the new Binge Watcher's Guide series from Riverdale Avenue Books.

Austin Worley has written everything from heroic fantasy to haiku, but *Law, Love, and the Whippoorwill* marks his first foray into romance. A native of Broken Arrow, Oklahoma, he fills his downtime with reading, music and stargazing. Some of his other short stories and novelettes have appeared in magazines and anthologies such as *Broadswords* and *Blasters #8, Unsheathed: An Epic Fantasy Collection* and *Fifty Flashes*. More short stories and poetry can be found on his DeviantArt profile, Legio-X. You can also follow him on Twitter @AMWorley_Writer

Other Riverdale Avenue Titles You Might Enjoy

Wickedly Ever after:
An Anthology of Retold Tales
Edited by Rachel Kenley

Dangerous Curves
Edited by Rachel Kenley

Women Who Love Monsters
Edited by Lori Perkins

Gone with the Dead:
An Anthology of Romance and Horror
Edited by Lori Perkins

Amorous Congress
Edited by F. Leonora Solomon

The Circlet Treasury of Steampunk Erotica
Edited by Cecelia Tan

Made in the USA
Monee, IL
23 October 2020

45893808R00177